T0126157

LETHAL CARE

A Chief Inspector Carol Ashton Mystery
The Final Chapter

CLAIRE McNAB

with

Katherine V. Forrest

BELLA
BOOKS

2017

Copyright © 2017 by Claire McNab and Katherine V. Forrest

Bella Books, Inc.
P.O. Box 10543
Tallahassee, FL 32302

All rights reserved. No part of this book may be reproduced or transmitted in any form or by any means, electronic or mechanical, including photocopying, without permission in writing from the publisher.

This is a work of fiction. Names, characters, businesses, places, events and incidents are either the products of the author's imagination or used in a fictitious manner. Any resemblance to actual persons, living or dead, or actual events is purely coincidental. The publisher does not have any control over and does not assume any responsibility for author or third-party websites or their content.

Printed in the United States of America on acid-free paper.

First Bella Books Edition 2017

Editor: Cath Walker
Cover Designer: Judith Fellows

ISBN: 978-1-59493-581-7

PUBLISHER'S NOTE

The scanning, uploading, and distribution of this book via the Internet or via any other means without the permission of the publisher is illegal and punishable by law. Please purchase only authorized electronic editions, and do not participate in or encourage electronic piracy of copyrighted materials. Your support of the author's rights is appreciated.

Other Bella Books by Claire McNab

Under the Southern Cross
Silent Heart
Writing My Love

Carol Ashton Series:
Lessons in Murder
Fatal Reunion
Death Down Under
Cop Out
Dead Certain
Body Guard
Double Bluff
Inner Circle
Chain Letter
Past Due
Set Up
Under Suspicion
Death Club
Accidental Murder
Blood Link
Fall Guy

Denise Cleever Series:
Murder Undercover
Death Understood
Out of Sight
Recognition Factor
Death by Death
Murder at Random

Kylie Kendall Series:
The Wombat Strategy
The Kookaburra Gambit
The Quokka Question
The Dingo Dilemma
The Platypus Ploy

Acknowledgments

Sheila Jefferson: There are not enough words to describe what you mean to me, so I will simply say—Everything!

Katherine V. Forrest: Accolades to my incomparable co-writer, who handled with aplomb the complex plot and a cast of characters seething with strong emotions. I expected co-writing would be stressful. I was wrong. I learnt and I laughed—a perfect antidote to stress.

Linda Hill and Jessica Hill: Publishers extraordinaire, you made the impossible, possible. Thank you!

Cath Walker: You edited *Lethal Care* with grace and skill. This was a considerable achievement as you were editing two writers—the legendary KVF, who has dealt with countless manuscripts over the years. And me, who has no idea why people fall about laughing whenever I declare, "I'm a dream to edit."

Jo Hercus: Thank you for your keen psychological insights and outstanding group editorial reading. And pasta.

Eileen and Mollie: My gratitude—and Carol's—for your steadfast, unshakable belief that *Lethal Care* would eventually exist.

Loyal Readers: Who waited patiently (or not!) for Carol to decide.

Dedication

For Sheila

FOREWORD

You ask: why is the name Katherine V. Forrest on this book? When Claire McNab, all by herself, is the internationally published author of the Carol Ashton and Kylie Kendall mystery series, the Denise Cleever espionage series, numerous romantic novels, an assortment of plays and short stories—forty or so books all told. When, under the name Claire Carmichael, she has written even more books: she is one of Australia's well known children's writers. Many of you won't know that in her spare time she taught an advanced fiction class for two decades at UCLA Extension, an instructor so celebrated that she was named Teacher of the Year and given the Distinguished Instructor Award by that huge institution.

So why am I a co-writer on this book?

That answer first took shape in 2008 when Claire received a diagnosis of Parkinson's disease. A diagnosis she dealt with in her usual fashion, continuing her writing and teaching careers undeterred. Until Parkinson's began to increase its grip in 2012 as she began work on what would be the final book in her most celebrated series. Today Claire is no less brilliant, no less accomplished, funny, and determined than she ever was, but the cruelty of this disease no longer allows her physical body to obey the commands of her brain.

During my years at the legendary Naiad Press, I was Claire's editor on *Lessons in Murder*, the first Carol Ashton mystery in a series that would go on to form part of the foundation of our lesbian genre literature. I've edited a number of Claire's books in the years since, and saw about 35,000 words of *Lethal Care* shortly after she began work on it. But nothing had come in since, and I assumed she was too involved in her career at UCLA and other writing projects.

I didn't catch up with Claire again until a rush visit to her in the intensive care unit at UCLA Medical Center in late July 2016. In critical condition, she required emergency surgery due to complications of Parkinson's. She came through that surgery but still another surgical procedure followed, and after that, many months in a rehabilitation facility. It is a tribute to Claire's heart and soul and will that she is even with us today. It was during this time that she agreed that I would work with her to complete the final book in the series most meaningful to her. I am happy to report that she is home today with her Sheila, and has continued daily involvement in the writing of this book.

The seventeen Carol Ashton books not only form the centerpiece of Claire's writing career, they encompass three decades of Claire's life as she gave us her highly entertaining and popular stories, her vivid images of the remarkable topography of Australia and life and death Down Under, all mixed into her ingenious plots.

It has been a privilege and an honor to work so closely with the remarkable woman who is Claire McNab on this final book in her equally remarkable and most beloved series.

Katherine V. Forrest
Palm Springs, CA
2017

ONE

"Madeline," said Chief Inspector Carol Ashton, rising from her chair. "This is an unexpected pleasure."

Madeline Shipley sank gracefully into a chair opposite Carol's desk. "I took a chance you'd be available this early in the morning."

Carol resumed her seat, nodding to the awestruck young officer who'd escorted her uninvited guest to her office. When he finally closed the door on his unblinking stare, she said, "What is it I can do for you?"

"You're looking good, Carol." She added with a silky smile, "Of course, I say that as one who has a weakness for cool and classy blondes."

Carol looked at her with frank appreciation. The passing of the years had treated her well. "And you, Madeline, are your usual sensational self."

Slim as always, with shiny copper hair and deep gray eyes, Madeline was well aware of the impact she made and skillfully deployed her magnetic charm. An aqua classic silk dress enhanced her figure with such effect that it seemed to gather all the light in the room. She smiled easily at Carol's gentle mockery.

Carol looked down at her functional navy blue suit tailored to conceal the weapon she wore. She was amused to see Madeline giving the government-issue furnishings a critical once-over, her glance lingering on the photo on the credenza.

"David's grown into quite the handsome young man," she noted approvingly. "But then," she said, surveying Carol, "why wouldn't he..."

"He's driving through Europe with his father at the moment," Carol said, her gaze settling affectionately on the photo of her joyous son taken in his graduation gown.

Nodding, Madeline continued her survey of the office, and from her expression she was unimpressed. "Your promotion to Chief Inspector has brought about a slight improvement in the standard of décor," she observed, "but the ambience is hardly welcoming."

Carol grinned. "You're expecting ambience at police headquarters? Good luck. There's nothing anywhere here that even approaches the luxury of the waiting rooms in your offices."

"I admit the network looks after me rather well."

The television network had every reason to do so. Madeline was one of Australia's most successful media personalities, the combination of her glossy beauty and formidable interviewing skills ensuring enviable ratings for her current affairs program, *The Shipley Report*. Even changes in format and time slots over the years had had minimal effect on its popularity, and she was now entrenched in prime time on Sunday evenings.

Carol checked her watch. She had a meeting in an hour. He was a stickler for punctuality. "Madeline, I don't like to hurry you, but..."

Madeline leaned back in her chair and crossed her legs with casual grace, and Carol was taken aback to feel a feather touch of awakening desire. It seemed eons since they were lovers; their lives had diverged and they hadn't spoken for some time.

"How's Sybil?" Madeline asked.

She wasn't surprised at the question, but even so, it irritated her. "You've dropped in expressly to inquire after Sybil's health?"

"It was more a status report I was after. Are you back together again?"

Carol pushed back from her desk. "I've a meeting in a few minutes—"

Madeline put up her hands. "Peace, Carol. The subject's closed. I'll tell you why I'm here. Have you been watching *Motives for Murder*, the *Report*'s current in-depth series?"

"I'm afraid not."

Madeline's frown was a mild rebuke. "That's a pity. We've scored excellent ratings with jealousy, personal gain, and revenge."

"In my line of work I'm more than familiar with the reasons people murder each other."

Madeline chuckled. "No doubt. But we're about to cover a topic I'm sure will be of particular interest to you."

On guard, Carol said neutrally, "And that would be…"

"Mercy killing. Did you know that euthanasia is Greek for 'easy death'?"

"I did," Carol said.

Madeline beamed at her. "Good-looking *and* smart. No wonder I adore you." When Carol didn't respond, she went on, "I've heard on the grapevine that you're taking over the Greta Denby case. Because of Inspector Rooke's sudden death."

An echo of the shock she'd felt at hearing of Rooke's death rolling through her, Carol was silent for a moment to gather herself. There was no point in asking where Madeline had obtained information about the Denby case reassignment ahead of the official announcement, so Carol conceded, "The grapevine is correct."

"This one, Carol, is going to be quite a challenge, even for you."

"I admit the media is no help." She added with a dry smile, "With the exception of you, of course."

The media frenzy over Greta Denby's demise had been predictable. Greta, a gracious, beautiful woman with an effervescent personality, and her husband, finance magnate Harland Denby, had been luminaries for years in Sydney's social and cultural circles as well as generous benefactors to select charities. The Denbys' son and daughter were also tracked by the press, though for less admirable reasons—their escapades and brushes with the law. After Harland's sudden and fatal heart attack, Greta had dropped out of sight for months. When she returned to the public eye, the celebrity media had seized on her once again and dubbed her The Merry Widow, noting that her escorts to the various events and fundraisers were unfailingly handsome and often appeared younger than Greta's adult son.

Ovarian cancer struck; and the socialite's considerable fortune funded expensive, experimental, and well-publicized treatments developed by the controversial Dr. Eduardo Valdez. After an extended stay at his Swiss clinic, Greta Denby, accompanied by the doctor, had returned to Sydney. With her cancer in remission, she had begun to attend social functions again, along with assisting Valdez in his accreditation process in Australia and introducing him to influential people who might be interested in supporting his proposal to open his first Australian clinic.

Then Greta Denby had been found dead. Eduardo Valdez had been vindicated in his adamant refusal to sign a death certificate and his insistence on an autopsy. When the cause of death had been revealed to be an excessive dose of Nembutal, the inquest had been adjourned pending further investigation. The nonstop gossip and innuendo that followed was fueled by speculation about inheritance-based conflict in the Denby family and rumors that despite Dr. Valdez's claims of imminent recovery by his patient, Greta Denby's cancer had returned to ravage her body. Although the media was careful to skirt Australia's strict defamation laws, there seemed to be a general consensus of speculation that someone close to the suffering Greta Denby had helped her die. This was the morass Ian Rooke had been assigned to investigate.

"I must admit a few of my colleagues did rather embellish Inspector Rooke's fatal accident," Madeline said.

"Embellish?" Carol said scornfully. "Is that what you call the journalistic invention of an entirely fictitious 'Denby Curse'?"

"What can I say?" Madeline lifted her shoulders in an elegant shrug. "Although I agree Wally Marston went too far when he claimed it was the Denby Curse that sent Inspector Rooke's car over that cliff, he was only reacting to the public's intense interest in anything to do with the Denby family."

"Oh, *please*! He was a fine, decent family man who didn't—"

"I'm sorry, Carol," said Madeline, suddenly serious. "In my profession it's all too easy to forget that what we cheerfully label an interesting story is to others a personal tragedy. Inspector Rooke's death was surely a devastating blow to his wife and two young children, and a shock to everyone who worked with him."

"It was a shock," said Carol, mollified, thinking again of the stunned disbelief all around her that had greeted the news.

She felt a singular connection with Inspector Ian Rooke. His career had paralleled her own rise through the ranks and although they'd never been close, they'd had a friendly rivalry over who would be first to take the next step up the promotion ladder. A very private man, Rooke had had a low-key manner attractively combined with a sly wit.

She knew only the surface facts: Around nine at night, driving to his home in the northern outskirts of Sydney, he'd failed to negotiate a hairpin bend in a hazardous stretch of road running through the wilderness of Galston Gorge. His decade-old Land Rover had smashed through the guardrail and plunged over a sheer cliff into the depths of a bushland ravine.

The first responder to reach the vehicle found Rooke's dead body penetrated by the shaft of the steering wheel. The mangled wreck had to be winched back up to the top before he could be extracted. No other vehicle appeared to be involved, nor were there any skid marks to indicate he'd braked suddenly to avoid hitting an obstacle on the road.

"Had Rooke been drinking?" Madeline inquired. "Or taking any medications?"

"I don't believe the lab results are back yet."

Madeline raised a perfectly arched eyebrow. "Really? I find that hard to believe. Here he is, the cop handling a sensational high society case that has rumors flying around town about how and why Greta Denby died. And suddenly he's dead himself. Surely that alone would put the lab results at the top of the list. And now, I gather, there are unanswered questions not only about the manner of his death, but also about the way he was conducting the investigation."

She chose to ignore the remark about Rooke's investigation and did not bother to enlighten Madeline that lab results took a minimum of two weeks no matter who you were, even longer depending on the width of the fishing net. She smiled and borrowed the metaphor: "It seems to me you're on a fishing expedition, Madeline."

"Not at all. I'm simply asking you to confirm information I've received."

"From your usual reliable sources?"

"As matter of fact, yes. For example, I'm reliably informed that Inspector Rooke had already decided that Greta's death was a mercy killing."

Carol flinched, and immediately wondered if Madeline had seen it. Years, she'd had years to get over her knee-jerk response to the stirring of memory the term evoked, but it still caused a visceral reaction. Aware that Madeline was studying her through narrowing eyes, Carol said dismissively, "Inspector Rooke had only been on the case for a few days. There was no way he would have gathered sufficient evidence to come to a definitive conclusion."

Madeline's expression, quizzical, skeptical, prompted her to add too forcefully, "The Denby death could be suicide. We're still putting facts together."

Carol was immediately sorry she'd made this comment. A large part of Madeline's success as an interviewer was her ability to read the subtle changes in voice and body language that indicated her questions were getting too close to home. Although there was no indication that Madeline had sensed anything, Carol added lightly, "Of course, to have it be suicide could be wishful thinking on my part."

"It has to be one of four possibilities—accident, murder, suicide, or mercy killing. Are there any others?"

"Apparently so," said Carol, smiling at Madeline. "Concerned citizens are reporting any number of speculations about what really happened. One popular theory has the pharmaceutical companies hiring a hit man to protect their cancer drugs from competition. Several amateur sleuths are convinced she was murdered by an enraged husband and father who lost his wife and children to the The Greta Denby Safe Haven for those fleeing domestic violence. And then, there are the psychics—"

"Psychics!" Madeline threw her hands up. "Just the mention of the occult gives me a headache. You would not believe it, Carol. I've had a parade of clairvoyants, spiritualists, mystics, telepaths, mediums, you name it—every last one claiming to know the real truth about Greta's death. They're utterly unfazed by penalties for slander and defamation, they freely share their supernatural visions and name names. The most popular candidate for dispatching Greta to a better place? Thalia Denby."

"Why?"

Madeline shrugged. "You're looking for logic here?"

Greta's daughter, whose wild teenage years had filled countless gossip columns, was now in her late twenties. It was Carol's impression that recently she had settled down and was involved in running her mother's charitable foundation. Perhaps at her mother's insistence, Carol thought. The newspaper coverage showed her always in the company of her mother. Shortly before Greta Denby's death, Carol had admired a TV ad featuring her efforts to establish satellite Safe Haven shelters in communities where domestic violence was widespread. Throughout her career Carol had seen the brutalized bodies of women and children, victims of a ferocious male anger—an anger that seemed ever present in so many women's lives—and she felt a personal regret over Greta Denby's death whatever its cause.

Madeline said, "You haven't met Thalia Denby yet, have you? Photos don't do her justice. In person, she's a knockout."

"I've barely had time to read the case notes. Now, Madeline, if you don't mind…"

"We're expanding our segment, 'Murder or Mercy,' to cover the Denby mystery in depth. I'll be doing daily bulletins reporting on the progress of the investigation."

Carol could feel her shoulders tensing. She picked up her gold pen and rolled it between her palms. "There's a real chance you'll be making much ado about nothing."

Madeline shook her head. "I'm putting my money on what I would call compassionate murder."

"Evidence?"

"Gut feeling." She leaned forward to say persuasively, "Carol, I need your help. I'm looking for a fresh slant. I'll attribute anything you give me to the usual reliable police sources so you'll be fully protected."

She had to laugh at Madeline's audacity. "A fresh slant? So that's why you're here? You can't be serious."

"I'm very serious."

Emphasizing each word with a sharp tap of her pen on the desk, Carol said, "No. No. And no."

"For old times' sake?"

"Give it up, Madeline!"

"How about substantial donations to your favorite charity?" She added with a sly smile, "Of course, the charity could be *you*."

"Are you aware I could arrest you for attempting to bribe a police officer?"

Madeline's laugh was her trademark, low and husky. "I was joking. Surely you realize that."

A knock on the door cut off what would have been an acid response. Carol was relieved to see Mark Bourke's pleasant, blunt-featured face. "Come in, Mark. Madeline's just leaving. Madeline, I'm sure you remember Inspector Mark Bourke?"

The pinstriped suit on his tall, well-built body matched in elegance Madeline's dress. He loomed over her slender figure and offered, "Nice to see you again, Ms. Shipley. It's been awhile."

"Madeline, *please*!" She bestowed on Bourke a thousand-watt smile. "Just the man I wanted to see. I believe your wife knows the Denby family well, and had been advising Greta on what to do with the Denby art collection."

It was not news to Carol that Pat James, Bourke's artist wife, had a link to the Denbys. As required, Bourke had reported a possible conflict of interest when he'd been assigned to the case. She remarked wryly, "I'll say this for you, Madeline, you never miss an angle."

"I try not to." Madeline returned her attention to Bourke. "I'm rather hoping your wife will be willing to talk to me about the Denbys. I'm simply after the human interest perspective."

He showed his discomfort by shifting his feet and running a hand over his stubble-cut hair. "Sorry, but under the circumstances, I don't think it's a good idea."

Unfazed, Madeline went on, "I know you're involved in the case, but I promise you I'm only looking for general background material. Certainly nothing that would impinge on the investigation."

When he shook his head, Madeline said, "Let's leave it for Pat to decide, shall we?" With one lithe movement, she was on her feet. She barely came to Bourke's shoulder.

"I wouldn't get my hopes up, if I were you," he told her pleasantly.

She flashed Bourke her charming smile. "I'm always hopeful, but I'm a realist too."

To Carol she said, "Since I'm here, I wonder if I might see Anne Newsome just for a few moments."

Anne Newsome, newly promoted to Sergeant Newsome, had been assisting Ian Rooke, so it was very clear to Carol why Madeline was keen to speak with her. "Not available, I'm afraid."

"Another time, perhaps."

"I'll see you out," Bourke said firmly.

Madeline looked up at him, her lips curled in a half smile. "You don't trust me to find my own way?"

"Standard procedure."

As Bourke held the door open for her, Madeline turned back to say, "Carol, we must have dinner sometime. Yes? We've got a lot of catching up to do."

Carol sighed as the door closed behind Madeline Shipley. Just one more complication to add to an ever growing list.

She rarely felt overwhelmed, but sensed it building now. Her entire life seemed to be a pyramid of concerns, professional and personal. The Denby case, along with awakening long-repressed memories, was already proving to be a challenge at many levels, not least of which was Commissioner Hindley's close interest in the investigation. There was Sybil—her feelings for Sybil, Sybil's feelings for her. The growing regret over the impulsive promise to sell her beautiful cliff-top home and buy a house jointly with Sybil somewhere else on the northern beaches peninsula. And there was Aunt Sarah. The woman whose support and advice and honesty she most valued, the one person she fully trusted to explore with her a multitude of conflicts and confusions, was haring off to South America just when Carol needed her most. She owed it to Aunt Sarah to remain silent, to see her onto her aircraft with a mind clear of Carol's anxieties and eager for her own adventures.

Leaning back in her chair, Carol absently twisted the black opal ring she always wore. She glanced around at the utilitarian furnishings Madeline had disparaged. They were simply window dressing—nothing more. And as for her exalted career, how was this promotion anything to be all that proud of? Success had bred success, as it had for officials around her, many of whom displayed a level of competence below any standard of hers.

If the concerns in her pyramid were amorphous, the one forming the base was distinct: bedeviling doubts about her career. It was her career that had created the minefield that lay between her and Sybil. Her career that had led her to this new position where she reported directly to the Commissioner. And the plague of weariness at the mere prospect of performing the delicate political dance necessary to protect subordinates from the judgments of a man she neither trusted nor respected, much less implement procedures in keeping with policing a diverse city. She felt a melancholy yearning for the familiarity of the job that was moving beyond her fingertips; she already sensed a new formality, a developing distance from colleagues with whom she'd worked in easy comradeship. Yes, she would have more control over their activities and the pleasure of being able to open to them wider opportunities. But in some ways she would have less control, and she wondered how she could manage to prevent her itching hands from landing on her squad's murder cases.

Except for this last one, which lay fully in her hands. The Denby case with its collateral tragedy of Detective Inspector Ian Rooke being inexplicably, troublingly dead. It was her brief to step with caution in finding out what Ian Rooke had done or not done and why. Inextricably woven into it was the death of Greta Denby, the case that may have taken some mysterious toll on Rooke.

No one in her life—not Aunt Sarah, not Sybil, certainly not her son—had any inkling of the deeply personal toll the Denby case might wreak on her as well.

TWO

Bourke came back into Carol's office shaking his head in reluctant admiration. "Madeline Shipley's a piece of work."

Carol nodded. "Compared to the media in general, Madeline's methods are positively refined."

"Too true," he said, grimacing. "At this moment I wouldn't want to be anyone associated with the Denbys. Right now, they're fair game."

"And so are we. All the time," said Carol, thinking how radically the content and presentation of news had changed over the years, the explosive growth of the Internet creating voracious demand for sensational stories and lurid details whether true or not. Now that anyone could find out almost anything about anybody and spread distortion and disinformation, it was increasingly difficult to distinguish between truth and fiction.

Folding his long body into the chair Madeline Shipley had recently vacated, Bourke said, "Ready for Clive?"

"As ready as I'll ever be." Although they had ample time, she didn't want to run any risk of being late for their appointment with the new Commissioner of Police.

"What did you make of Ian's notes on the case?" Bourke asked. "I've only had time to skim through them, but anyone would gain the impression he was a bit out of his depth. And that's nothing like the Ian Rooke I knew."

"Pressure can get to anyone," Carol said in a neutral tone, "and in a high-profile case like this and early days, Ian was getting it from all sides."

Bourke put his hands behind his head and stretched out his legs. "Particularly from our newly minted head of police. Greta Denby's death is the first big case on Hindley's watch. He'll be expecting us to tie it up in a neat parcel he can tuck under his arm as he steps into the media limelight."

"Poetic," said Carol in mock admiration.

"My intention exactly," Bourke replied with a grin.

She began to double-check the papers in her briefcase. The Commissioner had already established a reputation for abruptly demanding to see any documentation associated with the case at hand. She glanced over at Bourke, envying the way he seemed able to relax at will.

Bourke yawned. "Didn't get to bed until late because Pat and I had quite an argument about this case. She's all for assisted suicide and I'm not. Pat expects someone will be there to help when she needs that final exit. 'Don't look at me,' I told her. 'You're on your own.' She didn't take it well."

"Knowing her, I imagine Pat didn't," Carol said, hoping that Bourke wouldn't ask her own opinion.

"It's the thin edge of the wedge," Bourke went on. "One day it's assisted suicide, next it's mercy killing without the consent of the victim. It's a fine line. What do you think, Carol?"

Wanting to close the door on the topic, she stated definitively, "The law's clear. It's our job to arrest any person who assists another to die, or who decides to kill out of misplaced compassion."

"Yes, but what's your personal opinion?"

"I don't have one. Can we drop the subject?"

Bourke immediately got to his feet. "Subject dropped."

"Sorry, Mark," she told him. "It's just that Madeline's got to me. She's convinced Greta Denby's death was a mercy killing and she's planning to use her program to hammer the idea."

Bourke accepted her lie with a wry grin, offering in return: "You could say she's going to beat mercy killing to death."

* * *

As they approached Commissioner Hindley's office suite, Bourke pointed out that because of Carol's concern about being late, they were now fully ten minutes early. "Makes us look like eager beavers," he said. "Not an impression it's strategic to make."

"You're early," echoed the commissioner's personal assistant, a young man with a pinched, angular face and a peremptory manner. "He's got someone with him. You'll have to wait." He indicated an arrangement of plump black lounge chairs around a white marble coffee table. "Take a seat. I'll let him know you're here."

Critically examining one of the chairs, then surrendering to its leather embrace, Bourke remarked, "Not bad. Did I tell you Pat has her heart set on a beige leather couch and chairs? I'm not keen, but Pat's mother is, and I've learned to never contradict my mother-in-law."

"Wise," said Carol absently; she was organizing her thoughts for the meeting.

"She can't make it tonight."

Now she paid attention. Pat was hosting a small, celebratory dinner to mark Carol's elevation to Chief Inspector and Mark Bourke's pending promotion to Inspector. "Sorry to hear it."

"Speaking of relatives, I saw Aunt Sarah and her Eco-Crones on the early news this morning."

"As you know, she's heading for the wilds of the Amazon Basin," Carol said glumly. "The delegation leaves next week. Aunt Sarah's confident she can bring home even more ecological onsite evidence to conclusively prove the link between rainforest destruction and global warming."

"Good luck with that in this political climate," Bourke commented.

Carol groaned. "I have a vision of myself trying to spring her from some fetid South American jail."

"I noticed she was introduced as Sarah, president of the Eco-Crones. She's now a one-name celebrity, like Beyoncé or Oprah."

Carol's response was a rueful, admiring headshake. The Eco-Crones, an activist environmental group of older women, had become internationally known for fearlessly challenging the environmental policies and actions of powerful individuals, huge corporations, and governments of countries large and small. Under Aunt Sarah's enthusiastic leadership, and employing her previous experience in the theatrical world, the Eco-Crones had expanded their use of flamboyant street theater. Featuring elaborate costumes and dramatic dialogue, the extraordinary tableaus and mini-plays they staged at demonstrations never failed to generate wide publicity, particularly on the Internet where videos of their colorful exploits tended to go viral.

"The news had clips of Aunt Sarah's street theater performances," Bourke said. "They showed my favorite, the golf course demo. Remember?"

"My aunt wearing huge yellow wings and performing a butterfly poisoned by toxic run-off from the fairways? Hard to forget," Carol said, smiling as she visualized her aunt's long-time-dying routine. "Just when everyone thought Aunt Sarah had fluttered her last flutter, she'd start up her dying routine all over again."

"Nice to see my officers can find something to laugh about," said the commissioner, ushering an impeccably groomed man in a pearl-gray suit out of his office. Carol recognized him: Simon Sykes.

With a practiced smile, Sykes murmured, "Chief Inspector Ashton, my warm congratulations on your promotion."

"Let's dispense with the pleasantries, I've got a full schedule," ordered the commissioner, cutting them off mid-greeting and impatiently beckoning Carol and Bourke into his office. His harsh, disagreeable voice delivered words in a strangled tone as if they were being squeezed through his larynx.

As he slid into his desk chair, Carol looked at him in distaste. Clive Hindley was a humorless, intolerant, tenaciously single-minded individual, with a pugnacious bulldog face and a square, heavy body. His graying hair was clipped short, not in an attempt to disguise approaching baldness but to enhance his spare, no-nonsense demeanor. She disliked him comprehensively. He served to reinforce her continuing misgivings about accepting her new rank as Chief Inspector. She grudgingly had to admit that for good or ill he was effective, a consummate political animal in the use of power, keenly aware of favors owed and reprisals to be meted out. He had proved to be a formidable enemy and, to those who had ceased to be of use, an unreliable friend.

Once they were seated, he said, "Hot potato, the Denby case. Got your work cut out for you. That's why I'm bringing in Sykes to coordinate PR."

Carol managed not to show her instant dismay. She'd worked with Simon Sykes before, when he'd headed the media unit of the then commissioner. His deferential manner was a false front over his arrogance, intrusiveness, and tin ear for the nuances of police work. When Sykes left to form his own public relations company, she had been pleased to see him go.

Bourke, who shared her opinion of the man, said, "Is it really necessary to bring in someone from outside?"

The commissioner's expression darkened. "You should know that the Premier is taking a personal interest in this case. Greta Denby was a close friend." If Commissioner Hindley was new to the top job, he was far from unfamiliar with his obligations to those who had put him there. He had established a network of influential backers, and the support of the state's premier had been a key element in his success. Strings were obviously being pulled in the Denby case. Carol resigned herself to this new reality.

"So that's settled. Sykes handles PR. Newsome can join Upton and Oatland on your team, since she's already familiar with the case. Not that she'll have much to contribute—Rooke had hardly got started."

At these staff assignments, Carol's mood elevated slightly. "I have copies of Inspector Rooke's preliminary interviews, as well as his notes," she said, indicating her briefcase.

"No time. Unless he's got anything on Eduardo Valdez?" He added with a sneer, "Calls himself Dr. Ed, did you know? Jesus Christ!"

"All I could find was a notation that Dr. Valdez had expressed concern about the confiscation of his cancer medications."

The Commissioner gave a derisive snort. "Valdez has been doing a song and dance about safeguarding his precious secret formula. Rooke told me the responding officers found him removing items from the bathroom. He put on a real show when he was forced to put them back exactly as he found them. Threat of arrest for compromising the scene of a police investigation was the only thing that shut him up."

Carol said, "I have details of the prescription drugs Greta Denby was taking, but I don't yet have an analysis of Dr. Valdez's specific medications."

"That's because Valdez was threatening legal action about proprietary rights. An injunction, no less. His lawyer talked some sense into him, and he dropped the whole idea but there was a delay. I'll see you get a copy, but it's no surprise. The doctor's precious, life-saving formula contains vitamins, minerals, herbs, and some concoction he orders from New Zealand."

"Not a miracle cure, then?" said Bourke, raising his hands in mock despair.

Hindley gave Bourke a sour smile. "Con artist, like the rest of them with these too-good-to-be-true cures. Handsome, foreign accent, white coat, swears he has the magic formula—he makes millions from deluded, desperate people, no sweat."

"But he is certified to legally practice in Australia," Carol pointed out.

"Damn shame," Hindley rumbled. He leaned forward to rest his elbows on the desk, his suit jacket straining across his meaty shoulders. "Well, Chief Inspector, you're taking over someone else's very high profile case. That's no picnic. What's your schedule?"

"To begin with, I've arranged to see Thalia and Kenneth Denby at their home this afternoon."

The commissioner gave an exasperated grunt. "It's a bloody nuisance, Rooke getting himself killed and muddying up a major investigation."

Resenting this callous remark, Carol observed, "I don't imagine he did it deliberately to irritate you."

Bourke looked over at her, obviously startled by Carol's tone. The commissioner, however, seemed amused by her comment. "Don't imagine the poor bastard did."

His chair creaked as he shifted his weight to reach for a folder. "The media can't get enough of the Denby case. Last thing I want is to give those baying hounds anything to run with." Shoving the folder across the desk to Carol, he said, "That's why we're releasing only selected details of Rooke's p.m."

As Carol glanced at the contents of the post mortem, he went on, "Preliminary. But you'll see there's nothing out of the ordinary in the blood work so far. Rooke hadn't been drinking and no drugs, legal or otherwise. One odd thing—the report shows a recent needle puncture in his right thigh even though he was in excellent health. The wife wasn't much help. Vague about whether he'd seen a doctor recently and couldn't think of any reason why he'd have an injection."

"I can't imagine Ian Rooke using anything illegal," Bourke stated. "Maybe a painkiller? I know Ian lifted weights."

"I'm expecting answers from you, not questions," the commissioner snapped. "It'll take another goddamn bloody week before we get the detailed analysis of Rooke's body fluids."

He jabbed a forefinger repeatedly at them both. "In the interim, I expect you to personally make sure this particular loose end is well and truly tied. Interview his wife again—maybe her memory's improved—and anyone else close to Rooke. We've gone over what's left of Rooke's vehicle—nothing wrong with the brakes or steering but it's worth a second look. You check through everything in that car. A wad of chewing gum, a used Kleenex—every bloody thing. If you uncover even a hint that something's not kosher, get back to me immediately."

Carol said mischievously, "Madeline Shipley was in my office this morning with queries about Inspector Rooke's death."

As she anticipated, the commissioner's face reddened with anger. "That bloody woman! Nothing but trouble. You don't need the distraction. Leave her to Sykes."

Carol could scarcely blame him for his animosity. When the Premier had released the short list of candidates for Police Commissioner, Madeline had been scathing about Clive Hindley's inclusion. In the *Report* she had questioned his qualifications and his suitability to be the state's top cop. Since his appointment, Madeline had continued to snipe at his performance, and had made clear that she would second guess every step and detail any missteps he made.

"Until we know definitively, Sykes will be feeding the media the official line," said the commissioner. "Inspector Rooke was a dedicated cop working long hours who simply fell asleep at the wheel." With a grim smile, he added, "And that's probably the truth of it."

Carol couldn't help taking a smidgen of pleasure in being the bearer of more bad news for Sykes to handle. "There's more. *The Shipley Report* will be doing an in-depth feature over several days portraying Greta Denby's death as a mercy killing."

"Jesus!" The commissioner slapped his thick hand on the desk. "And if we don't come up with the same conclusion, Shipley will blame it on police incompetence or a cover-up. That's all we need—one of the bloody woman's hatchet jobs."

He glared at Carol and Bourke. "This case needs to be wrapped up and out of the headlines as quickly as possible. I've given you the resources, authorized weekends, overtime. Now I want results and I want them fast. Got it?"

"Got it," Carol said, reaching for her briefcase.

Outside the commissioner's office, Simon Sykes was waiting for them. "A quick word with you?" he said smoothly. "It'll only take a moment."

Carol and Bourke followed him down a corridor to an empty conference room. Carol smiled to herself when she saw Bourke checking out the high quality furniture, expensive light fittings and plush carpet. Having recently bought an old Federation house, he and Pat had become refurbishing junkies, redoing the place room by room.

"Do sit down," said Sykes, pulling two chairs from the long, highly polished jarrah table. "What can I get you? Coffee? A cool drink?"

"You can get to the point," Bourke said, sliding into a chair.

"Of course." He strode around the table to sit across from them.

Although his well-cut suit was designed to disguise the fact, Sykes had put on weight since Carol had last seen him. His jawline had softened and his dark hair was lightly streaked with gray. The obsequious manner that had so aggravated her in the past seemed to have been replaced with something almost as annoying, a supremely self-satisfied air.

Sykes gave a small cough. "No doubt Commissioner Hindley has explained how I may help your investigation. I'm hoping to liaise with you both on a regular basis."

Carol had forgotten his maddening habit of giving a preparatory cough before speaking. But his voice, soft and insinuating, was exactly as she remembered. "How regular?" she asked, placing her hands flat on the table, feeling resistance building fast. She hadn't liked or trusted Simon Sykes all those years ago, and saw no reason to change her mind now.

"It would be preferable if we could touch base daily."

"I don't believe that will be necessary."

Sykes spread his own hands in a conciliatory gesture. "Chief Inspector, I'm here to assist you. I'm not talking about media conferences and the like, although I will be available to deal with any problems in that area. My concern is that the ramifications of this tragedy may be more serious than you imagine. Greta Denby has become the focal point of potential societal conflict."

Bourke chuckled. "Societal conflict? Now that *is* serious."

A shadow of irritation flickered across Sykes's face but he chose to ignore Bourke's jibe, continuing in an even tone,

"Already activists who support the so-called 'death with dignity' viewpoint are squaring off against various right-to-life and anti-euthanasia groups, most notably Canon Roger Armitage's organization, Cherished Life."

"Cherished Life?" Bourke's face hardened. "That name's a laugh. Armitage should have been locked up years ago and the key thrown away."

Sykes nodded gravely. "I couldn't agree more. As it is, he continues to infect his followers with his extremist doctrine, which in my opinion incites violence. Although naturally Armitage denies this."

"They're entitled to their opinions," Carol observed, fully aware that she was saying this simply to needle Sykes. She concurred with Bourke's view that Armitage belonged behind bars. The Canon's activities had been a severe embarrassment to the Anglican Church for some years, but never more so than recently when six of his followers initiated a terror campaign against Cherished Life opponents. They had bashed a young man in a family planning clinic so severely that he was now confined to a wheelchair. Security cameras had identified them, and when arrested, they claimed to be carrying out God's will as relayed to them by Canon Armitage. In court and under oath, Armitage, while attacking the deeds he claimed were perpetrated in the clinic, vehemently denied inciting members of his flock to attack anyone physically. The six acolytes, unrepentant, received lengthy jail sentences, while the Canon remained free of any charge of accessory, piously announcing he was praying for their immortal souls.

His expression grim, Sykes said to Carol, "It would be a serious mistake to take this too lightly. Having handled public relations for controversial clients, I'm very familiar with this type of volatile situation. My advice is that at the very least, you should prepare to face street demonstrations. At worst, you might consider your personal safety. I presume you will be armed at all times."

"We're accustomed to volatile situations," said Bourke, "but thank you for your advice anyway."

"I can't point out too strongly that everyone has an agenda," said Sykes, obviously put out by Bourke's attitude. "In Armitage's case it's to get as much publicity as he can. To be on the front page at any cost. And if that means inciting a riot, that's exactly what he'll do."

Carol got to her feet, indicating the discussion was over. Knowing that Sykes would be reporting back to the commissioner, she said, "About liaising—I'll call you on Monday."

Sykes remained seated to address her. "Inspector Rooke was hounded by certain members of the media, Madeline Shipley being one. As I recall, Chief Inspector, you know her as a friend. My advice in the circumstances is that you should put that friendship aside and avoid any form of contact with her."

"Too late!" Bourke said cheerfully, before Carol could slap Sykes down with a caustic comment. "Carol and I have both enjoyed long conversations with Madeline this morning. I know I resisted the temptation to tell all, but I'm not sure Carol did the same."

Sykes didn't respond to this baiting. His face expressionless, he rose to his feet and handed Carol and Bourke embossed business cards. "I'm available twenty-four/seven. Do not hesitate to get in touch with me. For my part, I will pass on to you any fresh information about Canon Armitage and his organization."

A few minutes later, as Carol and Bourke were returning to her office, Carol said, "Ironic, isn't it, Mark? People like Armitage beat the drum for the sanctity of human life while encouraging their followers to attack anyone who dares to oppose them."

Bourke nodded soberly. "I hate to admit it, but I think Sykes is right. He might dress it up with a term like societal conflict, but it all comes down to the same thing. Violence breeds violence. You said it earlier, Carol—we're in for a rough time."

THREE

"Thank you, Chief Inspector, for making time to see me."
Frederick Lowell took the chair Carol indicated. "As I'm sure
you know, I've handled the Denby family's legal matters for
many years."

If Carol had been casting the role of a family lawyer who
represented rich, influential clients, she would have chosen
someone very like Frederick Lowell. Tall and broad-shouldered,
he held himself ramrod straight. His thick silver-white mane
of hair framed a distinguished, aristocratic face, and he was
immaculately dressed in a dark suit, crisp white shirt, and
regimental tie.

Taking in his patrician presence, Carol decided not to put
more formality between them and took the visitor's chair beside
him instead of returning to her desk. "How may I help you, Mr.
Lowell?"

With a regretful shake of his head, he said, "This whole
brouhaha about Greta is so disturbing. She would have been
distraught had she known that those she loved would find
themselves in such an invidious situation."

Carol nodded sympathetically, wondering what Lowell's agenda might be. Ian Rooke had mentioned the lawyer in the first impressions he'd jotted down in his personal notes. *Devious* was one word that had caught her eye. *Pompous* was the other.

Lowell clasped his well-manicured hands. "May I speak freely?"

"Of course."

"Please believe me, this is difficult to say, but I must bring it to your attention. I have no doubt that Inspector Rooke was a dedicated officer. However, like all of us, he was only human. For whatever reason, it seemed to me that he came to the investigation with his mind already made up about the identity of the person he believed responsible for Greta's death."

"I'm very surprised to hear that," Carol asserted. She was not being defensive; she was startled by the accusation. It was hardly an unknown for police to be accused of bias, and preconceptions indeed influenced some investigating officers, but not seasoned ones. There had never been any suggestion that the very experienced and diligent Ian Rooke had been anything but open-minded and impartial on every case he'd handled. His arrest and conviction record was no less than exemplary.

"How did you come to this conclusion?" she asked, her voice carefully neutral. She was thinking: *Hell. What next?*

"Before I elaborate," said Lowell, "I must tell you that Greta was not merely my client. She and Harland Denby were my close friends. When Harland died, Greta turned to me for guidance."

Carol looked at him in wonderment that either Harland or Greta Denby would place any faith in this cartoonish ass.

"Harland left her the bulk of his empire. Greta was not familiar with the intricacies of the world of finance, and often asked my advice, which of course I freely gave as a friend."

"You provided *financial* advice?"

"Only in the most general terms," he said hastily, reacting to Carol's tone. "Harland's business enterprises have always required teams of specialists in the fields of accounting, contract and tax law, client relations and so on. Frankly, Greta was overwhelmed, and therefore more than happy to hand over the reins to the financial management companies her husband had selected."

Carol was anxious to get back to Rooke's alleged bias, but Lowell seemed intent on pursuing another subject altogether.

"Harland's will, of necessity, was extremely complicated. This was occasioned not only by his great wealth, but also by the number of financial instruments he owned and his business dealings in general. I was not privy to the terms and conditions of his last will and testament, so it was as much a surprise to me as it was to the family to discover the provisions for his son and daughter."

To hurry him along, Carol said briskly, "I've had only a few moments to skim through a summary of Mr. Denby's bequests, but I gather their share of the estate was to be held in trust until each turned thirty-five. They've been receiving a monthly allowance, drawn from the trust accounts."

It was plain that Carol's succinct summing up of the outcome had not pleased Lowell. "Correct," he snapped. "And the right to reside in the family home until marriage."

"Is this relevant?" Carol asked. "Inspector Rooke was not involved at that time of course, and Greta's will is the prevailing one now."

"I consider it important to provide background information, so that one might see the whole picture, as it were, however, if you insist..."

"Thank you, Mr. Lowell."

He barely concealed a vexed sigh. "In public, Greta always supported Kenny. Privately, she confided to me quite the opposite. I recall her saying, 'Kenny is outstandingly creative, but he has no head for money.' It worried Greta that he consistently overspent his allowance and abused his credit cards. Her greatest fear was that without her guidance he would quite easily be swindled in one of his many business ventures."

Lowell unzipped his thin leather briefcase. "Since that time, Greta made changes regarding the distribution of her assets."

"Mrs. Denby appointed you to administer the will?"

"Indeed." Lowell gave a satisfied little nod. "Greta's trust in me was very gratifying."

He extracted a document from his briefcase and passed it to Carol. "When she died, Greta was preparing to amend her will. These are my notes on the possible changes she was considering. That very morning, when she was found dead in her bed, I was to have a meeting with her to discuss the final points before I drafted a new will. In fact, I was on my way to Mosman when I heard the dreadful news."

Carol glanced at the pages without taking in any content—it was meaningless until she had more context. "This information wasn't given to Inspector Rooke. Why is that?"

Lowell lifted his chin. "I assure you I broached the subject with him, but Inspector Rooke didn't seem to find it relevant. Under the circumstances I didn't see any point in pursuing the matter."

Carol was astonished by this revelation. If Lowell were telling the truth, Ian Rooke had been breathtakingly negligent in ignoring information that might well indicate a motive for Greta Denby's death.

Suppressing her concern, she said, "This is a matter we can discuss later, Mr. Lowell, after I've read your notes."

"Of course. I'll treat this matter as confidential in the meantime." He spoke as one conferring a great favor.

"Thank you, Mr. Lowell. Let's move on to the issue of Inspector Rooke's alleged bias."

Deeply solemn, Lowell said, "It's clear to me that Inspector Rooke was quite wrongly and unjustly influenced by sensationalist media accounts. Before his investigation had even begun, the man had already formed the conclusion that Kenny was involved in his mother's death. I don't believe Inspector Rooke seriously considered any other person as a suspect."

Trying to fit this contention with the police officer she knew, Carol sat back in her chair and considered the man seated beside her. "This is a grave charge, Mr. Lowell. I must tell you there is no suggestion anywhere in Inspector Rooke's notes that he was convinced that Kenneth Denby was responsible for his mother's death. Do you have any hard evidence to support your view?"

Lowell frowned. "Hard evidence? No. But observing the inspector, I came to believe it to be true." He put up a hand to forestall Carol's comment. "I know what you're going to say, this is hearsay, merely my opinion. I grant you that, but I would be remiss if I failed to alert you that this could be an issue."

Even though she could not imagine a viable reason for Lowell doing so, she had to ask, "Are you intending to make a formal complaint?"

The lawyer permitted himself a slight smile. "Not at all. My opinion, though held in high esteem in some quarters, would have little weight in this situation. As you are now the investigating officer, I merely wished to counter anything Rooke may have put on paper. However, if there's nothing of that nature, you've answered my concern in that area."

"So the matter's closed."

He gave a brief nod. "It is."

"Mr. Lowell, before you go, may I ask you a question concerning Greta Denby's life insurance?"

He inclined his head graciously, and Carol said, "I understand Mrs. Denby's life was insured for ten million dollars, the money to be paid to her estate, and distributed according to the terms of the current will."

"That's correct. A pittance, in relation to the Denby assets. As the policy contains the standard suicide clause, payment will be withheld until the manner of Greta's death is formally established." He gave her a frosty smile. "And that would be your department, Chief Inspector."

"Mrs. Denby also set up a foundation to establish Dr. Valdez's cancer clinic."

"She did. Greta asked me to chair the foundation's board. Kenny and Thalia are sitting members. Greta also appointed Bruce Rowntree of Terrance and Rowntree as the foundation's accountant. We're in the preliminary stages of selecting a suitable site. In the meantime, a temporary clinic has been set up in rented offices. The initial funding for the permanent building totals twenty million dollars. Providing the clinic fulfills certain terms and conditions, the foundation will make available another ten million annually to cover running costs and so on."

"What is Dr. Valdez's position as far as these funds are concerned?"

Lowell's expression hardened. "In effect, he has no position. Greta wanted it that way. However, as director of the clinic, Valdez is already receiving a more than generous remuneration."

"So the doctor has no say in how the foundation's funds are used?"

Lowell gave a small, satisfied smile. "No say at all. Of course Valdez can petition the board for specific allocations, but there's no guarantee that the board will acquiesce."

Carol felt a momentary sympathy for Valdez. It was clear Lowell disliked him and had the power to make his life difficult. The future of his foundation appeared to be at best murky and at worst impossible. "There seems to be some controversy regarding Dr. Valdez and the efficacy of the treatments he developed in Switzerland," Carol remarked.

"Dr. Ed, as Valdez prefers to be called," Lowell said with disdain, "persuaded Greta that his radical regimen would cure her cancer. And for a time it appeared that her faith in him was fully justified."

"But her cancer returned."

"Yes, it did!" The lawyer's face flushed brick red. "I begged Greta to seek treatment in an established medical center with world-class cancer specialists but she refused to listen to me, or for that matter, to anyone else who tried to reason with her. She remained convinced to the end that Valdez could work miracles when the evidence apparent to all of us contradicted that belief."

Lowell took a deep breath, visibly collecting himself. "I'm sorry for the outburst, Chief Inspector, but I firmly believe Greta would have had far greater chances for survival but for Eduardo Valdez."

Lowell's power over the Denby purse had been trumped by Greta Denby's determination to oversee her own survival possibilities. But clearly, Lowell cared about his client and Carol said sympathetically, "Your responsibilities must bring you into contact with Dr. Valdez. I imagine it's difficult for you to deal with him, feeling as you do."

He nodded a dignified assent. "I concede it will be difficult, but it was Greta's decision to appoint me chairman of the board in good faith, and I will honor the trust she put in me. My personal views will not influence my decisions apropos the foundation."

He zipped up his briefcase and got to his feet. "Thank you, Chief Inspector. I won't take any more of your valuable time." He shook hands and took his leave.

Carol took out Rooke's papers to further refresh her memory on her colleague's impressions of Frederick Lowell. Rooke had additionally jotted down: *Check undue influence on G.D. The family his main meal ticket.*

She puzzled over Frederick Lowell's agenda in his meeting with her. What advantage would there be for him to bring up the issue of Rooke's supposed bias? To influence her thinking? To impress Kenneth Denby that Lowell was looking out for him? Or was it to emphasize how much Greta Denby valued Lowell's friendship and advice?

Deciding to follow up on Ian Rooke's notes, she called Lester Upton into her office. She was pleased to have him on her team, though not for his sparkling personality. Upton was, as Bourke had drily observed, dull to the point of genius. His face was usually impassive and his voice a monotone. What Les Upton did have, apart from a well-hidden but keen sense of humor, was a tenacious interest in anything to do with financial matters. Fine details and analysis, eye-glazing for most people, clearly delighted Upton. Carol had to smile at the flash of animation he displayed when given this task.

"Frederick Lowell? The Denby finances? I'm on it."

"Ian Rooke thought Lowell might have had an unwarranted influence on Greta Denby."

"Okay boss, I'll add it to the list."

She grinned as he left her office with a spring in his step. She reflected, as she often had before, how disquieting it would be for a potential suspect to learn that someone like Les Upton was in pursuit. He was relentlessly goal-oriented and never satisfied until he'd nailed the smallest detail and laid it all out with clarity and precision. If the Denby family had anything to hide in the financial sphere, Les would find it.

In preparation for her first meeting with Thalia and Kenneth Denby, Carol again went through the material Ian Rooke had collected on the case. Her initial scan of his interviews with Greta Denby's son and daughter had left her unimpressed. A closer reading deepened her concern. Rooke's questions—what they had observed in the hours before their mother's death and their own whereabouts—were on the whole routine and superficial. Even making allowances for their shock and grief, he had rarely bothered to challenge vague or contradictory answers. It was distressing to read such slipshod, unfocused work from a colleague, particularly one who had always held himself to the highest standards.

She put the interviews aside and glanced through the post mortem documents. The cause of Greta Denby's death was not in debate. She had somehow consumed a lethal dose of Nembutal along with the usual cocktail of prescription drugs including Dr. Valdez's unique therapy. But had she freely taken the fatal dose, with full knowledge it would kill her? Or was it forced upon her? Or had she unknowingly accepted it from someone she trusted?

In every suspicious death there were standard questions: Who had the means? The motive? The opportunity? Greta's usual medications were in plain sight within the bedroom suite, and the pill count in all the containers had matched the records of Greta Denby's caretakers. Greta could have asked someone to provide the Nembutal, a means of suicide reputed to be straightforward, uncomplicated. Or it could have been brought in easily enough. It was a barbiturate, once prescribed quite commonly but out of favor these days except by veterinarians where it was known as "the green dream." It was also the drug of choice for all the pro-euthanasia groups, and could be administered via an injection or taken orally.

She considered motive. If it was euthanasia, she thought, ruthlessly squashing sudden imagery of her own mother's death, the motive began and ended there. If it was out and out murder, then motive seemed obvious—the deceased had been an extremely rich woman and the provisions of her will affected many lives. Money was a primal urge for murder, and in families that urge was frequently triggered by deeply held, seething resentments. Rooke's notes indicated his sympathy for Greta Denby, whom he characterized as a benevolent dictator whose control of the family and household had been slipping away as her cancer progressed. Without her steadying influence, conflicts, previously hidden, were surfacing, and speculation about her two primary beneficiaries more frequent in the press.

Opportunity was a key issue. If only reality mimicked mystery fiction, Carol mused, where time of death often established definitively who in the cast of characters would have had a chance to carry out the crime, some investigations would be so much simpler. The pathologist who had examined Greta Denby's body at the scene and did the post mortem, even with the benefit of hard science—ambient temperature, internal body temperature, the onset of lividity, the stage of rigor mortis, and knowhow gained through years of experience—could only provide the usual three-hour window. Greta had taken her last breath somewhere between one and four in the morning. The fatal combination of drugs would have had to be administered approximately a half hour to an hour earlier than her death.

Carol agreed with Rooke's calculations: during a window beginning at midnight and running until about four in the morning, the deceased had ingested the drug that ended her well-publicized life.

In Greta Denby's celebrity status, a creation of the gossip columns, she seemed equivalent to a minor version of one of the Kardashians accustomed to and flourishing in the glare of the limelight. Carol had known her name and been aware of headlines carried by the media, but otherwise Greta was just a public face frequently photographed at social and cultural events. In recent months she had become a woman who had triumphed over cancer and was fighting to survive its recurrence. Now she was a case number, the victim in the center of an investigation that was stripping her of any semblance of privacy, reduced to facts and figures, a puzzle to be solved. How and why did this woman die? Who benefited from her death?

Memory suddenly overtook Carol again, anguished thought at how different was the choking grief when death took someone beloved. It had always haunted her that her own mother had died before dawn. Was that the time to relinquish life, in a darkness that held a thousand griefs, a thousand regrets?

FOUR

With Mark Bourke tied up on finishing work for another case and unavailable, Carol took Sergeant Anne Newsome with her to the Denby family home. Anne had worked many cases with Carol as her mentor, and Carol was gratified and delighted by her well-deserved promotion to sergeant.

As soon as Carol got into the passenger seat, Anne handed her a Starbucks coffee and a deli wrapped sandwich. "I reckon you haven't had time for lunch. My treat."

"Anne, thank you. The coffee alone is a lifesaver."

Carol wasn't hungry, but she dutifully ate the roast beef sandwich. Glancing across at Anne negotiating the heavy Friday traffic on Military Road with her customary skill, Carol diverted her thoughts into searching for a summary word that would describe her. Anne's movements were neat and economical, her work painstaking, her contributions to discussions on an investigation well thought out and concise. She always looked consummately professional in her choice of plain suits, wore her chestnut brown hair in a short, easy-care style, had a trim, well-cared for body and flawless olive skin that Carol secretly envied.

Failing the search for a summarizing word for Anne, her thoughts inevitably returned to the Denby case. Carol said, "Madeline Shipley dropped in this morning. She'd heard I'd been appointed to investigate Greta Denby's death. When she didn't get anywhere with me, she asked to see you. I told her you were not available. Has she tried to contact you?"

Anne grinned as she deftly changed lanes. "Nope. I wouldn't have thought I was high enough on the pecking order to interest Ms. Shipley."

"Do you know if she spoke with Ian Rooke? There's no mention of it in his notes."

Her voice dropping into a serious tone, Anne said, "There were several voice mail messages asking Inspector Rooke to call her but as of the final time I saw him, he didn't ring her back."

"Madeline's never been the type to give up easily," Carol said, adding *Check phone logs* to her mental list.

Making a right turn into Raglan Street, Anne said, "We're being followed."

"Media?"

"I'd say so."

They were entering an even more exclusive part of the already exclusive suburb of Mosman. A few minutes later they drew up at the entrance to the Denby estate, its front boundary protected by a substantial sandstone wall. As they turned in, a nondescript car passed them slowly, a bearded young man in a T-shirt leaning out to get clear shots through his large telephoto lens.

"And so it begins," said Carol. "There'll be a pack of them by the time we leave."

Stone lions snarled down at them from both sides of the heavy wrought-iron gate. Carol scanned for cameras, locating them between the front paws of each lion. The gate was open, but ahead the way was barred by an obviously new boom gate, manned by a uniformed security guard. He smiled at Anne, recognizing her from previous visits, but checked Carol's credentials and noted her name before raising the barrier and waving them through.

The long, winding drive was bordered by a variety of fragrant eucalypts, some in vibrant red and white flower. Signs admonished drivers to not exceed a speed of ten kilometers per hour. Anne slowed down even further, crawling along to allow Carol to assess the place.

Looking through the greenery, Carol caught glimpses of a wooden fence painted dark brown. "Is that part of the perimeter fencing?"

"Yes, and it's all in good condition, though at two meters high it wouldn't provide much of a barrier to a determined intruder."

The Google satellite view on Carol's tablet showed two entrances to the property. Vehicles were limited to the gate they had just come through but pedestrians had the choice of walking down the long drive or entering from a narrow one-way road through a gate close to the house. She checked with Anne that the same keycard was used for both.

None of this information had appeared in Rooke's notes, leaving Carol to wonder what else he had disregarded. "It's basic in a case like this to establish the level of security. Inspector Rooke seems to have virtually ignored the subject. What gives?"

Her expression troubled, Anne glanced over at Carol. "I'm not sure how to describe..." She paused, then said in a rush, "Something was definitely wrong, but I don't have any idea what it could be."

"Wrong in what way?" When Anne didn't or couldn't reply, Carol said, "If Ian Rooke's behavior has had any impact on this investigation, it's imperative I know about it."

Anne was silent for moments more as if choosing her words. "I had the impression he wasn't much interested. That he was detached and just going through the motions. Like there was something so heavy on his mind it was more important than anything else."

"Any idea at all what it could be? Trouble at home, perhaps?"

Anne shook her head. "He wasn't about to confide in me."

As Anne continued her slow way down the drive, Carol turned to her. "Anne, think back and visualize your time with Ian Rooke. Did he appear ill, or in pain?"

Frowning, Anne deliberated. "He wasn't sick," she said, "and he didn't show any sign he was in pain."

"How about his emotional state? Was he depressed?"

"Maybe. He didn't talk much. He wasn't moody, more like just very quiet. Until that last day before he died. Then he seemed...I don't know..."

"Give me one word to describe how he was."

"Relieved," she said immediately. "As though something had worked out better than he'd hoped."

Thinking of Lowell's accusation of bias, Carol said, "I saw Frederick Lowell earlier. He believes that right from the start of the investigation Rooke had decided Greta Denby's death was murder and Kenneth Denby was the guilty party."

Anne threw a shocked glance at Carol. "He said that?"

"Is it possible...could it be Ian was relieved because he'd discovered hard evidence to validate his previously unsupported opinions?"

Obviously perplexed, Anne focused on the roadway for a few moments, then offered, "My impression is that Inspector Rooke wasn't interested in anyone in particular around Greta Denby. I know he disliked Kenny Denby, but not with any real emotion, not with accusation. It was a sort of cold disdain, if you know what I mean."

"Kenny Denby?" said Carol. "This morning, Frederick Lowell started off referring to Kenneth Denby, but soon it was Kenny. What's with that, Anne?"

"Practically everyone calls him Kenny. He's a grown man still with a kid's name. You'll see why when you meet him."

"Let's get back to the security issue. I know the house has an alarm system."

With a sweeping gesture that encompassed house and grounds, Anne said, "A very comprehensive one, covering just about every way an intruder could enter the building. Unfortunately, most evenings it isn't switched on. Apparently Kenny kept forgetting the alarm was programmed to come on line at seven o'clock every night, so when he came home late—which was often—he'd set it off. Not only would it wake the house and neighbors, the nearest patrol car would arrive within minutes. As you can imagine, the whole routine got old fast, particularly for the cops."

Carol shook her head. "There's always time to punch in the code and cancel the alarm. It's not rocket science."

"Evidently it is for him. He never once managed to deactivate the system in time. It seemed easier on everyone not to set the alarm at all and rely on lights and cameras. It definitely wasn't working the night his mother died."

Carol added Kenneth Denby's curious inability to master such a straightforward procedure to her mental list. "What's the schedule for the security guard at the entrance gate?"

"It's manned for a twelve-hour period, seven in the morning to seven at night. The rest of the time the gate's locked. Everyone in the household enters with a keycard. Visitors using the intercom are picked up by surveillance cameras before being buzzed in by someone in the house."

"Okay, so that entrance is reasonably secure. What about the perimeter fence? If someone climbs over, what happens?"

"Other than motion-sensitive lights, basically nothing," said Anne, pulling into a parking area signposted *Visitors & Tradespeople Please Park Here*. "Thanks to Mr. Lowell. He put the kibosh on any new security claiming there was enough."

Out of habit, Carol checked her surroundings. There were no other vehicles in sight. A carved wooden pelican with the words THIS WAY on its extended beak pointed down a gently sloping pathway of crushed stone, which must lead to the Denby mansion.

Her attention was caught by the movement of a surveillance camera as it panned the area from the top of a metal pole. "Do you have a diagram giving the location of all the cameras? I didn't see anything in Ian Rooke's files."

"It's in my briefcase. Do you want to see it now?"

"Tomorrow will do. Before we get out of the car, tell me how Lowell got himself involved in anything to do with security."

Amusement lighting her face, Anne said, "Talk about a soap opera...I was with Inspector Rooke in one of the downstairs sitting rooms taking preliminary statements from anyone who'd stayed overnight in the house. Dr. Valdez had just finished and we were waiting for Thalia Denby to appear when there's commotion in the hall outside the room. I hear Dr. Valdez say, 'What are you doing here?' A moment later, Mr. Lowell's in the doorway with Dr. Valdez yelling, 'Ask him about Greta's security. It's his fault she's dead.' Then he shoves Mr. Lowell into the room and slams the door behind him."

"High drama indeed," said Carol entertained by the image of the very dignified Frederick Lowell with his feathers ruffled.

"Mr. Lowell just gathered himself and acted as if nothing unusual happened. Inspector Rooke introduced himself and me. So Lowell hands over his business card, says he'd had an appointment that morning with Greta Denby and was on his way when he heard the newsflash about her. As the family lawyer, it was more than proper for him to be present, to serve the family as needed."

"What was his manner? Did he appear at all upset about Greta's demise?"

"He looked rather stunned but who could tell?" said Anne. "He's very old school. Very formal."

"Good description," Carol said, smiling.

"Inspector Rooke asked what Dr. Valdez meant when he said it was Mr. Lowell's fault Greta Denby was dead. After muttering some comment about unreliable and over-emotional Mediterranean people, he gave us the whole story. Six months ago Dr. Valdez told Greta his life was at risk. Every evening when he left the clinic he was followed home. He'd not been able to get the license plate, but was absolutely sure it was the same vehicle. Claimed he'd made corporate enemies due to the success of his cancer treatments and suspected that as the source. He feared for his safety."

"It's quite a jump to go from simply being followed home to physical harm or death threats."

"Well, Greta took him *very* seriously. She had the passenger compartment of his car fully armored. Next, she instructed Mr. Lowell to engage the best possible home security company to assess his place and its surroundings and install an impregnable system. She made it plain the cost was irrelevant where the doctor's safety was concerned."

"Has any of this work been done?"

"Not a thing. Mr. Lowell freely told us he didn't believe Dr. Valdez was in any kind of danger, so the whole thing was a total waste of money. He intended to stonewall until Greta came to her senses."

"Why didn't Valdez didn't go to the local cops?"

Anne chuckled. "He had the best excuse and Mr. Lowell was delighted to quote it verbatim: 'Do not ask me to beg the police for help. I cannot. To do so would make me less of a man.'"

Shaking her head over what this could possibly have to do with Greta Denby's demise, Carol opened her car door into a eucalyptus-infused blanket of midafternoon heat. A welcome breeze wafting up from the cool water of the harbor greeted them as they made their way down the path and she slowed to enjoy it.

Then she ordered herself to focus—she was on a case. It was so rare for her disciplined mind to wander, her whole concentration directed toward establishing *who? how? when? why?* She wondered at the distracting tendrils of thought constantly disrupting her work. What among them was ascendant that she couldn't marshal her thoughts? Madeline raising the issue of euthanasia and long-banished images from the past invading her mind? Sybil and the dilemma she presented?

Carol raised her face to the sun. She loved the warmth soaking into her skin and the way the intense light revealed everything in stark reality. She had always preferred the certainty of sunlight to the ambiguities of darkness. How appropriate, she thought. This affinity for light in a detective whose task it was to reveal the truth hidden in the shadows.

How pretentious, she decided, amusing herself by creating an avatar Carol who strode like a warrior princess into utter darkness, holding aloft a torch as dazzling as the midday sun. She gave her imaginary self a sword of righteousness to brandish...

"What's so amusing?" Anne asked. "It's got to be good, to light up your face like that."

Somewhat embarrassed, Carol wiped the big grin off her face. "Just something I thought of," she said, attempting a dismissive gesture.

But Anne, half-smiling, was looking sideways at her, questioningly. Fortunately, they had reached the end of the path. Carol halted to take in the structure before them. "All that's missing is a moat and drawbridge," she remarked.

It was a storybook version of a castle with a sheer front wall crowned with faux battlements and a crenellated tower. The elaborately carved front door, embellished with brass studs, sustained the medieval illusion. Although the heavy brass knocker was in the shape of a gargoyle's grinning head, a discreet notation above a modern push button read *Please Ring*.

As they waited, Carol said, "I almost expect some ancient, stooped retainer to open the door."

"You're out of luck, Chief Inspector," said a husky female voice behind her. "No ancient, stooped retainers here."

FIVE

"I don't want Carol to sell her house to please me," Sybil Quade declared. "She'll resent it forever if she feels I made her do it."

Aunt Sarah chuckled. "No one can make Carol do anything she doesn't want to, not even you."

Sybil smiled at Carol's aunt, gazing affectionately at the short, stout figure clad in her signature brightly colored overalls. Today's color, an odd shade of reddish-purple, was intensified by the contrast with her halo of white hair which seemed to burst from her scalp with an energy all its own. On her lap sat an entirely different color, the orange-blond ball of fur that was Jeffrey, Sybil's ginger cat, his green eyes half-closed, purring.

"Besides," Aunt Sarah pointed out, "it was Carol's idea that both of you sell your houses and buy one together. A new beginning in neutral territory was how she described it to me."

"I think Carol's regretting she ever made that suggestion. She'd be giving up so much."

"Carol's not the only one making a sacrifice," Aunt Sarah said sharply. The wide, gesturing sweep of her arm drew a complaint from Jeffrey when she brushed his ears. "Look what you'll be losing."

They were sitting in Sybil's sunroom high above the constant line of waves marching toward shore and disintegrating into foam as they met the beige sand. Towering headlands delineated the north and south ends of the beach. At the foot of each headland were worn down, jumbled sandstone boulders, testament to the ocean's relentless assault upon the land.

"I do love this house. But not the way Carol adores Seaforth."

Her expression unusually subdued, her voice pensive, Aunt Sarah said, "I too will be sorry to see it sold. Carol's parents built the house from the foundations up, so it's always been in the family. And Carol's lived a good part of her life there. After her divorce she moved back home to support her mother. Vi took Sid's loss very hard."

Carol had never talked much about her family—understandably, Sybil thought; all of them had been touched by tragedy including Aunt Sarah who, after a tumultuous marriage of some duration, lost her husband in a boating accident. Childless, she had lavished her nurturing ways on Carol and all her passion on the environment. Carol's father had had a sudden, fatal cardiac arrest, his death particularly devastating because he'd appeared to be in excellent health.

Her face creased with remembered sorrow, Aunt Sarah mused, "Grief killed my sister. Vi was diagnosed with breast cancer the year before Sid's heart attack, but she was in remission. With him gone, the cancer came roaring back."

"Carol told me her mother wanted to spend her last days at home," Sybil said, thinking of how Carol must have valued those final hours.

"Sid's life insurance paid for a full-time nurse," said Aunt Sarah, "otherwise it would have been impossible for Carol to continue working. As it was, Vi didn't survive more than a few short weeks."

She blinked away sudden tears. "It's so long ago now, but I can still see her full-time nurse—Leanne was her name—wheeling Vi out onto the back deck so she could drink in the beauty of the bushland. It was for the last time—" She broke off and then said chokingly, "My dear sister died early the next morning, listening to the magpies caroling."

A dark tide of sadness swept over Sybil. What precious memories Carol must have of growing up in her family home in such a beautiful setting, and how hard it must be to think of giving it all up to strangers.

And it's all my fault.

Aloud Sybil said, "I wish from the bottom of my heart I could live in that house. But now I can't even visit. Even after Carol had the place repainted and got all those alterations done and I had intensive therapy..." She shook her head. "I was so sure it was all behind me, the therapy worked and I was free. Now it's come back and I'm in treatment again." She gave Aunt Sarah a bitter smile. "Yes, rationally I know it's all in the past, but at times it seems only yesterday."

Aunt Sarah leaned over to pat Sybil's hand. This was one inconvenience too many for Jeffrey, who leapt off her lap and stalked off. "I understand, and so does Carol. You can't change what that bastard did to you."

Nightmare images of the attack again nibbled at the edge of Sybil's reality. She willed herself to watch the surfers riding the waves into the shore; to concentrate on the soaring gulls, the wisps of cloud in the sun-washed sky. She'd grown adept at banishing Philip Ular from her conscious mind, but all this talk about Carol's Seaforth house had stirred up hideous memories she would give anything to expunge.

Although she'd brought up the issue herself, now she wanted to drop the whole subject. The details of the torture she'd endured seemed at times to be a horror story that happened to somebody else. No matter how hard she fought to keep this illusion, the images still seeped into her consciousness, overcoming any defense she put up. She seemed condemned, forced to live it again, over and over...

She became aware that Aunt Sarah was regarding her with deep concern. "Sybil? Are you okay, dear? You're very pale."

In an attempt at levity, Sybil said, "I'm always pale. It's the Celt in me."

"True, you redheads do have delicate skin. I hope you are using a suitable, ecologically acceptable sunscreen."

Sybil breathed a silent *Thank God!* For the moment, Aunt Sarah had been deflected from concern about Sybil's mental health to her firmly held opinions on naturopathic skin care and how to avoid further sun damage.

Before Sybil could frame a suitable response, Aunt Sarah declared, "Physical health is important, but so is a balanced state of mind. So let's discuss where you are at the moment."

"There's nothing to discuss," Sybil attempted, knowing it was futile.

"It's plain you're still not coping with the fallout from that dreadful experience."

"I should be coping." Sybil looked down at her clenched hands. "I thought I was strong enough. But I was wrong."

Clearly surprised at Sybil's self-denigration, Aunt Sarah sank back in her chair. "There's no way you should be blaming yourself. As I understand it, successfully treating post-traumatic stress can take some time."

"That's what my psychiatrist says."

Too late Sybil recalled that psychiatry was one of the many areas where Aunt Sarah held entrenched opinions.

"Your psychiatrist!" Aunt Sarah's face reflected her abhorrence. "Quacks, every last one of them!"

Feeling obliged to defend her doctor, Sybil said, "Nancy Fitzgerald is highly regarded."

"By whom? Her colleagues? That's no recommendation, considering the whole bunch of them are mad as hatters."

A smile tugged at Sybil's lips. "That's a bit extreme."

"Extreme? By no means. It's outrageous that after all these psychiatrists—how many have there been?—you're back where you started."

"Three," said Sybil. "Dr. Fitzgerald is the third psychiatrist I've seen."

"And I very much hope the last," declared Aunt Sarah, looking militant with her erect posture and clenched fists. "Is she doing you any good? Are you still having flashbacks?"

The very word made Sybil shiver. Flashbacks had proved to be the most disturbing element of PTSD. Wanting to get off the subject, Sybil said neutrally, "Occasionally. It's no big deal."

"That's not good enough. You shouldn't be having them at all." Aunt Sarah rummaged in her capacious pink bag, which carried the emblem of the Eco-Crones and the exhortation, CRONES OF THE WORLD—UNITE!

Finally locating her mobile phone, she said, "I'm going to find you a reputable psychotherapist who specializes in PTSD."

"Thank you for being concerned, but—"

"Don't you argue with me, Sybil. Your psychiatrist has had her chance, and she bungled it. I'll canvass the Crones— they're a wonderful resource. I guarantee someone will know a therapist—*not* a psychiatrist—skilled enough to get you over this post-traumatic thing for good."

Why not? "I suppose it wouldn't hurt," she conceded.

"Wouldn't hurt? It's essential! You stay here in the sunroom and relax. I think better on my feet, so I'll admire your garden while I make a few calls."

Left alone, Sybil rotated her shoulders to relieve the tension that always built up with any discussion of her PTSD. She'd been assured many times that her inability to overcome the symptoms did not reflect weakness of character or lack of resolve, but she couldn't help feeling to some degree she was at fault. Why couldn't she control her own mind? Wasn't it simply a lack of willpower on her part?

Still feeling strung tight as a wire, Sybil shut her eyes to concentrate on the rhythmic, muted sounds of the waves breaking on the beach. She felt her muscles relaxing as she pictured herself standing ankle-deep in the foaming water of a gentle surf, watching it run up the sand with a soft hiss, then flow back to join the next incoming wave.

She heard Aunt Sarah downstairs and then a door slammed. *A door...the front door.*

With a sudden, sickening jolt of fear, Sybil found herself sliding into the loop of images she had fought so hard to obliterate. It was no help to know it was a trick of her mind, a dramatization of a traumatic experience in the past that was over and finished. Nothing could stop the horror movie unwinding with terrible inevitability behind her closed eyes...

A beautiful morning. Bright sunlight pouring onto the back deck, birds singing in the trees, a breeze wafting up the cliff from the blue-green water of the harbor.

Carol's gone to supervise final details of a trap to capture a serial killer, also to attend the funeral of one of his victims. Sybil's connection to the suspect—they'd discussed her being in possible danger. Carol's convinced he's taken the bait and is about to strike on the other side of Sydney. So no warning, no premonition.

Suddenly realizing she'll be late if she doesn't get a move on. Jamming her supplies for school into a canvas tote. Checking there's food and water in the cat bowls. Snatching up her car keys. Hurrying to the front door.

Opening it to a man in faded jeans and a T-shirt reading DAVE'S FENCING. In one hand a battered toolbox, in the other a heavy silver revolver. He smiles at her gasp of recognition. "Hello, Sybil. Quite a surprise, eh?"

Trying to slam the door in his face. But he's too fast, shoving it so hard she's driven back a step. He pitches the toolbox into the hallway and steps inside. Evades her wild swing with the canvas tote. Seizes it, tosses it to the floor.

Trying to turn to run, but he has one arm around her shoulders in a parody of an embrace and the gun jabbed hard into her ribs. "One sound, and I'll blow you away."

Pushing the front door closed with his foot. "You're going to walk down the hall, slowly, with me right behind you. Cooperate, and maybe I won't hurt you."

Helpless terror closes her throat. Knowing he's killed so many without mercy, knowing it's pointless to try and talk him around. Her sole hope to seize any opportunity, however slight, to get away from this monster.

As if she's spoken aloud, he says, "Don't even think of trying to escape. You're not going anywhere."

"What do you want?" Making an effort to keep her voice steady.

"Revenge," his cheerful reply. "Surely that's clear to everyone by now?" Picking up his toolbox, prodding her. "Walk."

Him right behind her, the revolver pressed against her spine. They reach the sitting room, halting. "What now?"

Putting a hand on her shoulder, spinning her around. "You'll learn who's boss." Raking the barrel of the gun across her face.

Pain blossoms, filling her eyes with tears. Her nose gushing red blood. The cold metal of handcuffs securing her wrists.

"Down on the floor, legs straight out."

Shoving her into a sitting position on the rug, her back against the couch. Dizzy, nauseated, forcing her chaotic thoughts into some semblance of clarity. What options does she have? Even if there's something close by she could use as a weapon, getting to her feet is an impossibility. And now he's handcuffed her.

A loud scream? She'll only have time for one. The house next door isn't close, will Jenny even hear? Somewhere she's read that shouting "Fire!" got an instant response. As soon as he's distracted...

"In case you're wondering," he says, "I've already called your school and told them you're too sick to teach." Rummaging in the toolbox, coming up with a brown glass bottle. Unscrewing the top. "Just a little medicine to make you feel better."

Amused when she presses her lips together and shakes her head. "Don't be like that. Just a few drops, to begin with."

Keeping her mouth clamped shut. All humor vanishing from his face. "Refusal isn't in my game plan. If I have to hurt you, I will."

"Sybil? Sybil? *Sybil!*"

She could feel Aunt Sarah shaking her shoulder. The images shattered and whirled away and the comforting textures of the real world came rushing back. She managed to say in a shaky voice, "I'm okay."

"A flashback?"

She tried to smile. "Dr. Fitzgerald calls them episodes."

"Forget about Dr. Fitzgerald," Aunt Sarah said with a dismissive flick of her fingers. "The Crones, as always, have come through. I have the perfect therapist for you—Jayleen

Smith. I've left a message, asking her to schedule an appointment ASAP."

"Jayleen Smith?" Sybil frowned. "I know that name…"

"A little trouble with the law," said Aunt Sarah airily. "Don't give it a thought. The important thing is that this is the therapist who has the skill to make you whole."

"What sort of trouble?"

"A citizen exercising her rights. Nothing to do with her therapy practice."

With deep misgiving, Sybil said, "Carol isn't going to approve, is she?"

"I'd be astonished if she did," said Aunt Sarah with a laugh.

SIX

"Chief Inspector Ashton, I'm Thalia Denby." She extended her hand and gave Carol's a firm shake, then turned to Anne with a welcoming smile. "And Sergeant Newsome. So nice to see you again."

Madeline had described Thalia Denby as a knockout, and Carol could see why. Striking rather than beautiful, she had a slim, athletic body, black curly hair, a strong angular face requiring little makeup, with definite eyebrows arched over dark eyes and a full-lipped, sensual mouth. She wore white shorts with a magenta top and high-heeled sandals.

Even in this brief exchange with her, Carol could feel the force of the woman's physical magnetism and almost palpable charm. "Thank you Ms. Denby, for making time to see us at such short notice."

"Please call me Thalia." She added, playfully, "Naturally, I will show the proper respect and continue to refer to you as Chief Inspector Ashton."

Having come up from behind them, Thalia didn't invite them into the house, as Carol expected. "It's a gorgeous day, so we're having coffee on the terrace."

Broad stone steps led to a matching stone balcony that ran around the side of the house and down to a slate terrace. Shaded by a large umbrella, a handsome dark green cast-iron table with matching chairs was arranged to give the best possible view of an inlet of Sydney's sparkling blue-green harbor, Mosman Bay.

Sprawled on one of the chairs was a masculine version of Thalia Denby. He, too, was thin and had curly dark hair; however, it fell raggedly over his ears and down to his collar. The lines of his face were softer and his mouth held a discontented droop.

"My brother, Kenny," said Thalia.

Looking him over, Carol thought: *You certainly haven't dressed to impress.*

His once white T-shirt was stained and threadbare, his tattered blue jeans stiff with dirt. He wore a single flip-flop. Its mate, useless because of a broken strap, lay discarded under the table.

Perhaps I'm supposed to see this faux poverty as endearing little boy grubbiness. Then, wryly amused with herself: *Don't get complicated. Maybe he's just a natural slob.*

He raised one hand in a casual wave. "Hi. Forgive me if I don't get up."

Thalia said with an enigmatic smile, "As you can see, he's the ne'er-do-well of the family."

"Saint Thalia," said Kenny, putting his hands together as if praying, "forgive me my sins, oh patron saint of hypocrisy."

Ignoring her brother's remark, Thalia said to Carol, "Please enjoy the view."

"It is lovely," said Anne, walking to the sandstone balustrade at the edge of the terrace. Carol silently agreed, gazing at a vista of bushland and deep green water. The wake of a ferry departing from the wharf at the head of the little bay sent ripples to the shore. The sun was warm on Carol's shoulders, its heat tempered by a light sea breeze.

In contrast to the peaceful scene, tension was crackling between brother and sister. There seemed no sign of grief in them over so profound a loss as a mother, but she of all people knew appearances could vary in the extreme when it came to grief. She and Anne returned to the table as Kenny said something to Thalia in a low voice.

"Go to hell!" she snarled. Her face was flushed, whether from anger or embarrassment Carol couldn't tell. Glowering at her brother, she snatched up what proved to be a small wireless intercom. "Bea, please bring the coffee."

Carol deliberately took the chair next to Kenny. He gave her a lazy grin. "So you're the famous Carol Ashton." He looked her up and down. "Not bad."

Carol recalled Ian Rooke's brief notes made after his initial meeting with Thalia's brother: *Kenny (Ken?) seems cooperative in manner but deflects questions—manipulative—unreliable witness—has never held down a job—calls himself an entrepreneur—allowance funds various schemes—little success so far.*

"I understand you're an entrepreneur, Mr. Denby?"

Carol's cool question wiped the lazy smile off his face. He straightened in his chair. "That's right."

"An entrepreneur?" Thalia scoffed. "Kenny and my mother are the only ones who ever thought so. And she was beginning to have her doubts."

Anger washed across his face, but before he could respond his sister said, "Here's Bea. Let's not quarrel in front of her. You know how upset she gets."

A stocky middle-aged woman dressed entirely in black, a stern expression on her broad face, was approaching with a tray and a determined gait from the other end of the terrace.

Carol regarded her with interest. She knew that Beatrice Parker, Greta Denby's live-in nurse-companion, had discovered the body when she'd gone into the bedroom to wake her patient for breakfast. Ian Rooke's notes indicated that Bea, as she was known to the family, had quickly agreed to stay on for the next six months to help run the household and to deal with the fallout from Greta Denby's death.

Bea Parker slid the tray, laden with china cups, a silver coffeepot and a plate of assorted pastries, onto the cast-iron table. She acknowledged Anne with a nod. When Thalia introduced

Carol, the woman's doughy face remained impassive. "I've heard of you," was all she said.

When everyone had coffee, she indicated the pastries. "Freshly baked," she said, then added, as if ready to be challenged, "I've just made them."

Out of politeness, Carol took the smallest. Just as her mouth was full of raspberry scone, Bea Parker said to her, "I suppose you'll be wanting to speak with me."

The timing, Carol knew, had been quite deliberate. She finished consuming her mouthful and replied evenly, "That would be very helpful."

"Helpful? Is that what you call it?" Her resentment undisguised, Bea went on, "I've already been as helpful as I can possibly be. I told that other inspector, the one who died, everything I knew, which wasn't much. Makes no sense to answer the same questions all over again."

"I know it's an inconvenience," Carol said, "but I'm afraid circumstances have made it necessary."

Kenny gave a snort of laughter. "The circumstances being that the last cop did a Thelma-and-Louise dive off a cliff."

Carol channeled her wrath into a tight grip on her coffee cup. She did not have to look at Anne to know she would be struggling with her own anger. How had this kid survived this long with his punch-me-in-the-face insolence?

"Tsk, tsk!" Bea Parker gave him a small, indulgent smile. "You know very well, Kenny, in the movie those girls committed deliberate suicide. Inspector Rooke, poor man, died in a horrible accident."

He raised a shoulder in a half-shrug. "Whatever."

The nurse's smile faded as she shifted her attention back to Carol. "I'll be in the kitchen if you want me. But I'm warning you, I don't have anything new to add to what I said before. So it'll be a waste of your time."

"Good old Bea," said Kenny, watching her walk away. "Tells it like it is. But if you cops are expecting the truth from Bea about Mum, you're in for a disappointment."

"Don't believe a word my brother says, Chief Inspector. Kenny's a congenital liar. When you interview him, please remember that." Thalia raised her coffee cup in a mocking toast. "Here's to duplicitous brothers."

Kenny Denby mimicked her gesture. "I'll drink to that." He turned to Carol with a naughty little-boy smile. "Thalia's trying to discredit me before you ask a single question."

Carol raised her eyebrows. "Why would that be?"

"Surely it's clear, even to you. Classic misdirection. She intends to cast me as the chief suspect, when it was Thalia herself who murdered Mum."

With a dismissive wave at her brother, Thalia smiled thinly at Carol. "Welcome to the Denby family."

* * *

"Ms. Parker?" Carol said softly to avoid startling the woman.

Bea Parker turned from the kitchen sink where she had been washing her hands. Her expression was instantly hostile, her body language—feet planted, thick body braced against an expected attack—made it obvious to Carol that the defiance she displayed in front of the Denby children had not been purely for their benefit. Greta's nurse had very little intention of being cooperative with anyone.

With a baleful glare at Carol, she said, "So you've chosen to waste your time, and mine too." Giving a nod in Anne's direction, she went on, "She was present at my interview. She could fill you in on the details."

Carol said pleasantly, "I would prefer to have those details directly from you. May we sit down?"

"If you like, but I've got a meal to prepare. I can only spare a few minutes."

The kitchen reminded Carol of the one in her aunt's cottage in the Blue Mountains. This one was far more elaborate, with exposed beams, copper utensils suspended on metal hooks and a terra-cotta tiled floor artfully sloped to ensure that when washed, the water would flow into the depression that held the drainage grate. But the meticulous replicas of the stove, refrigerator, and porcelain sink with draining board, together with the heavy wooden table and substantial wooden chairs, re-created a kitchen belonging to the first half of the twentieth century. No matter how true to the past it appeared, Carol had no doubt that the innards of the stove and refrigerator were state-of-the-art, and that if she opened the old-style cupboard doors she would find all the latest culinary accoutrements.

With bad grace, Bea Parker gestured Carol and Anne to the table. A weighty kitchen chair screeched against the tile floor as she pulled it out. "Well?" she said, sitting down and folding her hands in her lap. "I haven't got all day."

Taking a seat across from her, Carol said, "You found the body at eight o'clock?"

The nurse blinked at Carol's blunt approach. "I found Greta, yes. I took over from Iris fifteen minutes early because Greta had mentioned it was an important day and she wanted my help to prepare for it."

Anticipating Carol's question, she added, "And don't bother asking. I have no idea why Greta said it was an important day."

She glowered at both Carol and Anne as if preparing herself for her next words. "Iris told me Greta had slept right through after her midnight meds and was still asleep. I went in to wake her for breakfast, and found she had passed away."

"Did you touch her?"

"How else would I know she was dead?"

"Was her skin still warm?"

"I don't recall."

That's one lie. "Did you touch anything on the bedside table?"

The nurse glared at Carol. "What are you implying? That I tampered with a crime scene?"

Carol said smoothly, "But at that time you didn't know it was a crime scene, did you? So if you saw something that was out of place—a pillbox, a piece of paper, a note—I would expect you to pick it up."

"There was no note, no nothing. And I didn't touch anything."

"But you *did* touch the body?"

A reluctant nod.

"Although you can't recall if your employer's skin was warm or cold."

Carol's reference to "employer" was intended to anger Bea Parker, and it succeeded.

Her cheeks flushed, she exclaimed, "My *employer*? I was much more than nurse and companion! I was Greta's *friend*!"

"She would discuss personal problems with you?"

"Of course. To Greta, I was a member of the family."

"Did you discuss any particular worries she had in the last week of her life?"

"No," she said evenly.

The sudden spurt of anger had dissipated too quickly. Carol changed the subject. "Iris Kemp had been on duty since the evening before?"

In this familiar territory Bea Parker became more expansive. "Her shift was eight to eight. Greta had an intercom by her bed, and all she needed to do was press a button if she needed a magazine to read, or a hot drink—just minor things. For anything serious, Iris was instructed to wake me immediately."

"By serious, you mean medical issues?"

"Iris has no nursing qualifications. In fact, no qualifications of any kind." Bea Parker's coarse features reflected the derision in her voice. "If Greta complained of pain or couldn't sleep, I would give her the appropriate medications according to my instructions." She added irritably, "And yes, of course I kept meticulous records. I had to. That doctor of hers was forever changing what she took."

"And Iris Kemp had no reason to wake you that particular night?"

Pointing at Anne, Bea Parker snapped, "Ask her. She took my statement. It's all there. Of course she woke me. To administer the midnight meds. Then I went to bed, I went back to sleep, I got up in the morning and discovered Greta had died. I'm not going through every detail again."

"We'll return to that later," said Carol, knowing that once she had time to look more closely at the preliminary statements of those who had been in the house that night and the next morning, she would have many more questions for everyone. "I take it Mrs. Denby was completely bedridden?"

"No. But she could not get out of bed or go to the bathroom without assistance."

The interview continued with Bea Parker brusquely providing basic information: her nursing qualifications; how long she had been the live-in nurse-companion for Greta Denby, her daily routine.

"These were all prescribed by Dr. Valdez?" Carol asked.

"Yes. I followed his directions precisely. However much they changed."

"Do you have an opinion about the doctor's somewhat controversial treatments?"

The nurse grimaced. "Greta totally believed Dr. Valdez had saved her life once, and could do it again. I was in no position to judge whether or not this was true. As far as I'm concerned, the jury's still out."

After painstakingly establishing the prescription drugs and other treatments Greta had been taking, her daily dosage schedule, the location of all the medications, and who had access to them, Carol turned to a question she'd noticed hadn't been asked in the earlier interview.

"How was it you obtained this position with the Denby family?"

The chair creaked as Bea Parker shifted her bulk. "By recommendation. For clients of this standing, it's the only acceptable way."

"May I ask who recommended you?"

"Mr. Lowell," she snapped. "I suppose you know who he is."

"I've already spoken with the family lawyer," Carol said. "How was it that Mr. Lowell knew you well enough to be confident you would be suitable for the position?"

The nurse immediately bristled. "There was nothing underhanded about it."

Anne looked up from the notes she was taking. She seemed as intrigued as Carol by this defensive reply.

After a moment's silence Bea Parker said, "Fred knew me because I worked for his brother Will."

Hiding her amusement at the casual use of "Fred" to refer to the very patrician Frederick Lowell, Carol asked, "It was a position similar to the one with the Denby family?"

Carol noted the nurse's demeanor had changed. A moment before she had been full of prickly indignation. Now her expression was bland, her overall manner down-to-earth as she said, "Will's wife, Ellen, was well advanced with Alzheimer's. She needed constant supervision."

"But when this job came up, you were available. How did that come about?"

"Ellen passed away about the time that Fred was looking for a nurse-companion for Greta."

Carol thought: *She's rehearsed these answers.* "Your patient succumbed to Alzheimer's?"

Bea Parker clasped her hands and leaned forward, deeply sincere. "A tragic accident. Ellen was easily confused and had problems with balance. She fell down a flight of stairs. Hit her head. Died instantly."

Anne and Carol exchanged a look. Anne too had picked up that the nurse's responses were well-prepared, even if her dramatic skills were not up to the task.

At Carol's slight nod, Anne took over the questioning. "Your patient was fatally injured while she was under your supervision?"

"Ellen wasn't under my direct supervision at the time," she said with emphasis.

Just like Greta Denby, Carol thought.

"She was not my responsibility during my afternoon break. Her husband took over her care for the thirty minutes I was off duty. He thought she was sleeping, and was on the phone when he heard Ellen scream, then the dreadful sound of her falling down the stairs." She added dolefully, "Poor Will. I don't think he'll ever forgive himself." To reinforce the heartbreaking circumstances, the nurse maintained a mournful expression as she shook her head.

Carol wished she could share her thought with Anne: *Forget the theater audition, Bea—I'd hang on to my day job if I were you.* She did look over at Anne, who was studiously straight-faced as she made a note. "Let's move on, Sergeant Newsome."

Anne referred to her notes. "After you left the terrace this afternoon, Kenneth Denby indicated that we would be disappointed if we expected that you would tell us the truth about his mother's death."

"That's Kenny." Bea Parker wore the same indulgent smile Carol had noticed earlier. "He says the first thing that comes to his mind. You shouldn't take him seriously."

"Even when he states—" Anne broke off to turn over a page in her notebook. "Quote: 'It was Thalia herself who murdered Mum.'"

The nurse shrugged. "Kenny's having fun at your expense. He's jerking you around. Can't you see that?"

"What I can see," said Carol, "is that Mr. Denby appears to be taking his mother's death rather lightly."

Her cool observation wiped the smile off the nurse's face. "What are you insinuating? That Kenny doesn't care?" Indignation mottled her cheeks. "Nothing could be further from the truth. Kenny was shattered by Greta's passing. What you see isn't him. What he shows to the world isn't him. He grieves in private. Why, the night after Greta died, Kenny cried in my arms, and—" She broke off abruptly, her look of chagrin suggesting she had said too much.

Deciding not to pursue this issue for the moment, Carol said, "On another matter, because of your profession, I imagine you feel a special obligation toward your patients."

Carol's polite inquiry elicited an impatient snort. "Of course I feel a special obligation. Are you suggesting I've failed in my professional duties?"

"By no means. However, Greta Denby did die in suspicious circumstances."

The nurse sat back in her chair and looked at Carol with weary contempt. "They're only suspicious circumstances because you people make them so. You're as bad as the others, trying to turn Greta's death into some great mystery you're going to solve."

"It's not a mystery to you?" Carol offered in a tone of mild surprise.

"I think that doctor did it accidentally with that stuff he was making her take. She was taking frequent doses of his special concoction. He bumped up her vitamins or whatever he claims he gave her and maybe he even mixed in some Nembutal and called it a vitamin—who knows? And her system couldn't take it anymore."

"Yet he was the one to call for an autopsy."

"Nothing he's ever done has ever made any sense to me," she said in the same weary tone. "Why should this be any different?"

Carol said, "I don't believe you mentioned this scenario to Inspector Rooke and Sergeant Newsome when they first interviewed you."

"In fact, Ms. Parker," Anne broke in to say, "you stated that you had no idea what had happened." She glanced at her notes, then continued, "Your actual words were: 'I last saw Greta alive at midnight. I went to my room and didn't leave it until the next morning. I don't know how or why Greta died. That's all I can tell you.'"

"How do you explain this discrepancy?" Carol asked, expecting another prepared answer. And it came:

"I was the one to discover Greta's body. Frankly, I was in shock, and couldn't put my thoughts in order." As she had before, she clasped her hands and leaned forward, saying earnestly, "I've nursed many very sick patients, so it could only be expected that some have passed away while under my care. But because Greta had become a close friend as well as a patient, her death was a particular blow to me, so much so that I couldn't think straight."

"And now, when you've recovered your equilibrium," Carol said with a touch of skepticism, "you have the sudden insight that it's Dr. Valdez who did this, is that what you're saying?"

"When I consider all the possibilities, it's the only explanation. Greta hadn't been sleeping well, was very fatigued. But hopeful, even so, right to the end. She never lost faith in him but I believe he'd gone panicky over his treatment."

"An interesting hypothesis, but you gave her her last medications," Carol pointed out.

"Yes, that he'd changed so many times—" Then Bea Parker slammed a hand on the table. "Are you insinuating that *I* did this?"

"Just asking how Dr. Valdez would manage what you're saying."

"Well, it's your job to figure it out, isn't it?"

"So this is simply your opinion. You offer no supporting evidence?"

Annoyed by Carol's clear skepticism, Bea Parker snapped, "It is my *professional* opinion from observing Greta. As such, it has more weight than most."

"Did Frederick Lowell tell you he believed Inspector Rooke had already decided Kenneth Denby was materially involved in his mother's death?"

She hesitated, then said, "He may have mentioned it."

"And it was about this time you came to the conclusion that Dr. Valdez was the explanation?"

Shaking her head, Bea Parker said firmly, "There was absolutely no connection."

"This is not an attempt to protect Kenneth Denby?"

"Protect Kenny? That's ridiculous. There's nothing to protect him from. He didn't do anything. I didn't do anything. End of story."

"You were the last person to see her alive."

Bea Parker's face darkened. Then her eyes grew damp.

Carol looked at her, wondering if her angry demeanor might simply be a protective veneer over grief. "And Thalia Denby—what about her?"

After another long pause as the nurse gathered herself, she said, "Thalia was always closest to her father—Greta told me that time and again. Thalia and Greta had some issues. That's all I care to say." She got to her feet. "I've no more time to give you."

Outside the kitchen as they walked back toward the terrace, Anne said to Carol, "Wow, nice little slip in the knife job on Thalia."

"Yes," said Carol, "and add that to Kenny's accusation—even though he claimed he was only joking—and Thalia seems to be the suspect de jour." Not to mention, she thought wryly, the consensus vote of the psychics besieging *The Shipley Report*.

"Maybe Bea and Kenny are working together," said Anne, "so Thalia takes the fall."

"Fall? That reminds me of Nurse Parker's unfortunate patient who fell down the stairs and broke her neck. Check it out, Anne. I have a feeling Nurse Parker may have been a little careless with the truth."

SEVEN

"Mother's bedroom," said Thalia, opening the door and ushering Carol and Anne into the airy, light-filled room where Greta Denby had died.

"I personally tidied up after your crime scene people had finished with everything. They took a lot of Mother's personal things and all her medications—even the aspirin and eye drops in the bathroom cabinet. I'd like to know when they'll be returning her laptop. There are irreplaceable personal photos and videos on it."

"If it contains material evidence, it may be some time," Carol said.

"Material evidence? On my mother's computer?" Thalia's full lips curved into a disbelieving smile. "If you're hoping to find anything like that, I'm afraid you're going to be very disappointed."

Carol hadn't seen any mention of a laptop in Rooke's notes, nor in the list of evidentiary items removed from the crime scene. She raised a quizzical eyebrow at Anne, who responded with an affirmative nod. Carol made a mental note to call Liz Carey, head of the SOC team.

"What a charming room this is," she said to Thalia.

Carol had examined the crime scene photographs and a floor plan of the suite and already knew that adjacent to the bedroom was a lavishly appointed bathroom and a dressing room and walk-in wardrobe, so she had expected the suite to be luxurious. But she was not prepared for its warm, welcoming atmosphere. French doors opened onto a stone balcony crowded with greenery in ceramic pots. The fronds of delicate ferns trembled in a gentle breeze blowing from the harbor. Even a quick glance confirmed that the view of Mosman Bay from this third-floor balcony was spectacular. The pale blond furniture looked sculpted, each piece obviously handcrafted. Carol particularly admired an elegant rolltop desk and its graceful chair. "That's beautiful," she said, moving toward it.

"It is lovely, isn't it?" Thalia, following, ran her hand sensuously along the chair's curved back. "It's polished until the wood is smooth as silk. Made to my mother's specifications. She designed every piece of furniture, with one exception." She gestured at the white-and-chrome bulk of the hospital bed, which stood in stark contrast to the refined accoutrements of the room.

"It became a necessity in the last few months. Mother was debilitated by the new regimen Dr. Valdez prescribed for her."

Carol veered away tactically from the obvious follow-up question about the new regimen to observe, "It surprises me a little that Dr. Eduardo Valdez prefers to be called Dr. Ed. It's not a name that rings with authority."

"You're not the first to make that observation. Eduardo always has the same answer and I can quote him verbatim. 'People today don't want authority figures, they want friends. And that's what I am, Dr. Ed, a physician who is also a friend to all my patients.'"

Anne said with the trace of a scoff, "I've heard that Dr. Ed has ambitions to be a media star."

Thalia's contralto laugh was infectious. Carol found herself smiling too as she said to Thalia, "It's rather a leap from pioneering cancer specialist to media celebrity."

"Eduardo is nothing if not ambitious. It's rather disarming, really. At the moment he has one small clinic in Switzerland and one just underway in Barcelona. His vision is to establish from these two little footprints a chain of international treatment centers where the success of his innovative cancer treatments will bring him further fame and fortune. My mother, as I'm sure you know, agreed to finance the clinic here in Australia."

"Mr. Lowell explained to me how the foundation your mother established will be providing funds to set up and run his clinic."

Carol was fascinated to see white-hot rage—a split-second flash—on Thalia's face. But Thalia continued in her amused but faintly derisive tone, "As for Dr. Ed, media star, Eduardo Valdez pictures himself taking America by storm. He's actually looking for a ghostwriter for his future best seller, *Dr. Ed's Recipe for Health and Long Life*. He'll have to come up with something a lot snappier than that."

Carol said, "How did you feel about Dr. Valdez? Were you confident his treatment would be effective in helping your mother overcome her cancer a second time?"

Any trace of humor vanishing from her face, Thalia shook her head. "Kenny was the smart one. Kenny never believed it would work. But he kept quiet, knowing it would upset Mother if she knew what he thought. At the beginning I was very hopeful, but two months ago, when Mother began to suffer nausea and fatigue to the point that she had to spend most of her time in bed, I admit I lost faith."

"Your mother knew this?"

"She heard me arguing with Eduardo. I wanted the top Australian oncologist for ovarian cancer, Dennis O'Malley, to give a second opinion. Not surprisingly, Eduardo was totally opposed. And as I soon found out, so was my mother. It was very clear she trusted Eduardo completely, nothing I could say would change her mind. Drop the subject, she told me, and never mention it again." Thalia spread her hands in a gesture of defeat. "So I gave up. I know I shouldn't have."

"I don't know that you could have done anything against your mother's will. By this point she was very ill?"

Thalia looked directly into Carol's eyes. "Have you had someone close to you die, little by little, day by day?"

"Yes."

Disconcerted by Carol's response, Thalia frowned. The silence that followed was broken by Anne. "In this situation, some people consider euthanasia a way to end pointless suffering."

Her words fell like stones. Carol felt as if her heart had stilled, her breath trapped in her throat. She heard: *"Please darling, it would be so easy."* Her own mother's whispered voice. And her own: *"No!"*

Anne was speaking. Carol forced herself to listen. "...so it appears the last person to see your mother alive was Bea Parker."

Carol focused on the planes of Thalia's arresting face. She was saying, "Iris took over from Bea at eight that evening. Mother was asleep. When Eduardo and I came by an hour later, she was wide awake and waiting for a toasted cheese sandwich Iris was making for her. Bea gave her the last scheduled meds at midnight."

Anne said, "When her services were not needed, Ms. Kemp spent her time in another room. Is that correct?"

"Yes, we'd set up a sitting room for Iris, with television, computer access, a small kitchen and her own bathroom."

"How did they communicate?" Carol heard herself ask.

"Two ways," said Thalia. "A button by the bed rang a bell in Iris's room, or Mother could use a wireless intercom to speak with Iris. It's the same as the one you saw me using on the terrace."

"Perhaps I could have a demonstration?"

"Of course."

Anne remained in the bedroom to operate the bell and intercom. Greta's suite dead-ended a long hallway and Carol noted the movement sensor mentioned in Rooke's notes. It would turn on lights automatically, if it were operational, as soon as anyone stepped into the hallway. Rooke had noted the switch in the off position. Perhaps not to disturb a sleeping Greta Denby, Carol reasoned. Or perhaps for another reason.

Iris Kemp's room was next to Greta's suite, only a few meters away. At the door, Carol asked Thalia if Iris Kemp had instructions to leave it open or closed.

"I've no idea. Why?"

"If it were open, it would be possible for her to see anyone approaching your mother's suite."

"Iris didn't say she saw anyone after Eduardo and me." Thalia opened the door. "At a guess, I'd say she kept this closed, particularly when the TV was on in case it disturbed my mother."

Carol had read Iris Kemp's initial statement. She confirmed that Thalia had looked in on her mother at eight and returned an hour later accompanied by Dr. Valdez, and Greta had been awake and sitting up in bed. Iris had served Greta her snack, provided coffee for everyone, then had gone back to her room. She didn't know exactly when Thalia and Valdez had left. When she came to collect the coffee mugs, the visitors had gone and Greta was asleep. She heard Bea come in at midnight.

Iris had checked on Greta at regular intervals throughout the night. She couldn't say exactly how many times she'd looked in to find her charge sleeping peacefully. When Iris was asked if it were possible she had dozed off at any time during the night, she had stated indignantly that she had remained awake and on duty. There had been no mention in the statement of the door to her room being open or closed.

Iris Kemp's room was small, but nicely furnished. There was no bed, but the reclining chair facing the flat-screen TV was well-padded and comfortable. Carol thought how easy it would be to relax in the chair and drift off to sleep in the long, silent hours of night. However, when Anne rang the bell from the other room, the harsh jangle was loud enough to convince Carol that it would jolt Iris awake if she had been dozing.

The intercom was equally efficient. Anne's voice was amplified above a normal speaking level, and would be next to impossible to ignore.

"So Iris should be in this sitting room, or tending to your mother in the bedroom. Would there ever be a reason for her to leave this area during the night?"

"None at all," said Thalia. "Iris knew that if there were an emergency, she was to call Bea immediately. Then, if necessary, Bea would contact Eduardo, Kenny, or me."

Thalia at her side, Carol returned to Greta's suite and walked into the dressing room directly adjacent to the bathroom. It was a deep room separated by a partial wall, half of it presumably once used by the deceased Harland Denby and now taken over by Greta Denby's vast collection of clothes, shoes, and hats.

Carol was primarily interested in the dressing room shelf by the entrance, converted, according to the crime scene photos, into the staging area for Greta's various treatments. One of those photos had shown a large, multichambered plastic pill dispenser on this shelf, collected into evidence by SOC. From the size of the compartments, Greta took many pills at the set hourly intervals noted on each chamber of the dispenser, and recorded on a chart, also taken into evidence. The number of pills in the dispenser compared with the remaining levels in the pill bottles checked out exactly, matched the records exactly. So Greta's fatal dose, administered by someone between midnight and four a.m., had come in from outside. Somehow.

She checked the view of the grounds from the window of the suite. She'd memorized the main details of a site map, and realized she was looking down at the drive leading to the extensive garage at the rear of the house.

She mused, "A person standing here could observe all vehicles coming and going from the garage."

"Not mine," Thalia said with a faint smile. "I don't park my car there."

Before Carol could ask why, a strikingly handsome man strode confidently into the room. "Thalia, here you are. We can't be late, you know, for the rehearsal. Not even fashionably late." He switched his attention to Carol and Anne. "Hello!"

"Eduardo." Thalia's tone was hardly welcoming. She turned to Carol. "Allow me to introduce Dr. Eduardo Valdez, also known as Dr. Ed. Dr. Ed, this is Chief Inspector Ashton. You of course remember Sergeant Newsome."

"Dr. Valdez," said Carol, extending her hand.

He flashed a very white smile as he enclosed her hand in the moist warmth of his. "Chief Inspector Ashton! What a pleasure it is to meet you. A true pleasure. And to see you again as well," he said to Anne.

He had a charming accent, glowing dark eyes, black hair, and olive skin. The cut of his dark gray suit was subtly foreign enough to add a touch of the exotic. Valdez was a little shorter than Carol, but he stood tall, spine straight and shoulders back. She wondered if he wore lifts in his shoes.

"Thank you, Dr. Valdez," Carol said drily. "It's rare to have someone express quite that degree of pleasure when meeting us in our official capacity."

The doctor's smile disappeared. "Yes, Greta's death is, of course, a tragedy. And a mystery. I have not the slightest doubt about your ability to solve that mystery expeditiously."

"Thank you, again, Dr. Valdez. It would be of help if you could make yourself available to go over your initial statement with me and clarify some areas where I have questions."

His warm smile returning, he said, "Anything I can do to help. Unfortunately, the earliest I can make myself available is Tuesday morning."

He gave Thalia an even warmer smile. "Thalia and I will be fully involved in carrying out Greta's wishes, overseeing the fundraising and awareness week for Greta's foundation, The Greta Denby Safe Haven. Tonight is the gala opening."

Carol was amused to see how he ostentatiously displayed his gold Rolex as he checked the time. "Under the circumstances, Thalia, you really should change your mind and arrive early in case there are any unexpected problems," he chided. "As you know, with so many volunteers involved, things can go wrong."

Her face was a cold, expressionless mask. "Eduardo, you really can be a proper bastard."

He raised his eyebrows and conferred on her an indulgent smile.

She turned to Carol and surveyed her with a bold, lengthy, admiring, unmistakable gaze. "Please stay as long as you like. I hope you don't mind seeing yourself out."

Watching Thalia's retreating back, Valdez said, "She is fire and ice. Yes?"

When Carol remained silent, still absorbing Thalia's potent stare, he said, "You think me impossibly romantic? I have hopes that Thalia will become my wife."

* * *

"Did you catch Thalia's micro-expression?" Carol asked Anne as they walked along the gravel drive that ran below Greta's balcony. "When I mentioned the foundation her mother had set up for Valdez's clinic."

"No, I missed it. At a guess I'd say it wasn't overwhelming happiness."

"Pure rage."

Anne valued such revelations as much as she did. Only a trained interrogator could pick up some of these lightning-fast facial expressions that were involuntary, reflecting intense emotion, impossible to fake. Surprise, sadness, happiness, disgust, contempt, anger, fear—all flashed across the subjects' faces with a swiftness that was revealed only in slow-motion film. The majority of law enforcement bodies had yet to develop interrogation techniques to analyze and capitalize on micro-expressions and similar phenomena.

"So what sparked Thalia's response?" Anne asked.

"Take your pick. I'd mentioned Frederick Lowell, Thalia's mother, the clinic's foundation."

"My money's on the clinic and the smiling Dr. Ed," Anne said. "He's almost too good to be true—handsome and personable and a life-saving doctor to boot. And don't forget that Spanish accent."

"If we take his words at face value, he has ambitions to marry Thalia," Carol said. "As I recall, there was some talk of Dr. Valdez marrying Greta Denby."

Anne rolled her eyes. "That has to be a joke. No one can be that shallow."

Carol shrugged.

"She inconveniently dies, so the good doctor switches to her daughter," Anne mocked. "Even if the doctor's delusional enough to believe it, think there's a chance in hell Thalia will cooperate?"

"When it freezes over," Carol replied, remembering Thalia's account of her efforts to wrench her mother from Valdez's influence and her savage reaction to his mild request that she arrive early at the fundraiser. And the clear implication in that stare she'd focused on Carol.

They halted and looked up to the third floor location of Greta's suite. In keeping with a storybook castle theme, the sandstone wall was crowned with an elaborate stone parapet.

"It wouldn't be all that hard for an expert climber." Anne indicated a point directly above the bedroom's balcony. "Gain access to the roof, secure your rope, play it out gently until it reaches the third floor, clamber down, drop silently onto the balcony, through the French windows and you're home." She grinned at Carol. "Simple, really."

"If you're Spiderman. Or, you could just walk along the hall and through the bedroom door."

"There's that," Anne conceded with a grin. "So long as he or she manages to get past Iris Kemp. She's very gregarious. When I interviewed her, it was difficult to keep her on track."

"I'd like to see Iris Kemp as soon as possible, Anne. I'll be available any time she—"

Engine roaring, a red Porsche convertible came skidding around the corner of the house throwing up a spray of gravel, and braked to a stop beside them.

"Hey," said Kenny, raising his gold-rimmed sunglasses to peer at her. "How's the detecting going, Chief Inspector? Arrested anyone yet?"

"I have some questions for you, Mr. Denby. When will you be available?"

"I'm really not sure." He gave Carol a cheeky smile. "I'll call you."

"We'll set a time now. In my office at police headquarters at precisely nine on Monday morning."

Kenny shook his head. "No can do. Too early, for one thing."

"You prefer to be arrested?"

His smile faded. "What for?"

"Impeding a police officer in the execution of her duties."

"Can you do that? Have me arrested?" He studied Carol's face, dropped his sunglasses back over his eyes, slapped the steering wheel with both hands. "Jesus! All right!"

As the Porsche took off in another spray of gravel, Anne said, "You sure fixed his insolent little arse. That implacable expression you get—I wish I could master it."

"Years of practice," said Carol, "and a hard heart."

EIGHT

Sybil had no opportunity to research Jayleen Smith online, so all she could recall was a vague impression from newscasts of a slightly built woman with grayish hair, frequently being led away in handcuffs from anti-corporate demonstrations.

Aunt Sarah filled her in as Sybil drove through ever-thickening traffic toward the Sydney Harbour Bridge. Once across and into the city, they would be a kilometer or so from Jayleen's office in cosmopolitan, historic Darlinghurst, part of Sydney's original settlement.

"I admit I know Jayleen only as a very effective environmental activist," declared Aunt Sarah. "She's fearless, well-informed, and has a knack for publicity."

"That description could fit you." And didn't exactly fit the vast majority of therapists, she thought with misgiving. Plus she was scarcely prepared to meet this one. She'd been unexpectedly given an appointment for this afternoon due to a cancellation, and she'd had to hurriedly assemble details of medications and progress reports from previous treatment. "Being an effective activist doesn't make her an effective therapist."

Aunt Sarah loosed a frustrated sigh. "It isn't enough to have glowing reports from two Crones who've had close members of the family in therapy with Jayleen?"

"I suppose…"

"Perhaps this will persuade you. When I called back to ask Franny Giaconi—" She broke off, mortified. "Never use real names. Protect the client. How many times have I heard that?"

"Did you mention someone's name?" said Sybil, hiding a smile. "Sorry, didn't get it. I was concentrating on the traffic."

A believable excuse. At this time of day most of the bridge's lanes were given over to the vast majority of cars fleeing Sydney for all points north, including the northern beaches where Sybil lived. For cars driving south over the bridge, it was a case of jockeying for position, all incoming traffic funneled into two lanes before crossing the water to the city.

A subdued Aunt Sarah said, "I'll be brief. A Crone's family member was an officer in the Australian Army. Served in Iraq. Came back with PTSD. Therapy with Jayleen was very effective. The officer occasionally attends the monthly PTSD support group."

As four lanes began collapsing into two, a red sports car, top down, driven by a balding, middle-aged man, roared past several vehicles, then, horn blaring, forced Sybil to brake as he pushed in front of her. His passenger, a young blonde, turned around and mouthed, "Sorry."

"Tsk," said Aunt Sarah, "a textbook case of midlife crisis. Rather pathetic how he's convinced himself that driving recklessly in a sports car, plus dating someone less than half his age, will magically make him young again. I could set him straight—but there is no way he'd ever listen to an old crone like me."

"Really?" said Sybil. "I was under the impression VIPs from all over the world clamor to speak with you and listen to your advice. A balding bloke with a midlife crisis would have to be impressed, wouldn't he?"

Raising her eyebrows, Aunt Sarah said, "Do I detect a note of sarcasm?"

"Irony," Sybil said with a grin. "I'm an English teacher. We never use sarcasm, being aware of its notoriety as the lowest form of wit. With us, it's always irony, possibly with a touch of sardonic humor thrown in."

Her smile vanished when Aunt Sarah checked one of the many dials on her huge new watch. "Excellent! We'll be a few minutes early. First impressions are important, don't you think?"

* * *

Sybil's first impression of Jayleen Smith was reassuring. Slender and below average in height, with brownish shoulder-length hair lightly streaked with gray, she exuded an aura of calm confidence and authority. She greeted Aunt Sarah warmly, congratulated her on the interviews she had given to the media earlier in the week, then ushered Sybil into her office.

There were two chairs and a small sofa in the room. Gesturing for Sybil to take a seat in the comfortably upholstered armchair, Jayleen took the more spartan chair opposite. Beside them were two end tables; between was a low glass table holding an exquisite little crystal box in which a single orchid nestled in polished river stones. For a few moments, a ray of sunlight shone through the crystal, splashing a rainbow of color on the table. Recessed lighting cast a warm glow over the walls, unadorned save for certificates of license and professional achievement. There were no curtains—broad plantation shutters were angled to catch the late afternoon sun and create patterns on the pale beige carpet. Sybil liked the office.

"Each session is recorded in its entirety with no breaks or editing," Jayleen Smith told her, seating herself and meeting Sybil's eyes. "You'll be given an encrypted copy of the video when you leave, or you may prefer to download it from our secure website service. We use only first names here. I'm Jayleen and you are Sybil, unless there's some other name you'd prefer. Before you answer, what name do you use when you talk to yourself? Say you wake up at two in the morning—who are you?"

"Sybil," she said without hesitation.

"Okay, Sybil, two questions. Try to answer them off the top of your head. One, what do you want of me? Two, what do you expect to get?"

Sybil heard herself say, "I want you to free me from these unbearable images. I don't expect you to be much help." She put her hand to her mouth. "I'm sorry—I didn't mean to say that."

Jayleen smiled. "You gave an entirely honest answer. Don't apologize."

"I could have been more tactful."

"You were honest. And I thank you for that honesty." Speaking with quiet intensity, she continued, "My hope is that you'll find this a place of safety, a place where you can be without fear, where you can always be honest. Now let's get a few more basics out of the way..."

* * *

With remarkable restraint, Aunt Sarah was silent until a break in the traffic allowed Sybil to join the crush of cars on Oxford Street. "Well? What did you think of Jayleen?"

"As a person or as a therapist?"

"Don't play games, dear. If you truly believe she can't help you, then we'll have to find someone who can. Just give the word."

"For pity's sake!" Sybil groaned. "I'll stick with Jayleen. I should give her a fair go, anyway."

"I don't want any details—"

"Hah!"

Aunt Sarah smiled sheepishly. "Of course I do, but I don't expect them."

"Most of our session was taken up by symptoms—what triggered my flashbacks, difficulties in sleeping, depression..." Sybil exhaled a long sigh. "Let's not talk about it now. I need time to process everything that happened this afternoon. I do feel overwhelmed," she admitted. "But I can say this much—Jayleen impressed me. I like her. I feel comfortable with her, encouraged. I feel confident she can help even though she made it clear it's not going to be a quick process. It's worth a try."

It was Aunt Sarah's turn to sigh. With relief. "I was beginning to wonder if I'd pushed you too hard to choose her as your therapist."

"Choose? You mean I had a choice? How careless of me not to have noticed."

Seeing the faint smile on Sybil's lips, Aunt Sarah said facetiously, "I judge that to be an English teacher's ironic comment."

Sybil shook her head. "Wrong. That was sarcasm."

NINE

Pat and Mark Bourke's house was in Cronulla, an old, established beachside suburb south of the city. With the main roads choked with Friday evening traffic, Carol was thankful to leave the clogged thoroughfares for the quieter streets of suburbia. So far she hadn't detected any media, and when she turned off the main road and no one followed, she finally felt confident she wasn't being tailed.

She'd been to the Bourkes' new house several times, so she hadn't used the dashboard's navigation system. But glancing at the blank screen, she was reminded of a missing ingredient in the investigation. She pulled over and called Liz Carey, whose Scene of Crime team had processed Greta Denby's suite.

"Liz, it's Carol. Apologies for calling you at home on a Friday night, but I've got a question about the Greta Denby crime scene."

"About to call you." Liz was her usual brusque, efficient self. "Found a thumbie in a large bottle of aspirin we collected from the Denby bathroom. Funny place to put it, eh?"

"A thumbie? You mean a flash drive?"

"That's the one. Crazy, eh? Les can give it to you tomorrow."

"Les Upton?"

"Yeah. He's right here. Want to speak to him?"

Carol was more than surprised. Les Upton and Liz Carey made an odd couple—if indeed they were a couple. "No thanks. Tell Les to line up tech support to analyze the flash drive. I'll be in my office by seven thirty tomorrow morning. Les is to report to me as soon as he has the information."

"Will do. Okay, back to you, Carol. What's your problem?"

"Apparently there was a laptop in Greta's bedroom, but it seems to have disappeared."

Liz said without hesitation, "Custom-made job in a scarlet case. When I last saw Ian Rooke he'd activated it and was staring at the screen. 'Anything interesting?' I asked him. 'Nothing apparent, but haven't had time to really look,' he said and shut it down quick smart and sealed it up for me to take. Have to say it slipped my mind after that, what with all the medical stuff we had to process. That Denby woman had enough pills around the place to choke an elephant. I'll get it to you."

"Thanks, Liz."

"Carol, about Ian Rooke...the poor guy had a lot on his plate. Hindley was putting all sorts of pressure on him to come up with the right answer fast."

"The right answer? What would that be?"

"The hell I know!" Liz's raucous laugh was followed with, "Whatever, Carol, the baby's all yours now. Have fun."

Bourke's place was on a tree-lined street ending in a cul-de-sac. As Carol parked, still mulling over why a flash drive would have been stashed in an aspirin bottle, who would have put it there and what could possibly be on it, she saw that Bourke was waiting for her in the driveway. He looked relaxed and casual in navy blue slacks and a white shirt with its sleeves rolled up to the elbow. Behind him, built on a slight rise, the red brick house looked down on them, lights blazing from every window. Its architecture was typical of the Federation style: brick chimneys rising out of a roof of red tiles; a flight of stone steps leading to a wide veranda; a substantial front door with a stained glass inset and matching glass panels on either side.

"Just a quick report before we have to go and make nice," Bourke said.

"Something interesting about Ian Rooke?"

"Something interesting about his wife, Rosalie. She neglected to mention earlier that Ian had his life insured for seven hundred thousand, and she was the sole beneficiary."

"Recent policy?"

"Five years ago when their first child was born. They decided the family would be best protected by having a substantial life insurance for Ian, as he was the main breadwinner. Rosalie's self-employed. An artist."

"Yes?"

He grinned at Carol's skeptical tone. "Works featuring ethereal beings with flowing robes against a background of mist-shrouded trees."

This seemed frivolous to her but she was hardly any judge of the art scene. "Successful?"

"Pat's agreed to make a few phone calls—help out with her own contacts."

Carol nodded, her suspicions about Rosalie's artwork neither confirmed nor refuted. Pat moved within the upper echelons of the art world where she was highly regarded, and she was a very kind person. "A news item from Liz Carey." She told him about the flash drive and its location.

A headshake and a muttered "Bizarre," was his response. "I've a news item for you too," he told her. "Anne checked on the death of the woman under Bea Parker's care before she came to the Denby family. It seems Ellen Lowell applied some sort of oil to her hands and arms, reached for the banister as she took her first step down a flight of stairs, her hand slipped and down she came. Could have happened to anyone with or without Alzheimer's."

Carol nodded. If such a death had been staged, Bea Parker seemed to lack the wherewithal to do something so inventive. And to what purpose? Still, the husband, Frederick Lowell's brother, had been on the scene, and the death seemed too coincidental to be ignored.

"Here come Sybil and Aunt Sarah," said Bourke, raising a hand to greet them.

Even after these many years that she'd known Sybil, Carol still found her breath catching at the sight of her, the curvaceous body in an emerald shirt and white pants, her auburn hair burnished with gold highlights in the light cast by the house lights. She continued to be so very beautiful...

She had to pull her attention away as Bourke said, "One more thing, Carol. I asked about the needle puncture on Ian's thigh. She said she had no clue."

"Did you believe her?"

"No."

Before he could elaborate, Sybil and Aunt Sarah came up to them, Aunt Sarah announcing, "Through the Crone network, I've found Sybil an excellent therapist. *Not*, I might add, a psychiatrist."

"Who would that be?" Carol hastened to ask, with a smile at Sybil, knowing full well that her aunt needed no encouragement to embark on a diatribe about the evils of psychiatry.

"Jayleen Smith."

Carol stared at her aunt.

"Yes," said Sybil with a wry grin, "*that* Jayleen Smith."

"Excellent work Jayleen's done with No More Lawns." Aunt Sarah beamed approvingly. "Tear up the water-guzzling grass and replace it with native plants. Brilliant!"

"If memory serves me right, she and her NML group were arrested for vandalism," Carol said, looking at Sybil in dismay. "Something about using weed killer to write the initials of the group on areas of lawn."

"Areas of lawn?" Aunt Sarah repeated disapprovingly. "Carol, dear, that's so vague. Give NML some credit. They select their targets very carefully to maximize media exposure, namely the over-watered lawns of well-known personalities, public parks where the local councils should know better, and the disgraceful landscaping many large corporations favor where grass is the principal ground cover. My only regret is that golf courses were not included. As you know, pesticides—"

She broke off when Bourke and Carol laughed. "What's so funny?"

"Stricken yellow butterfly," they chorused. Bourke added, "With much fluttering."

Aunt Sarah had to smile. "Well, yes," she said, "I do admit that perhaps my dying butterfly may have gone on a little too long, but the Crones' street theater that day was a media triumph."

"Are you lot coming inside?" Pat asked from the top of the front steps. "Carol, use your authority and get them moving."

Carol smiled affectionately up at her. "We're lowering the tone of the neighborhood, are we?"

Pat chuckled. "Something like that."

Carol took Sybil's hand, letting the others move ahead of them. "Are you okay?"

Sybil gave her a resigned smile. "Aunt Sarah on a mission is like a human steamroller. I can't imagine anything standing in her way for long. She was determined to find me a new therapist, and to my astonishment, she did."

"Jayleen Smith? Are you serious?"

"Carol, she's an accredited therapist. I've checked. She's had excellent results with post-traumatic cases. And she's quite impressive in person."

Carol shook her head. "There's no way you can know that, short of meeting the woman."

"I did meet her."

"You're kidding me," Carol said, sure that Sybil was indeed joking.

"I'm not kidding. Jayleen's practice is in Darlinghurst. There was a late afternoon cancellation and I took it."

Carol knew her face reflected her incredulity. "Sybil, you have no idea whether this so-called therapist is—"

Sybil pulled her hand from Carol's. "Don't start. You don't have to approve. I'm the one with the problem, not you."

Taken aback by Sybil's flare of anger, Carol took a moment to marshal her thoughts. "It's *our* problem," she said. "Let's talk it over."

"I'm through with talking. It hasn't got either of us anywhere."

"Hey, you two," Pat called from the veranda.

"Coming," said Sybil, starting off for the front steps.

Carol followed, her feelings a confusion of concern and resentment. Along with the usual abyss of guilt. She took a deep breath. Tonight was a celebration. She'd worry about all this tomorrow.

Pat was organizing a tour of the house. "Carol, come on. Join the group, or you'll miss all the fun."

Carol obediently went to stand with Sybil, her aunt, and Eric, Pat's brother. Eric was tall and thin, like his sister. He had none of Pat's ebullience, but he did have a dry sense of humor. "Admire everything," he quietly advised Carol. "It's the safest route to take."

Carol thought what a good match the Bourkes were. Pat almost Bourke's height, but where he was solidly built, she was lanky. Her wide smile often segued into a full-bodied bellow of laughter. Competent and energetic, she was the ultimate can-do person who faced every problem with a cheerful confidence that it could be solved.

Bourke was more thoughtful and restrained, but his broad shoulders and height gave him a strong physical presence. His homely, comfortable face and calm demeanor hid a quiet intensity. People tended to underestimate Bourke. Which made him an excellent interrogator. Carol had often observed suspects dropping their guard as Bourke interviewed them in his quiet way, unaware of the trap hidden in his apparently innocuous questions until it was too late.

They trooped from room to room, making the appropriate admiring comments. In the dining room, while everyone's attention was on Bourke, who was pointing out the difficulties of restoring the black marble fireplace to its former glory, Carol glanced over at Sybil.

She looked tired and defeated, and Carol's heart turned over. She felt powerless—alien territory for her. What could she do, what could she say, to make things right? She had to face the bitter truth: the fault lay entirely with her. It hadn't been simply an unfortunate set of circumstances but her own misjudgment that had caused Sybil unspeakable suffering. The blame was hers. Thanks to her precious bloody career, Sybil had become collateral damage. "Blame me," Carol had said to her many times. Now she was bitterly aware her mea culpa had been superficial lip service. She had never truly accepted responsibility and had abandoned Sybil to a black hole of torment.

"Tour's over," Pat announced. "Suitable alcoholic libations, including my very own fruit punch, await you in the lounge room." She guffawed as she followed the mini-stampede down the hall. "Come on, it wasn't that bad, was it?"

Carol took the opportunity to take Bourke aside. "Why didn't you believe Rosalie Rooke when she said she knew nothing about the needle mark in Ian's leg?"

"Rosalie's someone who's not used to lying. She tried to hide it, but she was obviously uncomfortable when I brought up the subject. When I asked her point-blank, she answered almost before I finished speaking, then started talking about something else as quickly as possible."

"What was the something else?"

"Roses," said Bourke, looking a little embarrassed. "She has some beauties, and was giving me some pointers on care and cultivation. Roses happen to be Pat's favorite flower."

"Somehow I can't imagine you digging up flower beds and planting roses."

Carol said this lightly, but inwardly felt a stab of envy. Her own marriage had been misguided and mercifully brief, its one saving grace the birth of David. Bourke and Pat were so settled, so sure of each other. So happy. Would she and Sybil ever have anything near that certainty?

Shoving the thought away, she said, "Liz Carey told me Ian took a brief look at the laptop in Greta's room but—"

Pat came up to Carol and took her arm. "What's your wonderful son up to these days?"

Carol smiled at her, pleased to be asked. "David's having a wonderful time driving around Europe with his father."

"He keeps in touch?"

Carol laughed. "More or less. If I'm lucky, a call on Skype so I can see how he looks, but mainly emails or the telephone if it's urgent. In case you're wondering, 'urgent' translates as, 'Mum, I have this payment due on a credit card…'"

"David sends me postcards," Aunt Sarah said, "with a few scribbled sentences in some sort of teenage code."

"It's what they use for texting," said Sybil. "I get those postcards from him too."

"Brevity—that reminds me of the offer I got from Madeline Shipley." Pat chortled when everyone looked at her. "Well, that got your attention."

"When did Shipley contact you?" Bourke asked, frowning.

"Just as Carol arrived. You were outside talking. So," Pat said, clearly enjoying herself, "knowing beforehand what she's going to ask, I give her a fast, 'Sorry, not interested.' But Madeline is never fazed, as you well know. So she says, 'I'll get back to you with an offer you can't refuse.'" Pat broke off to laugh. "And I say—'As long as I don't find a horse's head in the bed.'"

"Nice one," chuckled Aunt Sarah. "There is a touch of *The Godfather* about that woman."

"What do you think, Carol?" Eric asked, grinning.

Carol said sharply, "In my job I see the worst of human nature. Madeline seems pretty tame after that."

A glance at Sybil's face made her regret she'd said it, said anything at all.

TEN

Before the get-together at the Bourkes' house, Aunt Sarah had packed and left her home in the Blue Mountains to travel to Sydney by train. Sybil had picked her up at the station, and it had worked out well that after her visit with Sybil and Sybil's therapy session, she and Aunt Sarah could continue on to the Bourkes' dinner party. Aunt Sarah would now be staying with Carol until the Crones set off for South America.

After the party Bourke had gallantly volunteered to move the luggage to Carol's vehicle, so Carol and Sybil stood by while Aunt Sarah supervised.

Staggering from the weight of one huge suitcase, he said, "My, you Crones do believe in traveling light."

"That's PR material," said Aunt Sarah. "It'll be shipped ahead of our delegation."

While Bourke, closely watched by Aunt Sarah, transferred the last of the luggage, Carol said to Sybil, "I didn't have a chance to speak with you all night. I'm sorry for the way I carried on about your new therapist. Please forgive me."

"It's strange to hear you apologizing, Carol."

Disconcerted by Sybil's cool tone, Carol said, "It is? Why?"

"You hardly ever do."

Carol was about to retort that she rarely did anything that required an apology, but fortunately her aunt intervened before she could make what she quickly realized would have been a flippant, grossly inappropriate remark.

"Carol, we're ready to go. Sybil, you look very tired. Take care driving home."

After a final goodnight to Bourke, Carol walked Sybil to her car. "Tomorrow night? Can I see you? We could have dinner together. If you like I'll pick something up on the way to your place."

"You're on a case."

"I'll make time."

Sybil sighed. "I don't—"

"Please."

Sybil looked at her for a long moment. "Call me. I'll be home all day."

"Sybil," Carol began, but Sybil said, "Goodnight," slid into the driver's seat and shut the door.

Discomfited, Carol waited until she had driven off, then got into her own car. She glanced at her aunt, who remained uncharacteristically quiet in the passenger seat. This suited Carol. She felt unsettled, anxious and angry, all at once. When they reached the familiarity of the main road, she could drive on automatic pilot while mentally reviewing the evening.

Sybil had seemed tired and edgy from the first time they'd spoken outside Bourke's house. Carol was still disturbed by the sudden anger on Sybil's face as she'd said she was through with talking. Inside they'd barely spoken. In fact, when she thought about it, Sybil had been almost silent the whole evening.

Until the end of the excellent lamb roast dinner.

"A toast," Pat had said, raising her champagne flute. "To Carol and Mark, for all your outstanding career achievements in the Police Service, we commend you!"

After the toast, the predictable cry of "Speech, speech," was raised.

"Something original," Eric called out.

Bourke got to his feet. "I think I can say, without fear of contradiction—" He broke off at the general groan. "What? Not original enough for you?" Laughing, he sat down. "Your turn, Carol."

Carol stood, looked around the table, and said, "Your commendations mean a great deal to me, and I'm sure to Mark. However, I must set the record straight. I would never have reached this point in my career without Mark by my side. As a friend, he is dear to my heart. As a detective, I can simply say that Mark is the best—the very best."

She was both touched and amused to see Bourke blushing. Saluting him with her glass, she said, "Inspector Mark Bourke— thank you."

Bourke, his face still red, got up to reply. "I have to say Carol has it 'round the wrong way. That is, I'm the one who owes everything to her." After an awkward pause he mumbled, "I'm not good at this…" and sat down again.

"You're telling me!" Pat boomed to much laughter.

Sybil stood. "I'd like to add something about Mark and Carol." She paused, then said lightly, "As you know, I initially met them when they were Inspector Ashton and Sergeant Bourke, and I was a high school English teacher. I met them under rather inauspicious circumstances—"

"I'll say!" said Pat.

"—being that I was their chief suspect in a murder case."

Amid an uproar of laughter, Carol relived in vivid recall the first time she had seen Sybil. She and Bourke had been conducting preliminary interviews at Bellwhether High where the murder had taken place—a bizarre killing with a power drill as the murder weapon. Shaken by the vicious murder and hiding her involvement with the victim, Sybil had held onto her composure by sheer willpower. Even though she was pale and drawn, with quite a spectacular bruise on her cheekbone, Carol had been struck by her beauty. During the investigation that followed, Sybil had endured the stress of being the chief suspect in a sensational murder case without breaking under the strain.

After the interview Bourke had made some laughing remark about how redheads had fiery tempers, and who knew what they would do if pushed too hard. But the redhead stereotype had never described Sybil, who in various situations over the years always displayed grace under pressure. Carol had believed that they understood each other very well. Looking back, she realized that even during periods of difficulty and estrangement, even when she and Sybil were in diversionary relationships with other women, she had somehow been confident of Sybil's love, took Sybil's love for her as a given, a constant. It appeared she no longer had the luxury of that belief.

She tuned back in to find Sybil speaking of Carol's absolute dedication to the Police Service, the professional partnership between Carol and Bourke as the epitome of teamwork. As Sybil touched on their success in solving high profile cases, Carol glanced over at Bourke, who seemed pleased but self-conscious. Beside him, Pat was beaming.

The assault that had caused Sybil's PTSD was different from the stress she had experienced at Bellwhether High, different to such an extreme that Carol sensed she was near to breaking. How could she have not seen this earlier? Once her physical wounds healed, Sybil had seemed the same as before, except for an aversion to spending any time where the assault had taken place at Carol's home. Although therapy had not been very effective in helping her with this issue, in all other ways she appeared to be her former self. She had accepted Sybil's apparent recovery without question. Or rather, if she were honest with herself, she had wanted it to be true, so she had seen what she wanted to see and had avoided delving too deeply.

Sybil was saying, "In conclusion, if you will indulge an English teacher a few high-flown words, Carol Ashton and Mark Bourke are the premier team, at the top of their game. In short, they are the quintessence, the embodiment of professionalism."

Everyone had clapped and cheered, and Carol had been both warmed by the praise and dismayed by the accuracy of Sybil's words. She had spoken glowingly only of Carol's professionalism, her total commitment to her career, nothing personal about the two of them. Once Carol would have argued that this was disproportionate and unfair; but now she admitted it was true. It had always been true. Her job first and everything else second. This, when Sybil, of all people in Carol's world, deserved her undivided and unreserved love.

Had she already lost Sybil?

She couldn't think about that now.

Aunt Sarah's revelations about Sybil's new therapist came to mind. Jayleen Smith would be the last person Carol would choose. Apart from the woman's notoriety, she couldn't believe Jayleen Smith was the most skilled therapist available. And for that matter, why hadn't Sybil stayed with her psychiatrist? Surely Aunt Sarah's unreasonable acrimony toward psychiatry hadn't persuaded Sybil to dump Dr. Fitzgerald.

Carol abruptly broke the silence in the car. "Whatever possessed you to recommend Jayleen Smith?"

Not at all put out by her tone, Aunt Sarah said mildly, "Well, dear, by all accounts, Jayleen's an excellent therapist. I'm afraid you're just influenced by the fact she's been arrested a couple of times."

Realizing she was feeling more and more angry and not sure why, Carol made an effort to keep her voice even. "And I suppose your approval of her fringe environmental group doesn't influence you?"

"Of course it does, Carol! For Jayleen Smith to spend energy, time, and money on environmental issues indicates her good character and her commitment to the planet."

"Her good character?" muttered Carol.

"Speak up, dear. What did you say?"

"Vandalism does not indicate good character," Carol said.

"I'll concede there are other, more lawful ways to get your message across." Aunt Sarah paused for a moment, then asked, "But that isn't the issue, is it?"

"What do you mean?"

"It's Sybil, what happened to her, and how you feel about it."

"Forget me," Carol said. "What's important is that Sybil get the right treatment, and she's already seeing a psychiatrist. Why would you think this Smith woman could help her more than Dr. Fitzgerald?" Before Aunt Sarah could answer, Carol added, "Please don't go off on a tangent about psychiatry."

Aunt Sarah clicked her tongue, but instead of chiding Carol for her peremptory tone, she asked, "Have you ever attended a therapy session with Sybil?"

"No, of course not." Out of the corner of her eye Carol saw her aunt shaking her head. "What? I should have?"

"Have you spoken with her psychiatrist?"

"No. But if Sybil had asked me—"

"If Sybil had asked you! Why should she need to? Carol, she's the one who's traumatized, who needs every bit of support those who love her can give."

Stung by her aunt's words, Carol said, "If you remember, Sybil and I haven't been a couple the whole time since…since the incident. Sometimes months passed without us speaking to each other."

"I'm well aware of that, Carol," she said severely, "but it's no excuse. Simply as a friend, you could have been there for her."

"It wouldn't have helped then, and it won't help now." Hearing the raw anger in her voice, Carol took a deep breath. "I'm sorry. This whole subject upsets me."

Carol expected Aunt Sarah to be combative, but instead she said quietly, "Perhaps you need to talk this out with a professional."

"You mean a therapist?"

"If need be."

"I won't do it. It's not as if I don't know what's involved. I've been through enough debriefings with the police mental health specialists."

Her aunt shrugged. "Tell me if you change your mind, Carol." With a wicked smile she added, "I'm sure Jayleen would find some way to fit you into her busy schedule."

Just as Carol was pulling into her carport her phone rang. Checking the caller ID, she said, "I have to take this, Aunt Sarah. It's the commissioner. You have your own key, go on in. Sinker will be thrilled to see you."

The commissioner didn't waste time with small talk. "Canon Armitage wants a meeting with you tomorrow evening. This is basically a PR exercise. Sykes is arranging the venue and will accompany you. He'll call with the details. After the meeting, Sykes will report back to me, and I'll liaise with you if necessary."

Carol grimaced. *There goes my evening with Sybil.*

"PR in what way?" she said.

"As I said, Sykes will brief you, but overall I want Armitage to view the Police Service in a positive light. I'm trying to get him out of our hair, Carol. Euthanasia is like a red rag to a bull as far as he and his bloody Cherished Life group are concerned. Assure him that your investigation will be thorough and if the Denby woman's death was a mercy killing, the culprit will be prosecuted to the full extent of the law. Is that clear?"

Without waiting to hear her reply, he rang off.

Irritated, Carol got out of the driver's seat and opened the boot. She stood there, thinking. She had been glad when Ian Rooke was assigned to lead this investigation—she didn't want to have anything to do with the case. It hit too close to home. Memories she'd pushed out of her conscious mind long ago were surfacing again. One scene in particular burned in her imagination. Were Sybil's flashbacks as vivid as this?

"Carol?"

She started, her hand going automatically toward the small of her back.

"Try not to shoot your only aunt," said Aunt Sarah from the sidewalk to the house. "Or Sinker."

Carol relaxed. "Sorry. I didn't hear you coming. It's reflex."

"I've got your collapsible handcart here. Those suitcases are too heavy for you to lift."

Carol's black-and-white cat wound around her legs, then sat down to observe the action.

Heaving the first of the suitcases out of the boot, Carol said, "How did you and Sybil manage at the railway station this morning with all this luggage?"

"No problem. Take one helpless little old lady and one gorgeous redhead, and watch the offers pour in."

"Sybil *is* gorgeous," said Carol, "but you're far from being a helpless little old lady."

Aunt Sarah cackled. "I'm no lady, I'll give you that." Then she sobered. "Don't ruin it, Carol. Don't lose Sybil."

"I don't possess her to lose."

"You're as obstinate as your mother."

"Mum?" she said with a smile, although she felt the chill of the past prickling her skin. "I could never beat her in that area."

No, never, said her inner voice. Carol, to whom compromise was weakness, cringed. "*Why? Why did you ask me?*" she silently asked her dead mother.

Some minutes later, with all the luggage deposited in Aunt Sarah's room, having changed into pajamas, Carol came into the living room and sank into a corner of the sofa, nightcap in hand, still brooding over the evening's events with Sybil. She had taken her second sip of scotch when Aunt Sarah, in a floral nightgown, settled into the armchair across from her. Carol closed her eyes briefly; she'd wanted these few minutes alone with her medicinal scotch.

"*Carol,*" said Aunt Sarah.

Carol's head jerked sharply, automatically, toward her aunt. On that rarest of occasions when the normally ebullient voice dropped an entire octave, it signified a topic of magnitude.

"We need to talk. About something we've not talked about before. You've not brought it up and I've been, well…afraid to."

Oh God. Carol felt blood draining from her face. *Mother's death.*

"Sybil," said Aunt Sarah.

Carol let out an audible breath, slumped down in the sofa.

Now her aunt was scowling, her lips tightening. "You don't want to talk to me about Sybil?"

"Of course, of course I do," Carol managed to utter in the sudden ebbing of adrenaline at her aunt's misreading of her reaction. "Put it down to stress. With all that's going on."

"I realize that, dear. But this is terribly important. With me leaving the country in a few days…and so much going on with Sybil with these hideous flashbacks…I just care so much about the two of you, too much to keep letting this go."

Carol nodded, closed her eyes briefly. "Yes," she said simply. Adding, "Of course we can talk more about Sybil."

Her aunt took a deep breath, leaned forward and said slowly, softly, "The day that monster Philip Ular forced his way into your house. Carol, what did he do to her?"

Adrenaline surged again, this time with the surge of memory, driving her to sit up on the sofa.

Only a warning instinct of some primordial origin had alerted her that morning and pulled her back home, away from her police task force. Away from the diversionary operation devised to trap Ular...

Even so, she had entered her very normal-seeming house unsuspecting of what awaited her.

A sound...a moan? Drifting down the hall.

The feel of the subcompact Glock instantly in her hand, its sturdy weight only faintly reassuring as she heard, "Come in." A light male voice taunting, "You're in time to see her die."

Standing rigid in the entrance to the sitting room with the Glock raised, tightly clasped in both hands.

Ular. Leaning against the breakfast bar. A silver large-frame revolver trained just as steadily on her. The monster of photos and her imagining, wearing faded jeans and a T-shirt with a depiction of a fading fence, the words *Dave's Fencing* stenciled across it.

Not taking her eyes from him but in a corner of her vision: Sybil. Slumped on the brightly colored mat in front of the couch. Face turned away. Handcuffed.

Ular grinning at her, triumphant despite her unexpected arrival. Gloating. Over his cleverness in obtaining his muscular Smith and Wesson forty-five on the Queensland black market. Over his setting up the police sting to lure her away. Over reporting to Sybil's school that she was ill, then moving her car to remove evidence of her presence in the house.

Hearing moans from Sybil. Sybil turning her head to reveal her nose and mouth bruised and bleeding.

Ular saying casually: "She fought taking her medicine."

"Her medicine?"

"Gammahydroxybutyrate. You cops know it as Fantasy."

Also as GBH. Grievous body harm. The designer party drug. Altered consciousness then coma then death. She had to ask: "How much did you give her?"

"I just held her nose and poured it down her throat. It took a while because she wouldn't cooperate. I don't know how much she got but I'm sure it's a fatal dose. That's the important thing."

Bargaining with him. Calmly. "Leave now, nothing happens. I won't follow."

Ular countering. "If you put down that gun maybe I'll let you call an ambulance."

She had to distract, destabilize him. Talking to him then. Reaching then for the bludgeon of Sybil's abortive disaster of a relationship with his brother.

An instant reaction: insane rage directed at Sybil: "The bitch has to die!"

"Die? I don't think so. She seems to be doing okay to me."

His reflexive glance at Sybil—all she needs. Three shots from the Glock. A bullet from his forty-five plowing into the wall near her head. He's collapsed but the gun's raised to Sybil...

One more shot and now he's down and she's able to kick his gun away...

And leap to Sybil and call for help...

Aunt Sarah said softly, "I remember she was in the hospital for two days."

Carol did not reply. Her throat had closed as she concluded the story, and tears were running down her face.

"Carol, oh my, oh my..."

Her aunt had never seen her cry. As she started to get up, Carol gestured that she was okay.

"He didn't rape her," her aunt offered, sitting back down. "Didn't cut her. Didn't torture her."

Carol found her voice. Whispering as much to herself as to Aunt Sarah, "It's not what he didn't do. All those things he might have done—that's what I've tallied up and told myself all this time. Protecting myself with what I saved her from—when what he actually *did* to Sybil is all that's ever mattered. I've been so blind...so stupid. Why ever would she want to be back with me?"

"You were *both* traumatized," her aunt said forcefully. "You *both* needed time. And Carol, you did need to protect yourself, this man's assault was every bit as much on you as it was on her—"

"We needed to be protecting each other!"

"Yes. Well," her aunt said and flung her hands up as if two extraordinarily dense people had finally realized what had always been in front of their noses. She said briskly, "You both can get started on that right now."

ELEVEN

When Carol arrived at work on Saturday morning, Les Upton was already there, waiting outside her office. "It was a video on the flash drive," he told her without preamble. "Got it set up in the conference room so you can take a look. Anne's on her way."

A few minutes later, Anne Newsome entered the conference room accompanied by Bourke.

"Take your seats," said Upton, "the show's about to begin."

"Have you got time to watch this, Mark?" Carol asked as she sat down next to Anne.

"For sure. Then I'm off to view what's left of Ian Rooke's vehicle. I gather it's a bit of a mess. Ian wasn't wearing a seat belt, so..."

Carol's grimace matched his. "It's always worse when you know them." She gestured to Upton. "Okay, let's see it."

"It was made in the States," Upton said. "Catchy title—*A Peaceful Ending*. Just the thing for a documentary on death machines." His face remained expressionless as he added, "A bit of an odd sense of humor, the director had. *Dying Your Way* is the subtitle and you'll notice when it comes up there's a snatch of someone who sounds a lot like Sinatra singing 'My Way' in the background. Funny, eh?"

In Carol's experience, this was as close as Upton came to making a jocular remark. "Very funny," she said. "Was there anything else on the flash drive?"

"Not a thing." He punched a button on the console before him. "Here we go."

The screen on the conference room wall showed a bucolic scene of rolling green hills dotted with distant cattle, accompanied by appropriately pastoral music. Next, a sunset spilling warm light over the rolling waves and the title, A PEACEFUL ENDING.

As Upton had pointed out, a voice that very well could have been Sinatra's crooned in the background as DYING YOUR WAY appeared.

Carol was amused to see that Upton seemed to have assumed the role of MC. "The first device we see is the very famous Dr. Jack Kevorkian's euthanasia machine."

"Infamous," said Bourke, meaning it.

Anne looked sideways at him. "Kevorkian provided a service people desperately needed. And still need."

Bourke opened his mouth, caught Carol's glance and shut it again.

"A Two-Minute Death" appeared on the screen. A warm, friendly female voice read the title, then continued with measured enthusiasm, "Dr. Jack Kevorkian's Thanatron—meaning death machine—is possibly the most famous, or some would say, notorious of the euthanasia devices. It is so constructed that the person wishing to die simply pushes a button to deliver a fatal dose of drugs and chemicals via an intravenous line."

As she spoke, an animated diagram showed three bottles, each connected to a single IV in the arm of the subject, represented by the outline of a cartoon figure reclining serenely in a lounge chair.

"The first bottle contains saline," the voice advised. "The second, to induce sleep, the barbiturate sodium thiopental.

The third contains potassium chloride, to stop the heart, plus a muscle relaxant to prevent spasms before death."

"Charming," said Bourke. "We wouldn't want to distress anyone with dying spasms."

"There are three steps," said the voice, hushed but sincerely positive. "First, Dr. Kevorkian starts the saline solution. Second, the subject activates the flow of barbiturates to induce sleep." The cartoon figure's eyes began to close, as she continued, "Third, release of the lethal drug begins, triggered by the falling arm of the subject as he or she falls asleep."

The cartoon figure, eyes shut and a faint smile on its face, demonstrated the arm drop. "A peaceful ending," the voice announced. "Once initiated, it will take approximately two minutes for the subject to enter a better world."

"A better world!" mocked Bourke.

"If you were dying in dreadful pain," Anne said, "and with no hope of recovery, wouldn't any world be better than the one you were in?"

"Pain can be controlled."

Not always, Carol thought. She rubbed her forehead. The faint headache she'd had all morning was intensifying.

"This next one is Kevorkian's Mercitron, meaning mercy machine," said Upton. "He had to develop it because he'd lost his medical license, so couldn't legally get the drugs he needed for the Thanatron."

The same warm female voice resumed the narrative. "The Mercitron is very simple. A canister of carbon monoxide is attached to a face mask by way of a plastic tube. The subject simply turns the valve of the canister on, or removes a clip so the flow of gas begins." In keeping with the ease of using this device, the animated illustration had the cartoon character calmly affixing a mask to its face and flicking a switch without hesitation.

"Subjects are encouraged to take a sedative, as death make take approximately ten minutes." A red CAUTION blinked at the bottom of the screen, followed by: *Please note that carbon monoxide is a hazard to those discovering the body.*

Bourke gave a derisive snort. "How bloody considerate to issue a warning."

Upton spoke over him. "Now here's something anyone can set up. Note the title, 'Quick, Reliable and Non-Explosive.' Who could ask for anything more?"

To Carol, the narrator seemed almost cheerful as she extolled the virtues of the Exit International euthanasia method. "The original death agent was helium, the gas used to fill party balloons. The improved device requires only a barbecue gas bottle filled with nitrogen, plastic tubing and a plastic bag large enough to cover the head completely."

The now familiar cartoon outline sat comfortably in a wheelchair next to a bulbous gas bottle, from which led a plastic tube, attached to the inside of a roomy plastic bag.

"Nitrogen is much preferred over helium," the voice continued, "because it is not flammable and will not explode, so those discovering the body will not come to harm."

Carol closed her eyes. Her headache had become the steady beat of a hammer inside her skull. She heard Bourke say to Anne, "Can you see yourself ever helping someone to die?"

"It's possible, depending on the circumstances. What about you?"

"It's premeditated murder."

The narrator advised, "First, buy an empty LPG cylinder from a hardware store and have it filled with compressed nitrogen. It's used quite commonly for home brewing. The recommended pressure is four hundred pounds per square inch. Attach one end of the tubing to the cylinder of nitrogen and tape the other end inside a plastic bag big enough to enclose the head of the subject. Then place the bag over the head, secure it around the neck. The final step is to start the flow of nitrogen. Consciousness is lost within seconds as the nitrogen begins to rapidly flush oxygen out of the blood stream. A peaceful death occurs within minutes."

Bourke said in disgust, "What the hell is wrong with these people?"

Carol rubbed her forehead. She had aspirin in her office and she'd have to take it soon, before this headache developed into a monster. "Is there much more?" she asked Upton.

"Just one, and we all know it well. Death By Computer, also known as the Deliverance Machine. It was used legally in Australia for a couple of years."

Carol didn't bother looking at the screen, or listening to the irritatingly upbeat soundtrack. She knew what she'd see—a laptop computer programmed with software called "Deliverance." The software asked the subject a series of questions. If the correct answers were given, a fatal injection of barbiturates was administered via an IV line after a button was pushed by the person wishing to die.

"Under the Rights of the Terminally Ill Act 1995," the voice droned, "the Northern Territory of Australia had made euthanasia legal. Four people took advantage of the device during the period 1995 to 1997 before the act was overturned and euthanasia again became a crime…"

"That's it?" Carol said, speaking over the narrator, who was advising her audience of the many resources available for those wishing to embrace a serene close to life.

"It seems there's nothing else recorded," said Upton, "but we'll know for sure when the techo's report comes in later this morning. So far all we have is a video downloaded from a website onto a flash drive anyone could have picked up for a few dollars."

We have more than that, Carol thought. Who had placed it in an aspirin bottle in proximity to a dying woman? And why? Had Greta Denby herself hidden it there, having viewed it on her laptop with the intention of suicide? She needed to look at that computer.

With markedly more enthusiasm, Upton added, "I'll get moving on the Denby finances and the family lawyer quick smart, and get back to you as soon as I can."

Walking back to her office, Carol said to Anne, "See you in twenty minutes?"

* * *

Two aspirins later, Carol felt the first slackening of the pounding in her head. She would call Sybil after she had spoken to Sykes about where and when they would meet with Canon Armitage that evening. Massaging her temples with her fingertips, she willed the headache to go. She wasn't looking forward to telling Sybil that yet again police work took precedence over everything else. Sybil would understand Carol had no option, as she could hardly disobey a direct order from the commissioner. But it would only add to the tension between them.

When Anne knocked on her door, Carol was reading through Iris Kemp's statement about her care of Greta Denby the day before her death and jotting down points of interest she would follow up.

"I've just spoken with Iris Kemp," Anne said, "and she's keen to see you at any time this afternoon or tomorrow."

"I've got her statement here. How did she strike you overall? Reliable? Truthful?"

"I reckon so," said Anne. "She's known the Denby family for a long time, they think the world of her. Her husband was the groundskeeper for years, and Iris was always on call to help out with dinner parties or take up the slack when someone on staff was away. After Bob Kemp died, Greta thought so much of Iris that she set her up rent-free in a flat nearby. And when Greta fell ill, Iris took over the role of companion, assistant—whatever you like to call it."

"Did you get the impression that there was tension between Iris and Bea Parker?" Carol asked.

"Not on Iris's side. Bea Parker always emphasizes that Iris has no medical credentials, which simply seems to amuse Iris. But then, almost everything does. You'll see what I mean when you meet her."

As Carol was asking Anne to advise Iris Kemp that they'd be there at two o'clock, Maureen Oatland came bustling in. She was an excellent detective, in Carol's opinion, her career before joining the department focused on sexual assault and juvenile crime. Large in every way, she announced in her penetrating voice, "Here's your laptop, Carol. Sealed, signed, and delivered." She carefully placed the evidence bag on the desk. She plunked a bulging cardboard container next to the laptop. "Doughnuts. You look peaky, Carol. Sugar's what you need. You too, *Sergeant Newsome.*"

Along with Bourke, Anne had had to put up with good-natured teasing about her promotion. "That's *Detective Sergeant Newsome,*" she said primly.

Maureen rolled her eyes. "Pardon me. Now dig in while they're still warm. All yours—I've got more, just for me."

Carol's usual breakfast of black coffee and toast had been some time ago. Now she realized that she was hungry. "Thank you, Maureen. This is good of you. Let's have coffee and doughnuts, the three of us. There's a couple of things I'd like to discuss."

Always expressive, Maureen's face showed her astonishment. "You mean here, in your office?"

"That's right."

She knew very well why Maureen was so surprised. Carol was on cordial terms with everyone in her department, but there was always an unspoken understanding that a line existed they could not cross. Bourke was an exception to the rule, as he and Carol had worked closely together for many years. To a certain extent, Anne also was an exception. No one else.

TWELVE

Late in the morning Bourke appeared at Carol's door.

"I see Maureen delivered the laptop," he said, gesturing at the sealed evidence bag on her file cabinet.

She nodded. "I didn't see much of anything on it beyond the photos Thalia Denby mentioned, so our techs need to take it from there, if need be. We had a talk about Ian Rooke. You know what a private bloke he was. He didn't socialize much with anyone here even though everyone liked him, so she couldn't tell me much. But she mentioned he worked out at the old Patterson Gym in Darlinghurst. That's where you go, isn't it, Mark?"

"A couple of times a week, if I can manage it." Bourke added with a rueful smile, "Full disclosure—since we bought the house, I'm lucky if I make it once a fortnight, if then."

"Was Ian on good terms with everyone there?"

Bourke rubbed his nose as he considered Carol's question. "He'd say hello to me. That pretty well sums up the extent of our conversation. He was so focused on the strenuous program he'd set himself that he didn't say more than a few words to anyone."

"What about the staff at the gym?"

"Same thing. Hello and good-bye was about it. But that's nothing unusual—people aren't there to chat."

"I'm hoping Maureen can dig something up," Carol said. "She gets on with everyone, always has a joke or a bit of gossip to share. I've told her to casually ask around about Ian. Did anyone notice anything unusual? Did he discuss the Denby case? Was he worried about handling the media? What about pressure from the commissioner? Anything Maureen can find out to shed some light on Ian's state of mind could be of help."

"Hope she has better luck than I just did." Bourke slumped in a chair, all humor gone from his face. "Ian's car is more like a hunk of crushed metal than a vehicle. No one could have survived that fall down into the gorge. The petrol tank split open, it was some kind of miracle the bush didn't go up like a bonfire."

"The mechanics didn't find anything suspicious the second time around?"

"Zilch," Bourke said, taking out his notebook. "With Ian investigating such a controversial case, they looked for any sign of tampering. Nothing. The steering column killed him right through the deployed airbag. The brakes were fine, same with the tires. No problems with the steering, no sticking accelerator. The vehicle had the oil changed and a checkup three weeks ago. To sum up, it was in good shape."

"If the vehicle checks out, what's left seems to be driver error," Carol said. "Ian swerved to avoid hitting something and lost control, or he fell asleep at the wheel."

"Falling asleep seems the most likely. If something suddenly appeared in front of him, there'd be skid marks on the road indicating where he stamped on the brakes and yanked the steering wheel. There were none."

"So the commissioner was right? Ian was very tired, he lost concentration for a few moments, or did fall asleep, with fatal results."

"Maybe," said Bourke, but his expression conveyed doubt. "I managed to get hold of the leader of the rescue team who climbed down to the wreck. Most of the glass had been smashed to pieces, but the driver's window was intact enough to show it was down at the time of the crash."

"Maybe because he'd started to feel sleepy."

"That could be. It was a cold night, and Ian had the climate control turned to heat. He could have felt drowsy. Whatever, he wasn't wearing a seat belt."

She shook her head. "No seat belt, on that road—hard to believe. Could the belt have failed? There must have been tremendous G forces when the car was somersaulting into the gorge."

"It checked out. Nothing wrong with the belt. He wasn't wearing it."

One more element that didn't make sense. "He was so meticulous about everything..." Carol again shook her head. "For any cop, putting on a seat belt is automatic."

"Not this time." Bourke looked morosely at his notes. "Hindley asked us to check exactly what was found in the car. Short answer, nothing much. Stains in the passenger compartment that had to be dried blood..." He winced. "I told myself it would have happened so fast that Ian was dead before he could feel much of anything."

"That's probably true, Mark."

She had quoted from the standard words of comfort offered to relatives of homicide victims. She didn't believe them, had never believed them. She could too easily visualize Ian's nightmare plunge to his death into the gorge. Had the vehicle's headlights illuminated for him the depths into which he was falling? Or had they mercifully been smashed almost immediately?

Bourke looked down at his notes again. "The windscreen must have shattered when the vehicle hit the first of the trees growing out from the side of the cliff. There were various twigs, broken branches, leaves and bits of bark in the passenger compartment. Nothing personal of Ian's except his tie, which he probably took off when he got behind the wheel, and his personal mobile phone which the SOC team found in the glove box together with a flashlight. Both broken in pieces of course."

"His phone was in the glove box?"

"Well, he did have Bluetooth, but Ian hadn't used that phone for at least a week," said Bourke. "Received calls but didn't take them. The last call he made on it was to his dentist." With a faint grin he added, "And before you ask, yes, I checked it out. All aboveboard. Ian had his teeth cleaned two days before he died."

"How about the boot?"

"They did manage to pry it open. Empty."

Carol sat back in her chair, puzzling over Ian Rooke's last hours. "Why was there nothing in the car about the Denby case?"

"Beats me," said Bourke. "It's odd for two reasons. One, because I know he almost always took work home. In fact, his wife complained to me that he spent so much time on his cases, he hardly saw his family. And two, the Denby case is *huge*. Ian should have been spending every waking moment on it."

"Very true." Carol leaned forward and punched in Anne's intercom number. "Anne, would you check the appointments you and Ian Rooke had set up for the day after he died? And any scheduled for the rest of the week. Thanks."

"What are you thinking?" said Bourke.

"It didn't strike me before, but when I was given the Denby case, I found the files, Ian's notes, everything, all together waiting for me in the file drawer of his desk."

"He was a neat freak—everyone knows that."

"I've heard *you* described in exactly those words."

Bourke spread his hands. "What can I say? It's a trial to be so perfect."

She looked up at a knock on the doorframe. Anne came in.

"I'd already checked. Inspector Rooke had only one appointment for the rest of the week, for nine o'clock the day after he died. He'd made an appointment to see Frederick Lowell at his law offices."

"He didn't ask you go with him to take notes?" Anne shook her head. "Any idea why he was seeing Lowell?"

"Not really." Anne considered for a moment, then said, "It's funny, but I had the impression it was something personal between them. Can't imagine what it could be, since the Inspector made it clear he'd never met Lowell before this case."

"Yet another mystery," said Bourke, getting to his feet. He stretched and yawned. "I'm too old for late nights." Stifling another yawn, he headed for the door. "I'll do a preliminary report for the commissioner, in which I say that basically as yet there's no evidence of foul play but we're continuing to investigate."

"What about the needle puncture?" Carol asked.

"That bloody, inconvenient needle puncture," Bourke said, and Carol knew he was just as puzzled and uncomfortable about this death as she was.

Anne asked, "What about his kids? They're very young, aren't they?"

Bourke nodded. "They're with Ian's parents outside Newcastle. To shield them from the media. The kids are six and four—too young to really know what's going on."

"Ian's funeral is next week," Carol said. "I want to interview Rosalie Rooke soon."

* * *

Simon Sykes finally called Carol's mobile. She snatched it up from the charger on her desk. "I was about to call you, Mr. Sykes, regarding our meeting tonight with Canon Armitage."

"I can only apologize for my tardiness. I would have got back to you earlier had I not been with Commissioner Hindley."

Gritting her teeth at his unctuous tone, Carol offered a noncommittal, "I see."

"The commissioner asked me to advise you that there will be a Cherished Life demonstration outside the Denby home this afternoon. The word's gone out through their website and various social networks—Twitter, Facebook, the lot. Possibly there will be counter-protesters against Cherished Life. And of course the media will be there in strength."

"The Denbys have been alerted?"

"The commissioner himself advised them of the problem," said Sykes, adding with smooth assurance, "and he personally guaranteed a substantial police presence to head off any trouble."

"What rationale is behind the demonstration?"

Sykes gave a disgusted grunt. "Canon Armitage has brainwashed his deluded followers to the point that they merely parrot the slogans they've been taught. They denounce suicide, assisted suicide—euthanasia in general. Conveniently, Greta Denby's death appears to fit into all of the above."

"When's the demo scheduled? I'll be in the vicinity this afternoon."

"The time given on their website is two o'clock." In his annoying way, he emitted a little cough to clear his throat, then said with oily certainty, "Am I correct in assuming you're in Mosman to interview Iris Kemp?"

"Yes," Carol snapped, increasingly irked by his smug, know-it-all attitude.

"I may have something for you about Kemp. I'll email the material the moment I get off the phone. It's self-explanatory."

"If the subject of Iris Kemp hadn't come up, Mr. Sykes, just when were you intending to give me this material?" Carol inquired.

"In a timely fashion, of course, I assure you. This evening, actually." Sykes gave another delicate cough. "We're to liaise with Canon Armitage at the Cherished Life headquarters at seven forty-five."

Carol jotted down the details and established that she and Sykes would arrive at the organization's building a few minutes early to discuss between themselves any issues that might arise from the demonstration and the media coverage.

"One final thing," said Sykes. "I'm speaking in my role as PR adviser to the commissioner when I point out how injudicious it would be for you to be seen at, or indeed, near the demonstration this afternoon."

"Thank you for your advice."

Her icy tone impelled him to add hastily, "Naturally I have every confidence that you would always conduct yourself in a professional manner."

"Good-bye, Mr. Sykes." She terminated the call.

"Bloody hell," she grated. The meeting with Armitage might be completed in a few minutes, or it could stretch for hours. There was no way to know what time she'd be free to go to Sybil's place.

She had the unsettling conviction that what she said and did in the next few days would have a significant impact upon her future with Sybil. This unavoidable complication couldn't have been more ill-timed. She picked up her mobile and weighed it in her hand as she rehearsed what she would say and how she would say it. She was never this indecisive. "Oh, come on! Just do it."

She speed-dialed Sybil's number, and when she answered, took a deep breath. "It's me. Darling, I'm so sorry, but..."

It was a short, unsatisfactory conversation, ending with Sybil saying, "Come when you can and let yourself in. I won't wait up for you."

Carol sat morosely staring into space. What was that line from a song? Something about not knowing what you'd lost until it was gone.

The strident ring of her desk phone broke up her thoughts. She contemplated not answering it, but forced herself to pick up the receiver. "Yes. Put her through."

"It's Thalia, Chief Inspector Ashton."

"Yes, Ms. Denby?"

A throaty laugh came down the line. "Please, *please*, call me Thalia."

"Is this about the demonstration? I believe Commissioner Hindley has told you that steps have been taken to ensure your security."

"Nothing to do with the demo—it'll be a nonevent. Anyhow, I won't be at home this afternoon." Her voice warming to huskiness, Thalia went on, "Kenny and I will be live on TV this coming Wednesday in a special segment representing my mother about the work of charitable foundations for victims of domestic violence. An absolutely perfect way to end the fundraising weekend for my mother's Safe Haven foundation."

"Yes?" Carol said with a hint of impatience.

"I'd love you to be my guest at the celebration afterward. Very exclusive, I assure you." Thalia gave another cozy chuckle. "Rather forward of me to call you like this, but I know you'll forgive me."

It *was* forward. And arrogant, and irritating, and in terms of forgiveness, inconsequential. Before Carol could speak cool words rejecting the invitation, Thalia said, "Someone you know well will be there—Madeline Shipley's guest-producing the show. Did I say we're going live to air? Nerve-wracking, when Kenny's on camera. No one knows, least of all Kenny, what he will say next."

"I can well imagine," said Carol, diverted in spite of herself. "It's standard in live broadcasts to have a ten-second delay, so somebody will have a finger on the dump button."

"I'm relieved," said Thalia. "Now, where shall I send the limousine to pick you up?"

Irritation shifting to wry amusement at Thalia Denby's cheekiness, Carol said, "You won't, Ms. Denby. Thank you for the invitation, but I'm not available."

"Ms. Denby? That's so official, Chief Inspector."

Amusement shifted back to irritation. *I can't very well hang up on the woman.* But she did not have to respond.

"I can see I've done the wrong thing," Thalia said into the silence. "I apologize. It's just that I felt an instant connection between us. And you felt it too, didn't you?"

Clearly, Thalia Denby was accustomed to the twin battering rams of her physical beauty and celebrity knocking down all barriers. Carol said with ice-cold formality, "I'm a police officer investigating your mother's death. That fact alone precludes anything other than professional distance." Not to mention that Thalia Denby had not been taken off the suspect list.

"You've put me in my place," Thalia said, her amused tone conveying that she had not remotely moved to that place. "You'll find I never stay anyplace for long." Her phone clicked off.

* * *

In her sunroom Sybil glanced with indefinable emotion at the mobile lying silent on the round cane table. She wasn't surprised Carol couldn't commit to what time she'd be here tonight; she was embroiled in a major, high profile investigation and her suggestion of dinner had been pure wishful thinking. Sybil had expected the call she'd just received. What she hadn't expected was uncertainty in a voice that always conveyed assurance, the apologetic admission that her arrival would not be the early evening she'd hoped for.

She stood at the sunroom window absently watching the huge waves generated by a storm far out at sea smash themselves into boiling foam on the sand. Yesterday, during their first meeting, Jayleen Smith had said, "Always tell yourself the unvarnished truth. You can choose to lie to others—to yourself, *never.*"

What *was* the unvarnished truth? Could she really be totally honest with herself about Carol? Perhaps she was refusing to face a stark and inescapable fact: their relationship would inevitably end because of what had happened on that sunny morning when she opened Carol's door to Philip Ular.

It's not your fault, Carol. But—neither is it mine.

Even as she formed this thought, a resentful anger tightened her throat. Carol had to bear some of the blame. Didn't she?

Her thoughts went back to the day before Philip Ular, before the horrors of the next morning that would blight her life. She had just returned from an introspective and healing year in England, believing herself ready to give Carol her decision, that no reconciliation between them was possible. Carol's single-minded response had been to insist she stay at Seaforth that night, citing the danger the running-amuck Philip Ular posed to anyone he held responsible, however tenuously, for his brother's conviction and subsequent death in a prison riot.

Sybil had reluctantly agreed. Ular was a soulless sociopath, capable of the worst one could imagine.

The next morning, Carol had told her of the trap they had set for him. How very sure Carol had been that Ular would take the bait, certain that he would attempt to kill the judge who had sentenced his brother to a life term for murder. She'd given no thought to any other outcome.

In hindsight, Sybil had to admit that she too had been convinced that Justice Flint would prove to be an irresistible lure. By comparison, she herself had played only a peripheral role as a minor witness in the events leading to Ular's brother Reginald's arrest, and she had no connection whatever to the prison beating that had cost him his life.

They had all completely misjudged his intentions. Raining destruction on the life of Inspector Carol Ashton had been Ular's primary objective—and the torture-death of Sybil Quade had been the means.

Chillingly aware she could trigger another flashback if she kept agonizing about the past, she said to Jeffrey, who was sprawled inelegantly on his back exposing his ginger belly to a patch of sunlight, "You never worry about the past or the future do you, Jeffrey? It's always *now* to you."

Carol's call had interrupted her preparations for her next therapy session. Normally, she would not have seen Jayleen so soon after her first appointment, but the unfortunate man with the family emergency had been forced to cancel his make-up Monday session too.

Jayleen had emailed her a selection of material relating to new strategies for dealing with her PTSD and Sybil was reading through each article with a yellow highlighter. As a teacher, it felt strange to be on the receiving end of homework, but Jayleen had explained that she required her client to be well-informed and equipped to take a proactive role in her own treatment.

Sybil's realistic immediate goal for her therapy would be a reduction in the number of vivid flashbacks. Jayleen, however, had confidently stated that Sybil could expect more than that, assuring her she would be able to control not just the frequency but the intensity of the disturbing images.

Sybil remained doubtful, knowing from personal experience and from her reading how difficult PTSD was to treat. Even so, Jayleen had kindled a spark of hope that persisted through all chidings of herself that any expectation was very likely wishful thinking.

Jayleen's attitude was light years away from her experiences with psychiatrists. Each of the doctors she had consulted had taken a similar stance—the psychiatrist was the guide and Sybil the passive, cooperative patient. Looking back, she could see how she had been encouraged to play the role of a child, while the psychiatrist took the role of wise parent.

"Was I too abrupt with Carol?" she asked Jeffrey who was staring at her from his patch of sunlight. For a few moments he seemed to consider her question, then he blinked slowly. "I *was* too abrupt—is that what you're telling me?" There was no response. Her feline sage had gone to sleep.

She returned to the cane chair and table where she'd been sitting before Carol's call had set her pacing around the sunroom. To finish *Prolonged Exposure Theory: A New Approach to PTSD*.

THIRTEEN

Iris Kemp lived in a grand old house converted tastefully into separate flats within a few minutes' walking distance of the Denby estate's impressive front entrance. She was waiting for them at the front gate when Anne drew up to the curb. "She may be small," Anne had briefed Carol, "but she's dauntingly energetic."

Carol's mental image had been of a talkative but unassuming older woman conservatively dressed in muted colors and wearing sensible low-heeled shoes. Clearly a major revision was necessary. Small? She was miniscule. Carol felt like a giant towering over a diminutive figure with a mass of gray curls, alert brown eyes and a face animated by mobile eyebrows and an expressive mouth. She wore crisp white jeans and a luminescent pink blouse. Her white leather walking shoes were far from new but without a scuff mark on them.

"Knew you'd be punctual." Her voice was high and clear. "So, came out to meet you. Made a cake. Chocolate, everyone likes chocolate. You do, surely, Chief Inspector? You'll have a slice, won't you?"

"Ms. Kemp—"

"Oh, no, *no! Iris.* Everyone calls me Iris." With a giggle, she added, "So fortunate, since my name *is* Iris. Otherwise they'd call me something else, wouldn't they?"

Carol already felt exhausted. She caught the smile on Anne's face. If she'd been in a better mood, she too would have been amused. As it was, she needed to concentrate on the business at hand and not be distracted by worry over her conversation with Sybil.

"Have you spoken with anyone in the media?" Carol asked, thinking of the communication she'd received from Simon Sykes.

"Only if you count 'no comment' as speaking." Chuckling at her own witticism, she ushered them through the gate. "Reporters pestered me, popping up all over the place. Even followed me while I shopped at the supermarket. And the phone calls! A trial. The person they really upset was Sid McGowan across the street. One of those big TV trucks backed right over his snapdragons, would you believe? Mad as a cut snake he was!"

"I can imagine," Anne said, managing to sound sympathetic.

While driving to Mosman with Anne, Carol had discussed how to run the interview, how it should be tailored. Anne was a natural at interviewing. Like Mark Bourke, she used a casual, easygoing manner to disarm subjects and convince them that she posed no threat. Relaxed, their defenses down, they were unprepared for Anne to ask, in the same mild tone, the hard questions, and very often blurted admissions they might never have revealed to another interviewer.

"These flowers are glorious," Anne said, indicating the bloom-covered bushes on either side of the front path.

"I tend to the garden," said Iris Kemp with justifiable pride. "I have a green thumb. Even my late hubby said so."

Carol said, surveying the staid elegance of the building, "This is a very tasteful conversion. I gather Greta Denby helped you find this place?"

"And arranged to pay the rent on my flat. Greta's always been such a generous soul. Not to everyone, mind, but to those she cares about." Misery flooded her face. "I have so much trouble thinking of Greta in the past tense. I keep expecting to see her, hear her laugh…"

Carol had seen too many suspects mimic sincere grief and loss to be certain that Iris's sorrow was genuine, but her instant and raw emotion was convincing.

"It is a sad time," Carol said with sympathy. Then, shifting gears, "You've been associated with the Denby family for a long time, so I imagine you've seen Thalia and Kenneth Denby grow up."

Iris smiled nostalgically. "I've known those two darlings for their entire lives. My hubby, you know, worked on the grounds for goodness knows how long. Thalia and Kenny were beautiful children, but like all of us, I suppose, they've had a few problems as young adults."

A few problems? Carol exchanged a bemused glance with Anne. They could itemize rather more than a few. Thalia had been particularly wild, Carol had learned. Her police record included possession of controlled substances, drug-fueled altercations often resulting in the old reliable, resisting arrest. She had spent two stints in court-ordered treatment for substance abuse, all served in privately run luxurious clinics. Nothing in recent months; either she'd acquired self-discipline and impulse control—highly doubtful, Carol thought, remembering the phone call—or she understood her jeopardy. Probably the case here. Having used up all possible judicial leniency, brushes with the law would now draw jail time.

Kenny tended to show his uninhibited nature by means of fast, expensive sports cars. Breaking the speed limit was standard behavior for him. In the process he'd written off a Porsche and an Aston Martin, but he had remained relatively unscathed each time, aside from what surely had to be astronomical traffic fines and punitive insurance premiums. Carol considered it inexplicable that Kenneth Denby still had a driver's license. If in fact he did.

"I have the impression Greta's son particularly relied upon his mother," Carol remarked.

"Oh, *Kenny!* Runt of the litter, you know!" She paused to consider. "*Can* it be a litter if there are only two? Well, anyway, yes Kenny did rely on Greta for everything. He has such original ideas, all these games for computers and such, but none of them seem to ever work out that I know of. Kenny's a dreamer, but as they say, you can't live in castles in the air."

"And Thalia?"

Iris's disapproving expression was replaced with a smile. "She was *so* attached to her father. And likewise him to her. He was grooming her, you know, to take some sort of role in his businesses. I thought she'd never get over his death. I'm sure it's why she kicked over the traces and got herself into all that mischief with the law. But now she's turned into Greta's gift to the world and she'll be carrying on her mother's wonderful charity work."

Perhaps wishful thinking, Carol speculated, remembering Thalia's reluctance to fulfill a minor commitment to Dr. Valdez's event, and as for her attending her mother's fundraiser, odds on it was prompted by the presence of television cameras and Madeline Shipley.

The back fence had a gate secured by a simple latch. Anne opened it and peered out. "This is the lane that runs behind the Denby house, isn't it?"

Iris beamed at her. "It is!"

"Thalia told me she parks elsewhere. Would this be it?"

Iris nodded. "Oh yes! I don't drive, so my spot is free for her to use. The dear girl doesn't like people to know her comings and goings and she has a right to her own life. In the big house there's nothing private. Do you want to see the carport?"

She led them down the short driveway to the back of the building. "Thalia's out at the moment..."

"Isn't that an MG sports car?" Anne asked.

"It is! British Racing Green's the color. A vintage MG. When I was young—feels like a hundred years ago—any boy who drove a car like that, he was a *god*. Thalia parks next to it. We call the MG Mr. Beecham's folly."

"Why is it Mr. Beecham's folly?" Anne dutifully inquired.

"He's been restoring it bit by bit for years. Wife got fed up." She mimicked a high-pitched voice: "'Beecham, either the MG goes or I do.'" Iris added with a peal of laughter, "And *she* went."

Iris stepped briskly into the lane. "That's the Denby boundary," she said, indicating the dark brown wooden fence on the other side. "And down there," she said, pointing, "is the gate into the estate." Frowning, she cocked her head like a curious bird. "What *is* that noise?"

"Cherished Life is staging a demonstration outside the Denbys' front gate," Carol said as indistinct shouts and the muffled sound of a loud hailer were carried by the breeze. Added to this was another sound, the whop-whop-whop of approaching helicopters.

"They'll get great shots of the demo for the news tonight," said Anne. "Armitage will be happy. Like they say, you can't pay for that kind of publicity."

"It's a crying shame," declared Iris. "The family's in mourning, for heaven's sake! Canon Armitage has no respect for the dead. Or the living, either."

"You speak as though you've met him," Carol said.

Iris shook her head vigorously. "Me? No. Wouldn't recognize Armitage if I tripped over the man."

Carol and Anne exchanged glances, Carol's brief headshake a sign not to pursue this.

As soon as Carol and Anne were seated in Iris's spotless, uncluttered little flat, she bustled off to the kitchen.

Carol had imagined the place would contain old-fashioned furniture on faded wall-to-wall carpet with family photographs and knickknacks on small tables. Again, she couldn't have been more wrong. The décor was minimalist modern, with chrome and white leather chairs that proved to be a great deal more comfortable than they looked. Deep maroon rugs lay strategically placed on the polished hardwood floor. The only table in evidence was a low coffee table featuring brilliant abstract swirls of color in its heavy glass top.

Iris served tea and chocolate cake and would not countenance them taking anything less than a generous slice. Carol noticed Anne wolfing her cake down, and managed to successfully pick away at hers.

Washing down the last of it with good strong black tea, Carol prepared to start the interview. Anne took out her notebook and balanced it on her knee, giving Carol a nod to indicate she was ready.

"Ms. Kemp—"

"*Iris*, please!"

"I've read your statement covering the night and the early morning hours before Bea Parker discovered Greta Denby's body. I hope you don't mind going over it again."

"Oh, poor Greta!" Iris took out a lacy handkerchief and dabbed at her eyes. "I get so upset just thinking about what happened. But if I can be of any help…" She aimed a wobbly smile at Anne. "The interview with you and Inspector Rooke was very comprehensive, I thought. Can't imagine there's many more questions to ask me." She dutifully switched her attention back to Carol. "I'm ready."

"In general, during the night you would spend most of the time in your sitting room next to Greta. Is that correct?"

Iris's nod seemed careful, as if she were expecting some trap lurking in Carol's question. "Yes, unless Greta wanted my company, or something to eat or drink. Or needed help to go to the bathroom. And of course I would look in on her every hour or so to make sure everything was okay."

"Those times you are in your room, do you shut the door?"

Iris sat silent to give this some thought.

Carol said, "Are you finding the question difficult to answer?"

"Not at all. I often watch movies and the soundtracks these days can be so loud, don't you agree? I didn't want to run any chance of disturbing Greta's sleep, so I'd say I usually kept the door closed."

"So it would be possible for someone to enter the bedroom without your knowledge?"

"Possible, but very unlikely."

It would be quite likely with her door closed, Carol thought, but she'd detected defensiveness in Iris's tone and chose not to immediately challenge the statement.

"That night her visitors were Dr. Valdez and Thalia?" Iris nodded. "No one else, then."

"Well, yes. Bea, to give Greta her midnight meds."

"Did you see her, hear her?"

"The house is quiet at that hour and Bea takes pains to disturb Greta as little as possible. Greta's very tired from her day by then."

Carol took that as a no. In contradiction to her original statement that she heard Bea and would hear anyone who went in. "The hours must be long when everything is quiet and you're the only one awake," she observed.

Iris said sharply, "If you're about to ask me if I ever sleep on the job, I don't. And I didn't at any time fall asleep that last night."

"Let's look at that night," Carol said easily. "You relieved Bea Parker at eight o'clock sharp, when your shift began. Is that correct? I ask because precision as far as time is concerned is essential in an investigation."

Perched on the edge of her chair, Iris pursed her lips as if wondering how to answer Carol's question. "More or less correct. I arrived early because Bea asked me as a favor to check in at seven thirty."

"Do you know why?"

From her conflicted expression, Carol's question was not a welcome one. At last, when the silence had stretched to the point where her discomfort overcame her reluctance, Iris said, "I didn't mention this before because…because Bea asked me not to." Clearly embarrassed, Iris stared at the floor.

Carol murmured an encouraging, "Please go on."

"Bea rang me midafternoon. Said she had to leave early. Late that morning, Greta had an argument with Kenny over some scheme of his that Greta thought foolhardy. They were both upset, especially him. He begged Bea to meet him. Said she was the only one who could help him patch things up with his mother. It had to be seven thirty. He had some important appointment after that."

"With whom?"

"I've no idea."

Iris had answered so quickly, Carol decided the opposite was probably true. She asked politely, "Are you sure? Perhaps a name was mentioned…?"

She shrugged. "Maybe Mr. Lowell, about his allowance. I don't know." Her face again twisted into misery. "Poor Kenny, he must feel absolutely dreadful that an argument with his mother is his last memory of her."

"I'm sure," Carol said with sympathy. "That evening, did Greta mention anything about her nurse leaving early?"

Iris shook her head. "Actually, she'd dozed off, and didn't know Bea had gone." Clearly more at ease with this topic, she went on, "Of late, since Greta's become so weak, something as simple as a shower exhausts her. Bea said she'd fallen asleep over her evening meal even though Dr. Valdez was there." Iris gusted a heavy sigh. "It's horrible, seeing someone so vital become more and more of an invalid."

"Understandably, anyone in such a situation would be likely to be depressed."

With a touch of indignation, Iris said, "Not Greta, never. She had such a positive attitude. She viewed it as nothing but a temporary setback. It was incredible. I admired her so much."

"So she was asleep when you came on duty early, at seven thirty?"

"Yes, Chief Inspector."

Carol almost smiled at the respectful tone Iris had assumed. "You didn't see Dr. Valdez?"

"Not then. Later, when he and Thalia called in around nine o'clock. Greta was wide awake. She asked me to make her a toasted cheese sandwich and Thalia brought her a mug of coffee with lots of cream. It was her favorite snack. Bea would have been livid if she'd known—she's really bossy about healthy diets—but Greta couldn't eat more than a few bites, poor thing."

"I've read your preliminary statement," Carol said. "In it you say you looked into the bedroom at regular intervals throughout the night to make sure everything was in order. And as far as you were concerned, everything was."

Iris looked at her warily. "That's right."

"And on each occasion you went to the bedside?"

"Not exactly." When Carol raised her eyebrows, Iris hastened to explain. "Greta's night light provided easily enough illumination for me to see how she was without running the chance of waking her. A couple of times during my shift I did come right into the bedroom."

"What time was your last check?"

"I'm not sure. Somewhere between five and six. I didn't notice the time."

"Did you go to the bedside that time?"

"No. Greta seemed to be sleeping peacefully."

It seemed minimal that observing Greta Denby during the night would include verifying that her chest was moving up and down with her breathing. "The coroner estimates that Greta Denby was dead by four o'clock."

Carol's cold statement straightened Iris's back. "I was never employed as a medical professional," she said in an equally chilly tone. "I fulfilled my duties. It seemed to me that Greta was all right and I hardly wanted to disturb her. If Bea had been in my place, then perhaps she would have realized something was very wrong."

Assuming that Iris had no reason to kill her employer and friend, she'd more than likely been asleep herself between five and six o'clock. There was no point in challenging or antagonizing her. For now.

Carol glanced over to Anne, who took the cue from Carol's lack of follow-up and said, "When we spoke with Bea Parker yesterday, she mentioned several times that she was a fully qualified nurse, and that you—"

"Had no qualifications at all!" Iris finished with a smile.

"You don't mind?" Anne asked.

"Not one bit. It's just Bea's little way of puffing up her self-image."

"Oh?" Anne raised her eyebrows. "Really?"

Encouraged by Anne's apparent surprise, Iris dropped her voice as she said, "Truthfully, Bea's not all that good at what she does. Just ask Dr. Valdez. You know, I never can bring myself to call him a silly name like Dr. Ed, even though he says he prefers it."

"So Dr. Valdez wasn't pleased with Bea?"

"Far from it! More than once I've heard him telling her off for not giving Greta her medications at precisely the times he'd scheduled. And just a fortnight ago, when I arrived to take over from Bea, they were at it, hammer and tongs. He was saying he'd have her dismissed, and Bea was saying she'd been with the family for years and Greta listened to her and Thalia and Kenny were fine with her, so he should watch out. They both shut up when they saw me."

"I bet they did! Tell me, who would you back to win?"

Carol wouldn't have phrased the question this way, but she admired Anne's conversational just-between-us style, which had Iris responding freely.

"To win? Oh, Dr. Valdez, no worries! Greta thought he walked on water."

"And you? What's your opinion about his water walking?"

Iris gave this some thought. "I'd have to say I believe he's sincere. Not a crook, or anything like that. He really is convinced his treatment works and he and Greta both believed he could save her life. He was stunned on the phone and looked gobsmacked when he came in and found she was well and truly gone."

A reaction, Carol thought, not in evidence when she'd met him.

"It's my understanding it was Bea Parker who called Dr. Valdez after she discovered Greta's body."

"No, it wasn't. *I* had to call him. Bea fell to pieces. Panicked."

"You must have been astonished to see that," said Anne, adding without a sign of levity, "and she a registered nurse!"

Carol hid a smile. Iris laughed outright. "Fancy," she said, "all those qualifications, and here's Bea running around the room like a hen with its head chopped off."

Carol glanced at Anne to indicate she would take over. She said to Iris, "What was the reason for Nurse Parker's panic?"

Carol's stern tone instantly sobered Iris. She straightened in her chair. "Bea was hysterical over the idea that she somehow made some mistake with Greta's medications. Especially since Dr. Valdez had made yet another change in her dosage. I went over to the bed and checked Greta's pulse. She wasn't breathing, her skin wasn't cold yet but it wasn't warm. I knew she was gone."

This probably explained Bea Parker's inability to remember whether Greta Denby's skin was warm or cool. "There was no mention of Bea Parker's panic attack in anyone's statement."

Iris looked self-righteously at Carol. "It wasn't my responsibility to mention it. You're the first one who's asked. I slapped some sense into Bea, told her to pull herself together, and called Dr. Valdez. From the look of the pill dispenser it seemed she'd given her exactly what she was supposed to, but I knew it would be the first thing anyone would ask her, and it was up to her what she told them."

"An account she conveniently revised." Carol's tone was biting. Iris shifted in her chair. "You have withheld information that could be important to our investigation."

"I'm sorry, I didn't think anyone needed to know how silly she behaved." She bit her lip. "I mean, Bea can be careless, but not *that* careless."

"In your judgment."

"Well, yes. In my judgment."

Had Bea Parker been in a similar panic when her previous patient had fallen down the stairs? If so, why had Frederick Lowell recommended her for Greta?

"This is not the only information you have withheld, is it?"

Iris swallowed. "I haven't a clue what you mean."

Carol looked at her for a long moment, then said, "Have you ever been arrested?"

"I...No, never."

"And you've never met Canon Armitage?"

Iris remained silent. Carol waited. At last, Iris said, "I may have met Canon Armitage. It slipped my mind."

"And it also slipped your mind that you were arrested for making threats against Canon Armitage's life?"

Iris said quickly, "Oh, that. That was just hot air." With a defiant lift of her chin she added, "The magistrate thought so too. He let me go with just a fine and a warning to watch my tongue."

Carol regarded her thoughtfully. Simon Sykes had emailed a brief news clipping covering a demonstration outside a political meeting where Armitage had appeared to endorse a far right candidate for the Senate. As Armitage left the stage, he was accosted by Iris Kemp, who had entered the hall conservatively dressed to appear to be a supporter. There was an exchange of heated words, and Iris had reached into her bag for pig's blood to throw over the Canon but was instantly hustled away by security before she could act. She had been arrested for attempted assault, and uttering specific death threats the newspaper chose not to quote verbatim.

"On the subjects of death and dying," Carol said, "would it be fair to say you hold opposing views to those promoted by Cherished Life?"

Lifting her shoulders in an exaggerated shrug, Iris declared, "I don't give a fig about mercy killing or assisted suicide. It's abortion rights I'll do anything to defend. Every woman should have total control over her own body."

"But isn't the decision to die at a time and place you yourself choose also a matter of control over one's own body?" Carol asked.

Her face flushing with anger, Iris said, "Do you really believe I would help Greta end her life when doing so would mean I lost a job, an income, and a dear friend?"

"Perhaps, if you were in Greta's will. Perhaps, if you gained more than you lost."

Standing, Iris drew herself up to her meager height in full outrage. "I don't intend to answer any more questions until I receive legal advice. Please leave. Now."

FOURTEEN

Iris Kemp slammed the front door of her flat.

"I guess that means no more homemade chocolate cake for us," Anne said.

"Guess not."

Carol's flat tone signaled she was not in the mood for banter, and Anne did not miss the cue. They walked down the hallway in silence. Outside, the chatter of hovering helicopters indicated that the protest rally was still proving to be a newsworthy event.

"At least Armitage's followers are keeping the media occupied," Carol said, donning dark glasses to temper the rays of glaring afternoon sun in a cloudless sky.

"It would be interesting to know if Iris truly did restrict her attack on Canon Armitage to abortion rights only," Anne mused.

"That reminds me." Carol's mood darkened again as she slid into the passenger seat. "Simon Sykes. I'm going to spend a fun evening with him chatting to Armitage at the Cherished Life headquarters. Apparently it's more PR platitudes than interview, but I'll take the opportunity to ask the Canon if he remembers

Iris Kemp. As far as I can see, there's no reason why he should. Iris would be just another confrontation among many others."

The clatter of blades was becoming louder. One of the helicopters had peeled off and was headed their way as they drove off. Anne said, "Traffic's bad enough as it is. People from the demo will only make it worse."

She negotiated Raglan Street and joined the long column of vehicles clogging Military Road. "It's the weekend," she grumbled, "the weather is beautiful, everybody's out and about, the roads will be jammed. I'll go the back way," she decided. "It's longer, but quicker."

Carol's mobile rang.

"Simon Sykes here. There's been a change in plans, Chief Inspector. Might you be available now to meet with Canon Armitage at a different location?" Sykes sounded peeved, as though this change in plans did not suit him at all.

Carol was elated. She would be able to see Sybil this evening after all. After putting the phone on speaker so Anne could hear, Carol said, "In fact I would be. But at the moment I'm in Mosman, stuck in heavy traffic."

"Fortuitously, you're not far from our new meeting point. We've had to change location and have just arrived ourselves. It's a private residence, the home of one of the canon's most generous supporters. He and his family are away for the weekend, so the canon has full use of the house. Let's get this done now."

Sykes gave her an address in Kirribilli, a small harborside suburb nestling at the northern end of the Sydney Harbour Bridge. Carol recognized the name of the street. The houses there had panoramic, multimillion-dollar views of the harbor and the city.

"Why the change of venue, Mr. Sykes?"

"*Simon*, please." He gave a preparatory little cough before declaring, "Late this morning, Canon Armitage received what may be a credible death threat. He immediately contacted me—"

"Not the police?"

Sykes said sharply, "If you will allow me to continue, Chief Inspector, I was about to say that the canon refused point-blank to advise the authorities. He believes it may be a mentally disturbed individual affiliated with Cherished Life, so absolute discretion is required."

Carol shook her head. What difference would that make? None of it made any sense.

Grinning, Anne murmured to Carol, "Doesn't Mr. Sykes realize that by informing us he's advised the authorities and therefore gone against Canon Armitage's express wishes?"

When Carol repeated Anne's question to Sykes, he replied pompously, "No death threat should be taken lightly."

No *legitimate* threat, she thought. But she said, "Of course not. So what's been done to ensure the canon's safety? At the very least, does he have a personal bodyguard with him at all times?"

"I've been given no specific details," Sykes snapped.

"How was this death threat delivered? In writing? By phone?"

"I've no idea!" He took a breath, then said in a calmer voice, "Canon Armitage has emphatically assured me that all necessary security arrangements are in place."

"A private home is difficult to secure effectively," Carol noted. "He would be safer in the Cherished Life headquarters."

"I'll expect you in say, half an hour?" Sykes said, pointedly ignoring the remark.

"At best, given the parking situation in that area."

"When you arrive, please text me."

Carol disconnected with an impatient sigh. "What do you reckon, Anne? Armitage is suddenly and conveniently available for a meeting scheduled for this evening. He's got a demo well underway that's receiving at least minor press coverage. Now he's apparently got a threat on his life—we have no details— so he decides he'll be safer in an unguarded private home in Kirribilli instead of a building with security already in place."

"Bloody publicity stunt," Anne muttered.

"I'd say so. Especially if the media have been alerted."

Anne's ill-tempered reaction matched her own. Armitage had been suspected of similar ploys, misusing police time and resources. Saturation coverage of Greta Denby's controversial death was an opportunity for another of his trumped-up stunts and more waste of precious police resources.

Carol called the commissioner's private line. When voice mail kicked in, she left a terse message outlining the situation. She called in a request for a patrol car to sweep the neighborhood. Told it would be at least thirty minutes before a car would be available because of the Denby demonstration, she said wearily, "As soon as possible," then requested a text alert when patrolling began.

"This is rare luck," Anne said only twenty minutes later, swiftly backing into a tight parking spot on the Kirribilli street seconds after a silver Mercedes had vacated it. "It's always hell to park anywhere around here." She'd made exceptional time already via her alternate route.

Carol, who suspected she looked as grim as she felt over being roped into what looked to be a setup, tried to keep her tone light. "Our one bit of good fortune. I'm not expecting any more this afternoon."

"Shall I wait in the car?" Anne asked.

"And miss this wonderful opportunity to meet with Canon Armitage?"

Anne grimaced. "Of course not. I can't imagine what I was thinking."

They were parked three cars down from the address Sykes had given Carol, a meticulously restored nineteenth-century brick terrace house enjoying the prized corner position on the block. Its harbor view was magnificent, ships and ferries, launches, vessels big and small crisscrossing the blue-green water. And because it was the weekend, yachts of every size ran before the wind, their colored spinnakers bright in the hot, clear summer day. A five-minute walk from where they stood were the massive sandstone pylons supporting the soaring gray arch of the Sydney Harbour Bridge. Across the water, the towers of the city rose behind the glorious curving roofs of the Sydney Opera House.

The vista reminded Carol of what made this city so extraordinarily beautiful—the immensity of Sydney Harbour, its inlets and islands, its little bays and tiny beaches. She had lived in this incomparable place all her life, and knew she was unlikely to be happy anywhere else.

Out of habit she checked her surroundings, but now more acutely because of the death threat to Armitage, however spurious it might seem.

A steep narrow road choked with parked cars ran down beside the house toward the water. Across it the two pylons supporting the bridge were set in a broad grassy area with no cover for an attacker. The parked vehicles, however, provided ample opportunities for concealment.

They walked up the rise of the side road to check out the back entrance of the house. "They've even managed to squeeze in a garage," Anne remarked. Next to the securely locked garage door, a double green gate, also locked, was set into the high brick wall. "I'm guessing there's a patio in there," she said. "Or maybe a hot tub."

A breeze with a welcome hint of coolness blew off the water as they walked back down the slope to the front of the terrace. As instructed, Carol texted Sykes's mobile: *We're outside.*

She had her hand on the latch of the cast-iron gate when Sykes opened the front door. "Come in," he said tensely, with none of his customary arch courtesy.

Carol and Anne mounted four shallow steps leading to a small tiled porch spanning the front of the narrow building. "Wait here," Sykes ordered with an abrupt gesture toward a small alcove which held a bench seat and a hall tree with brass hooks for coats.

Carol told him, "Sergeant Newsome will be taking notes of the meeting."

Glancing at Anne in irritation, he snapped, "I'll advise Canon Armitage."

Watching his retreating back as he hurried down the narrow hall, Anne said, "What the hell is his problem? Isn't he supposed to be working for us?"

"The commissioner certainly—"

She broke off at the unmistakable flat crack of a shot.

Carol seized her Glock. Anne too drew her firearm as Sykes ducked his head out a doorway at the end of the hallway, yelling, "Someone's shot at the canon!"

"Is he hit?"

"No but—"

"Keep down! Call Triple-O! Anne, the back entrance."

Anne took off at a sprint and Carol ran past Sykes and into an area flooded with bright light, quickly noting that its sloping glass ceiling was not substantial enough to sustain the weight of an assailant.

To her left was a compact black-and-chrome kitchen, to her right an entertainment area and bar. French doors opened onto a sandstone patio that appeared deserted. The star pattern in the glass of one of the French doors showed the first and so far only shot, probably fired from an elevated position above the wall.

She called out to anyone in the house, "Take shelter till we tell you to move!"

She scanned the area in sections within the high brick privacy wall. To her left was the wall containing the wide dark green double door that they'd observed from the street a few minutes ago. Then it had been securely locked, although Carol knew better than to assume this was still the case.

A garage took up the back left corner of the area. Through its long window facing the house Carol could see the sleek lines of a luxury car, probably the creamy white Bentley that Armitage usually drove. Someone could be concealed in or behind the vehicle. A hot tub was set flush with the surface of the sandstone patio, its gentle bubbling loud enough to mask any slight sounds an intruder might make.

Seizing on the possibility that the weapon had been fired by someone looking down at the patio, Carol concentrated on the boundary walls, the roof of the garage, and in particular a substantial loquat tree on the neighbor's land, growing behind a creeper-covered back wall.

Sykes ventured out into the entertainment area. "Anything?"

She had enough to do without concerning herself with him. "Back inside, Mr. Sykes, you'll be—"

"I'm quite safe here," Sykes declared, walking toward her. "Surely he's got clean away by now. He'll be to hell and gone."

In the distance Carol heard the welcome wail of patrol car sirens. Then, from outside in the street, close to the gate, a male voice yelling, Anne's voice calling over his: "Got him! Open up!"

Carol, the Glock in both hands, her attention still focused on the possibility of another shooter, backed up until she could include the door in her field of vision. But Sykes was already there, fumbling with the lock, opening the double doors to reveal Anne behind a short, stocky, struggling man, her arm around his neck in a disabling hold. In her other hand was a lightweight bolt-action rifle she carried by the barrel to avoid smudging any fingerprints.

She loosened her grip and forcefully shoved her captive into the courtyard. The man, his wrists secured by nylon flexcuffs, staggered and stumbled and came to an abrupt halt at the sight of Carol's Glock aimed between his eyes. He wore a crumpled white shirt, faded jeans, and grubby tennis shoes. His nose was bloody and his expression was terrified.

"Solo act," Carol offered, securing her weapon in its holster.

"I'd say so. Choice of weapon alone." Anne deposited the rifle on the table, expertly patted down her captive, and added a wallet and car keys next to the rifle. "That's all. No spare ammunition."

She addressed her captive. "One-shot wonder, are you? Not even a telescopic sight. You're not an assassin's bootlace. Talk about amateur city!"

"Didn't do nothing wrong," he snuffled, blood and mucus dripping down his shirt.

"What happened out there?" Carol asked.

"Piece of cake," said Anne. "He's got his rifle still up on the wall, he's trying to scramble after it. I grab him. He resisted—so I had to get a bit rough with him."

Managing not to beam proudly at her sergeant, Carol nodded approval. "Is this your wallet?" she asked the man, checking through its contents.

"Yeah." He licked his lips. "Look—"

"You're Douglas James Fulton?"

"Yeah, but everyone calls me Lofty. Like, if I was real tall, they'd call me Shorty..." His eyes jerked around frantically, as if searching for someone.

"Do you need medical attention, Mr. Fulton?"

His lurching stare settling malevolently on Anne, he played tough guy. "For what? My nose? Ain't nuthin'."

Carol showed Fulton a keychain featuring a rabbit's foot. "Yours?"

"Yeah. The rabbit's foot's for luck."

Carol smothered a grin at this idiocy. Anne grabbed the keys, ducked out the door and pressed the Open symbol. A car parked directly outside obligingly beeped its horn. Very convenient parking spot, Carol noted.

Sykes muttered something to Carol about calling the commissioner, and turned to leave.

"Keep Canon Armitage in the other room for now," she instructed him.

"Canon Armitage!" Fulton called out. "You in there? You tell 'em we was just foolin' around—tell 'em it was a bit of a joke just like you said." To Carol, with conviction, "The canon will back me up."

The scream of a siren cut off as a patrol car skidded to a halt. Almost immediately more backup arrived. Within minutes the whole area was blocked off. The interested spectators grew rapidly, drawn by the promise of high drama on what had been a typically quiet day in staid Kirribilli.

Carol briefed the cops as they arrived. The house and surroundings were to be treated as a crime scene, and thoroughly searched. Although she had every reason to believe this to be an abortive publicity stunt, procedure dictated that the remote possibility of a second shooter had to be eliminated. Since

Fulton, the pea-brain of the operation, had the car keys, a co-conspirator would be on foot.

Leaving two cops guarding the suspect, with strict instructions not to allow anyone in the house to approach or speak with him, Carol and Anne went out into the street, Carol for overall assessment, Anne to have the suspect's car cordoned off.

Hearing Canon Armitage's name repeated, and someone opining at the top of her lungs that Greta Denby had every right to take her own life—a view that was challenged by a group of young men wearing Cherished Life T-shirts—Carol decided to reinforce the security particularly at the back of the house where the onlookers were concentrated. Mobile phones were held aloft, taking photos and videos of anything and anybody. Standing on friends' shoulders, some managed to get shots directly into the patio area. Carol spotted a small, anonymous drone zigzagging just above the crowd. It was breaking separation regulations with impunity because there was no way to identify the operator, who could be next door, or thousands of kilometers away.

By now all the social media sites would be flooded with the images. Carol had only a thin line of cops to control this mass of people. Reinforcements were urgently required.

"Here come the choppers!" someone yelled.

As if cued by an unseen film director, a police helicopter chattered into view, closely followed by three media 'copters, vying with each other for the most advantageous position to capture the drama on the ground. A reporter from a news radio station was there already, suspiciously early, microphone in hand, describing the scene in excited tones and asking for comments from spectators.

Joining Carol at the green door, surveying the crowd, Anne said, "Not looking too good."

A male TV reporter Carol recognized from Madeline's network accosted them at the gate. "No comment," she snapped before he had a chance to frame a question.

Anne completely ignored both the reporter and his cameraman. Chagrined, Carol realized she too should have acted as though he didn't exist. She had given them a police sound bite, however tiny, that would be played countless times.

As soon as they were back inside, Carol ordered everyone searching for a possible second shooter to redeploy for guard duty around the house. Then she called Commissioner Hindley, explained the situation while he listened without interruption. She asked for reinforcements, telling him, "Admiralty House is—"

"Christ, yes!" his voice burst in her ear. "The bloody Governor-General!"

The official residence of the representative for the monarch of Britain was a sandstone mansion at the tip of Kirribilli Point. Just around the corner. A ceremonial office to be sure, but should any damage be done to the residence, the individual appointed to represent the British Crown be endangered, the fallout would be unimaginable.

She heard him barking commands away from his phone, then he was back on the line, telling her the Riot Squad was arriving by water, landing at Kirribilli Wharf. "All this for a put-up job? Is that definite?"

"I'll put it this way. The weapon is small caliber, bolt action, no telescopic sight. A single gunshot. Then Sykes appears, yelling that someone's trying to kill the canon. Some of the press is already here—"

The commissioner snorted. "And how convenient to have you of all people right there on the spot."

"Not quite convenient enough, I suspect. Sergeant Newsome and I arrived before we were expected. I think Fulton was supposed to fire his shot at a preset time and get out of here, not be captured. Certainly not be hauled off the wall by a woman officer, no less."

His gravel voice held a note of amusement as he rumbled, "His goddamn church is going to need deep pockets. This pathetic little hoax is costing the Police Service—not to mention law-abiding taxpayers—a mint of money. I'll see to it that Armitage and his followers are billed for every cent. Sykes called to assure me he'd had no prior knowledge of the stunt. Believed at the time it was a genuine attempt, blah blah blah. What's your take on his involvement?"

"My take?" Carol said, surprised to be asked. "The opposite. Sykes was not happy when he saw me. I think he was roped in by Armitage late in the piece. Sykes probably played along only to avoid alienating a wealthy client."

Hindley grunted. Whether or not in agreement Carol couldn't tell. "A nut case is how Sykes described this Fulton fellow."

It would be to Sykes's advantage to have Fulton's statements branded as from an unreliable witness because of mental illness. "He doesn't seem very bright," Carol conceded, "but I wouldn't—"

The commissioner spoke over her. "The man's stupid, you're saying, but not certifiable. What's Fulton's story? Whatever it is, it'll be bullshit, I can guarantee that."

"He may be simply telling us what he believes to be true," said Carol. She'd been hearing his remonstrations from the other room during her call. "He has a touching faith the canon will back him up and agree it was a silly joke, no harm intended." She added, "I think it more likely that Fulton will be thrown to the wolves."

Unexpectedly, Hindley laughed. "That definitely takes Sykes off the hook. He'd never be involved in anything as amateurish. And he wouldn't schedule it on a Saturday when everyone's out and about and not glued to a bloody screen."

Carol described how relieved Sykes had been when it seemed the shooter had escaped, and his consternation after Anne had appeared at the gate with Fulton.

"Playing both ends against the middle," Hindley summarized. "Blew up in his face, didn't it."

Carol felt almost sorry for Sykes. The canon's harebrained scheme had had very little chance of success, and Sykes had apparently seen little choice but to support his client.

Carol mentioned the conflict of interest issue—on one hand Sykes was representing the Police Service and on the other hand Cherished Life and its leader.

"Sykes knows which side his bread is buttered on. He'll dump Armitage—too bad if that leaves the canon up the creek without a paddle."

Dismayed at the prospect of continuing to have to work with the man, Carol said, "You're not thinking of keeping Sykes on, are you?"

"What's your objection?"

Before Carol could form an answer to this loaded question, he went on, "Sykes knows I've got his nuts in a vise. One step out of line and he'll find himself facing a shitload of charges. Obstruction, conspiracy—you name it."

The glee in his voice was quickly replaced by his usual domineering tone. "Wrap up this debacle fast. I want you concentrating on the Denby case one hundred and ten percent. Got it?"

* * *

Watching Anne place the rifle into an evidence bag, Carol heard Canon Armitage's sonorous voice. "Chief Inspector, I've waited long enough! A word please!"

"Canon, I'll be with you in a few minutes."

"Right now." He bustled into the room, Sykes behind him. "You'll see me right now."

Carol looked at him with no attempt to hide her irritation. The impression he gave was very different from his television image of a leader, impeccably dressed, who spoke with the confident authority of one who truly believed he had been chosen by his God to fulfill a mission. Now his trademark white suit was wrinkled and smudged with dirt from wherever he had taken cover. His silver hair had little of its usual bounce, and his face, without benefit of professional makeup, showed dark circles under his eyes, flabby cheeks, and a sagging jawline.

"Canon Armitage!" Fulton exclaimed in relief. "You tell 'em who I am, how we was just foolin' around!"

The canon did not look at him as he said, "I've just realized I know this man. He's a member of my congregation."

"Do you know the man's name?"

He paused, as if searching his memory, then said, "I don't think so."

"You do!" Fulton, about to be taken out to a patrol car, his bloody nose having been cleaned and treated by a paramedic, his wrists now confined in regular police cuffs, stared despairingly at Armitage. "Fulton. I'm Fulton!"

"This poor, misguided man is indeed a member of my flock," sighed the canon after a glance at him. "But I would not place great reliance on anything he might say."

Douglas Fulton, increasingly agitated, hollered, "Tell them, Canon Armitage! *Tell them!*"

"Chief Inspector," Sykes said, "this man is clearly an out-of-control alcoholic whose every word must be suspect. I believe we can dismiss any accusations he makes."

"*We*, Mr. Sykes?"

He reddened at her tone. "I'm sorry. I misspoke."

Fulton pleaded, "It's a mistake, all this—"

"Mr. Fulton," Carol interrupted, "you'll have the opportunity to give your version of what happened this afternoon when you make a sworn statement in which you explain why you fired a rifle at Canon Armitage with the intention of wounding or killing him."

Fulton shook his head violently. "Nothing like that! It was all a plan, a—a joke. I just did what they told me to do when they told me to do it."

Indicating Armitage and Sykes, she said, "Do you recognize either of these two gentlemen?"

Fulton looked puzzled. "I belong to Canon Armitage's church. Sure I know him."

"He's clearly deranged," the canon said calmly. "I won't press charges, I'll have him looked after—"

Carol looked at him coldly. Of course he wanted this debacle swept under the rug. Legal proceedings would keep this embarrassment in the press indefinitely.

"Not going to happen," she informed him. "The attempt on your life is only one of the charges he's facing. Discharging a firearm, attempted flight, resisting arrest—"

"You can't do this!" Fulton yelled, straining at his handcuffs as an officer pulled him away. "Don't let them do this!"

Armitage turned on Sykes. "Deal with this mess. It's your responsibility, not mine. I'm leaving."

Carol said to Anne, "Take Canon Armitage to the front room. If he attempts to leave, arrest him. I'll interview him after I've finished with Mr. Sykes."

Armitage, his face flushed, marched up and confronted her. "This is an outrage. None of this is necessary. I'm taking this as a personal attack on me and my church. Believe me, I'll be holding you to account."

Holding her ground, she met his approach with an icy stare. "Are you threatening me personally for doing my job, Canon Armitage?"

"I'm defending myself." He stepped back but said emphatically, "In no way was I involved in whatever this ridiculous scheme was supposed to be. I believed it was a genuine attempt on my life."

Carol resisted the impulse to answer his provocation— there was a better tactic. She glanced at Sykes, who had lost his customary aplomb and was sweating profusely.

"I believe Mr. Sykes will have something to tell us about that."

FIFTEEN

Sybil had received an updating text from Carol that she could not estimate what time she'd arrive; a situation had come up with Canon Armitage.

Sybil had no need to wonder what "the situation" might be—it was featured on every newscast and covered widely across the Internet. With no firm basis on which to build a coherent narrative, name recognition alone had been enough to send the story viral, and Sybil had watched the mutation of rumor-driven headlines with bemusement.

THIS JUST IN! Killer stalks provocative founder of Cherished Life…Possible terrorist link…Canon Armitage statement from Intensive Care: "I pray for my attacker's soul."

BREAKING NEWS: Abortive assassination attempt…Canon Roger Armitage escapes…Manhunt underway…Suspect armed and dangerous.

By late afternoon, actual facts had emerged. An amateurish effort to stage an attempt on Armitage's life had been exposed, the actor's escape aborted by police on the scene. With each repetition of the story came the oft-repeated "no comment" statement by a grim-faced Chief Inspector Carol Ashton, clearly one of the referred-to "police" even if Sybil had not already known she would have been there.

Those media outlets whose initial reporting of the incident had been fiction were unapologetic, ignoring their previous pronouncements as if they had never existed, transforming the sensational assassination attempt into repeated accounts of a clumsy hoax perpetrated on the public to gain publicity and sympathy for the Cherished Life Church. The church's earlier demonstration at the Denby estate had been dropped from the news cycle as if it had never occurred, in favor of this much more dramatic story. The teacher in Sybil saw yet more examples of news gatherers catering to the appetite for the sensational at the expense of truth. The papers would give a more balanced and accurate account the next day, but electronic media increasingly served up immediacy—electric crowd scenes and a deluge of photos and videos sent from mobile phones.

Her interest in the transfigured story continued, layered with uneasiness over how much danger Carol might have been in during the capture of an armed man, whatever his intention.

Although the canon had issued a written statement implicating a mentally disturbed member of his congregation, speculation continued unabated about his own complicity. By early evening Armitage had obviously decided he needed to address the situation with a personal appearance at a media conference, which was about to begin.

Sybil immediately saw that he had stage-managed the event. He entered the room unaccompanied by any entourage, immediately put up his hand to quell the rising clamor of reporters and intoned, "Please, no questions."

He spoke from notes with the trained voice of an orator, and Sybil admired Armitage's skill in projecting a façade of sincerity tinged with regret. "The man responsible for the events of this afternoon is a sadly deluded soul who has carried out some minor public relations work for Cherished Life in the past. The police have made more of this incident than it warrants. His family have asked me not to reveal his name and I will honor that request."

Sybil laughed at this faux gallantry uttered by the figure on the screen. Douglas Fulton's name had been on the airwaves for more than an hour.

Then, with a dramatic gesture, Canon Armitage threw away his statement and addressed the camera directly. "It is a glorious, yet humbling experience to be the channel for God's mercy. Cherished Life will cover all legal expenses incurred by this unfortunate man who is a child of God. As for myself, I shall be spending the night on my knees, in deep contemplation and prayer."

Brushing aside the tumult of questions, he quickly exited the room.

Sybil's mobile rang and she seized it. Seeing the caller's name she decided to let it go to voice mail. Then, in a burst of ill humor at this grating addition to the events of the day, changed her mind and answered the call.

"Madeline, I can only assume you're trying to reach Carol. She isn't here."

"I know very well where Carol is. So does everyone in Sydney with a television. You're the one I need to speak with."

Sybil could not imagine why, but she was not about to engage her with a question, and remained silent.

"Carol isn't taking my calls," Madeline said quietly. "I've left message after message telling her it's extremely urgent—"

Urgent? I'll just bet. She said coldly, "I don't see how I can be of help, Madeline."

"Get in touch with her. She'll take a call from you. Tell her it's vital she get back to me."

Sybil said firmly, "If she doesn't want to talk to you—"

"I wouldn't impose on you unless it were something serious and dangerous to her—and it is."

This had to be a ruse to reach Carol. "And that would be…?"

Madeline emitted an exasperated sigh. "Tell Carol this: someone who would be in a position to know has just approached me with the accusation that Carol was materially involved in her mother's death."

It took some moments for Madeline's words to sink into Sybil's shocked mind. "Who on earth is this person?"

"I've already said too much on this line. I'll give Carol the details when she contacts me. Believe me, this is no joke. For security, tell her to ring this number on a landline, not her mobile. Thank you, Sybil." And she was gone.

Madeline had abandoned all her arch sophistication to deliver her message. This was real. Sybil sat staring at nothing while she marshaled her thoughts.

She thought back to her conversation with Aunt Sarah and reviewed the facts she knew. Carol's mother had died not long after her father's sudden death from a heart attack, and Carol had never talked about either death in anything but general terms. A reticence Sybil could understand—neither had she, about her own parents. There was permanent grief attached to death of a parent. There had never been any suggestion, not so much as a hint of anything untoward about Violet Ashton's death. And now, years later, someone was coming forward with this? *This?* It had to be a lie. A scam.

She was not about to call Carol while she was embroiled in a chaotic news event in the city even though it was open-ended as to the number of witness interviews and paperwork and follow-up Carol would need to conduct. News like this had to be delivered in person.

She settled back in front of the TV. She would wait for Carol no matter what the hour.

* * *

Sybil had been listening for Carol's car, and had the door open to welcome her. "Are you all right? One newscast had you risking your life to save the canon."

"Never happened. Anne took him down." Carol's taupe suit looked wilted, her face was drawn and she moved at this late evening hour as if she carried a weight on her shoulders. "I'm fine, just weary," she said, giving Sybil a perfunctory kiss on the cheek. "I'd love a scotch."

While Sybil went to the bar, Carol sank into a lounge chair and gazed blankly at the television screen. The sound was muted, but the news was still concentrated on the botched staging of the fake attack. They were rolling the tape of the canon making his statement. "What a contemptible piece of work you are," she snarled at the screen. "You deserve to be under the wheels of the bus where Sykes threw you." She picked up the remote and turned off the TV.

Sybil handed her a heavy crystal whiskey glass. "Scotch on the rocks, as ordered."

Carol took it with a faint smile. "Thanks."

"Want to talk about what I saw on TV all afternoon and evening?"

"Nope." Carol took a sip of her scotch.

"Madeline Shipley called a few hours ago."

"Looking for me, yes? I'm sorry she bothered you. She's left urgent messages—of course it's always urgent with Madeline—but I haven't got the time or inclination to deal with her."

"Carol, this seems very serious. Madeline said for security you should call her back on a landline."

Carol looked at her with a frown. "What exactly did she say to you?"

"That a person in a position to know has come to her with the story that you were materially involved in your mother's death."

Carol's suddenly still body, her silence, her pallor, chilled Sybil to the core. "Carol?"

Silence.

"It's got to be some sort of sick joke," Sybil finally offered.

Carol looked and sounded inexpressibly tired. "Darling, don't worry. I don't want to talk about anything tonight."

Taking the adjoining seat, Sybil said, "Will you call Madeline?"

"Tomorrow." She drank more scotch.

Sybil was all too familiar with that tone of finality in Carol's voice, the clear signal that this was not a subject she intended to discuss.

"Carol…"

"I don't want to talk about it now."

In a flare of anger Sybil snapped, "That's not good enough."

Carol looked at her with surprise. "What?"

"You can't just leave me with this. I have to know what's happening."

"Nothing's happening. I'll talk to you tomorrow after I've called Madeline." She pushed herself to her feet. "Mind if I get a refill? Can I get you something? Your usual?"

Sybil followed her to the bar and watched as Carol chose a bottle of red wine for her. Inwardly, Sybil was at war with herself. She was both hurt and infuriated by Carol's attitude, and felt impelled to have it out with her here and now. But would that be fair? Carol was obviously exhausted.

Unknowingly, Carol lit the spark: "So, later, okay?"

"It's always later, isn't it? But later conveniently never comes."

Taken aback, Carol stared at her, the bottle growing slack in her hand.

"You don't trust me, Carol? Is that why you won't tell me the truth about this right now?"

"Please, I really can't…" Carol's eyes filled with tears. "I can't…" She dropped the bottle on the bar where it began to roll.

Stunned to see Carol like this, Sybil said more gently as she rescued the bottle, "I know you're in pain. I don't want to add to it, but if you share it with me, perhaps I can help."

Carol shook her head. "No."

"This is the problem, Carol. The trap door between us. We'll never have a relationship if you never share anything important with me!" The words spilled out, fueled by so many other times in the past when Carol withheld herself, conducted herself her own way.

Carol wiped the tears off her face with the palms of her hands. "All right, if you really want me to spell it out, this is it in a headline: my mother, suffering intense and unrelenting pain, begged me to assist her commit suicide."

Carol took a deep, shuddering breath. "And I did."

"*What?*"

Shaken by the expression of resignation on Carol's face, Sybil exclaimed, "That cannot possibly be true!"

"That's the trouble, Sybil—I don't know if it's true or not." Tears again sprang to her eyes and she covered her face with her hands. "Oh, God!"

Sybil ached to comfort her but she remained still and silent, fearing that if she spoke or moved, Carol's extraordinary openness might end. Even in their most intimate moments in the past, Carol had never opened herself to this extent, had never shared any of her deepest feelings, her fears.

Sybil knew with a bleak, unsettling certainty that this time was very different. For this to happen, Carol had to be close a breaking point. Secrets she had kept close, truths she had hidden from herself, questions she'd refused to face and answer, seemed to have now overrun her.

Grabbing a handful of tissues from under the counter, Carol wiped her eyes. "Another scotch might help." She walked back to her chair, leaving Sybil at the bar.

"I'll keep you company, and switch to brandy and soda."

Somewhere within her shock from what she had just heard and seen, Sybil remembered the first time she said that she was changing from wine to a mixed drink, and Carol's playful mockery about drowning good liquor instead of drinking it neat over ice cubes as Carol did. Hard now to even imagine that teasing banter.

She placed on a tray a chilled glass, a bottle of Johnny Walker Gold and an elegant silver ice bucket and tongs—a gift from Carol when they'd begun this uneasy reconciliation a few months ago—and took the tray over to Carol. Then went back to the bar to make her own drink, returning to the comfortable, upholstered chairs where she and Carol had so often sat side by side watching television or movies. Now the flat screen was dark and the only sounds in the room were the clink of ice as Carol made her drink, and Jeffrey, who had chosen the corner of the sofa to embark upon a wash of himself.

Carol picked up her glass, then put it down untasted. "Those last weeks were dreadful. Mum's face just gray with pain—it haunts me to this day. Leanne—Mum's nurse—was there ten hours a day and on twenty-four-hour call. Aunt Sarah had moved in to help. I, of course, escaped to work every day."

Heedless of the tears that were again flowing down her face, Carol stared sightlessly into the room. "That last night, I went to see her as I always did, as soon as I got home. She was completely bedridden, not eating. I was earlier than usual, so when Leanne brought in my mother's evening meal—a plain roll and some kind of chicken broth—I said I'd have a go at coaxing her to eat."

Carol sighed. "I'm sorry, I can't—I don't want any more scotch," she said, rubbing her temples. "A mug of hot black coffee and some aspirin would be wonderful." Seeing Sybil hesitate, she added, "No, darling, I won't use this as an excuse to stop talking. I promise to tell you every single thing I remember."

Carol didn't speak again until they were both seated with mugs of coffee. "I remember I'd got Mum to eat a piece of bread dipped in the soup. She shook her head when I offered her more, so I asked if there was anything else she wanted—a cup of tea? She looked directly into my eyes and said, with the faintest smile, 'You can do something for me, my darling. Help me die.'"

Carol's hand jerked up and she clamped fingers over her mouth as though she could not bear to utter her response, then dropped the hand into her lap.

Sybil said, half to herself, "What answer could anyone give to that question?"

"'Mum, please don't ask me. I can't do it.' That's what I said. She took my hand. Her fingers were cold, so icy cold. 'Carol, what do I have to look forward to? Increasing pain and no hope.'"

Turning to Sybil, Carol pleaded in a choked voice, "You understand, don't you? I was a police officer, sworn to uphold the law. I couldn't—I wouldn't—help anyone die. Not only was it against the law, I believed it was morally wrong..."

Carol frowned at the mug in her hand as if surprised to see it there. She took one sip, then put it down. "She told me, 'Carol, it would be so easy. Leanne makes sure I'm comfortable, then leaves around eight. Unless I call for her, she doesn't see me again until morning. I know what to take and exactly how much. All you have to do is put the tray of medications within my reach. And I need something more than this glass of water to get the pills down.'"

Carol bit her lip. "Even through all this she'd kept her sense of humor. 'Gin and tonic would be nice, dear, but Carol, I suppose I'll have to settle for water. Then leave me. I'll do the rest.' I didn't know what to say. Mum was looking at me so imploringly, waiting for my answer... And then Leanne came in and saved me."

With a bitter smile, Carol added, "Like a coward, I couldn't wait to get away. 'I'll look in on you later, Mum,' I said. Then I left."

"Did you go back later?"

Carol shrugged. "I honestly don't know." Her face reflected her remorse, her anguish. "I took a bottle of bourbon and went outside into the darkest corner of the back deck..."

She stared at Sybil with an expression of utter misery and shame. "I think I drank half of it in one gulp. Last I remember, I was falling down drunk. I don't know if I went back to see her: I don't know if I helped her to die."

Sybil said very softly, "Do you remember anything else about that evening?"

"It's all a blur. I'd been outside for a while when I heard Aunt Sarah and Dr. Yates talking on their way to Mum's room. He called in to see her almost every evening, more friend than doctor."

"Were they discussing your mother?"

"I seem to recall it was something about magpies...or not. I was so out of it words were just part of the background noises of the night."

"Did someone come looking for you? Or did you stay there till morning?"

"I woke up on my own bed, still fully dressed. It was early, just before dawn." With a painfully managed smile, Carol said, "As you can imagine, I felt wretched. I dragged myself to the bathroom, threw up, then stood under the shower till Aunt Sarah knocked on the door. All she said was, 'Get dressed. Dr. Yates will be here soon.' I knew immediately, I just *knew* that Mum had passed away, and he was coming to sign her death certificate."

Sybil said firmly, "Darling, if you were that smashed, there's no way you could have done anything. How did you even make it to your room? Did Aunt Sarah help you?"

"I've no idea."

Puzzled, Sybil said, "You didn't ask her?"

"We've never ever discussed anything about that night."

"Why not?"

"Off limits." She grimaced. "Maybe we each thought—still think—the other had helped Mum die. And neither of us wants to risk hearing the truth."

She put down her coffee and sat back, her face slack with exhaustion and grief. "Now you know. I should call Madeline."

"Tomorrow," said Sybil firmly. She rose. "Come to bed."

If she could not confer absolution for this long-withheld confession, she could offer comfort. And love.

SIXTEEN

"Madeline, I thought I meant more to you than this. How can you run with a story that can't possibly be proved? My mother died more than two decades ago!"

Carol squirmed in shame. Again. Just as she had at tones in Madeline's voice she had never heard in all the years she had known her, even in their most intimate encounters. Or for that matter on any tragedy-ridden story of Madeline's on *The Shipley Report*. Madeline's words over the landline had been hushed, kind, measured, as she related her meeting with Leanne Gordon, with just a touch of awkwardness, delivered in the manner of someone offering condolences at a funeral.

Gripping her portable phone, staring sightlessly into the leafy gum trees surrounding the terrace of her house, Carol knew her protests were futile. Madeline had run with a multitude of stories that couldn't be proved. They were her stock-in-trade.

Madeline answered her plea with quiet exactitude. "Because of who you are, Carol. Leanne Gordon is credible. She presents herself with sincerity, has a stable job history. She's come forward with apparent total recall, pay records as proof she worked at your house, and no motive for making this up. She very earnestly claims she was so disturbed by your mother's death that over all these years she kept the written instructions from a Doctor Yates about dispensing pills to her, claims she overheard conversation between your mother and you, claims there were pills missing that morning. This Doctor Yates looked after your mother, yes?"

"Yes, but her records are no proof of anything! He looked at everything, he reviewed those records. He signed the death certificate. She could be accused of this herself!"

"You're right, of course. Even I know that much about evidence—"

"Then *why*? You—of all people!—doing this to me!"

"She came to *me* with this and you're damn lucky she did," Madeline said, her voice hardening with each staccato word. "Otherwise it'll be someone else and I guarantee you, they'll run with it, the story will be out there. In case you haven't noticed, Carol, I'm in a cutthroat business. My producers know I know you. If I don't go with this, they'll fire me for bias, favoritism. For turning down a very big and credible story involving a high-ranking media star of the New South Wales Police Force. You've been visible for years in this city, and now you're Chief Inspector—even more of a story magnet."

"Good for you, you get to keep your job," Carol said gratingly. "I lose mine." She continued in flat despair, "I'll be forced to resign, Madeline."

"It won't come to that," Madeline said, again in that funereal tone. "Trust me on this. We're still researching this woman and her claims, and I'll take the best care of you I can. I deserve points, don't I, for bringing this to you before we go to air tonight?"

"*Tonight!*"

"Tonight. Before someone else gets wind of it and scoops us on some bloody Internet site. But you're right that she's got a claim that's unprovable, an inexplicable time lapse of years before she came forward, and of course there's your denial it ever happened—you are denying it, aren't you?"

Carol slammed the phone off with a fist. And doubled over in anguish. To have this story come out extended far beyond her. It was a defiling of her mother. Violet Ashton's last day of life would be laid bare, her privacy violated for countless strangers to speculate over in the most sensational, garish manner. On top of that—in the most profound, gut-knifing betrayal, her own life was being turned into a commercial property, a *scoop*, by a woman who had been an intimate presence in her life.

No question, she would have to resign. She could not survive professionally and Madeline knew it better than anyone. She had been complicit—if not the death-dealing instrument—in the demolition of many careers and reputations.

When it came to certain accusations, being deemed not guilty was never proof of innocence. A story like this—the hypocrisy of a high-ranking police official mercy-killing her own mother—was an indictment that could be neither proved nor disproved. It was akin to an accusation of child molestation. The story would hang over her in perpetuity, clouding and undermining her authority and reputation. Her credibility with the rank and file serving under her would disintegrate. Those confident words from Madeline about taking care of her were a delusion. Madeline Shipley could not conceivably protect her.

She stared at the phone in her hand as if it were a malignancy.

She had needed to be in her own place for the call to Madeline and had risen early, explaining this to Sybil as she donned one of the suits that she kept at Sybil's house. Aunt Sarah was a late sleeper and Carol knew she would not disturb her, would make the call to Madeline from her terrace—the place where she would need to be regardless of the presence of her aunt. Another very real reason was that she did not want Sybil to witness her hearing the outcome she dreaded, the nightmare scenario that had played endlessly in her mind during the night while she lay uncomforted by Sybil's arms.

Sybil was anxiously awaiting her report on the conversation with Madeline, and Carol remained on the terrace and used the same landline to call. Afterward, she stood at the railing, the buzzing phone in her hand, with no recollection of how long the call had been or of most of the words spoken between them; her mind had been too engaged with the realignment of reality, her new reality. She, who had spent her professional life exposing other people's secrets, was about to have her own life laid bare. She remembered only her first words to Sybil, the unequivocal statement: "I'm finished. My career is over."

She went into her house to let herself out before her aunt awakened. Placing the phone back in its cradle and reaching for her car keys on the counter of the wet bar, she thought: there really must be a Denby Curse.

SEVENTEEN

From her car outside her house, Carol made two calls on her mobile. The first to Rosalie Rooke asking if it was convenient to visit her. Then to Bourke informing him she had decided to interview Rosalie Rooke unaccompanied on this Sunday morning, explaining into his silence that an informal conversation might draw out some information from Ian Rooke's widow that would buttress their final report. Bourke had not argued. But hearing something in her voice he'd asked: "Not fighting off a cold are you?" *Dear Mark* was all she could think while she'd reassured him she was fine.

Now she was retracing the path Ian Rooke had taken to his house that final time, slowing her Camry in very light traffic along the spectacular Galston Gorge for a solemn, respectful moment on the fatal curve that had snuffed out his life. In a way, today would be the last day of her own life too, she reflected. Her life as she had known it.

With her team away from the Denby case for a well-earned break on at least one day of the weekend, she had determined that she would spend as much of the day in solitude as she could manage. After seeing Rosalie, she would closely review the Denby case files in the quiet of her office, a task that would serve as a distraction as well as a vital step in the investigation. That much more essential when her summary notes and hypotheses might well be among her last official acts.

But what she had told Bourke about Rosalie Rooke was in large part truthful. The few casual interactions she'd had with this young second wife of Ian's at police functions had imparted a vague impression of an introvert out of her comfort zone with her husband's colleagues, who smiled too anxiously at even the smallest courtesies extended to her.

She pulled off the road in front of Ian and Rosalie Rooke's house in Galston and gathered herself. She had done her best during the hour-long drive to cut through her despair over Madeline's call and plan her approach to Ian Rooke's widow. It would be somehow fitting if one of her last acts as a police officer was to put in place a final report on the respected colleague with whom she'd shared parallel careers. Both careers ending, she realized, in a bolt of lightning.

She had never been to Rooke's house, and had imagined that Ian would be able to buy a nice property up here out of the expensive city. But it was quite modest, an old Californian bungalow well off the road, with a veranda covered by an extension of roof. Its narrow plot of land was fronted by a low hedge and separated from its neighbors by thick, varied, well-tended foliage. It was pretty here, she decided as she made her way between a profusion of perfumed roses up to the house, and she envied the Rooke family the silence, the privacy, the peace here in this agricultural enclave among the earthen smells of eucalypts and flowers. She wished she could spend the day here.

A roof-hung swing came into view amid outdoor furniture on the veranda, along with two little bright blue tricycles arranged neatly against the gray clapboard. Melancholy gripped her as she thought of her own son when he was little. At least he'd always had two parents in his life, unlike the two small children who lived here. She remembered hearing from Bourke that the youngsters had been taken into the temporary care of Ian's parents. She wondered if they would be at their father's funeral in the coming week and have that memory scarring their young lives.

She climbed the four steps to the veranda and halted; through the living room window she could see Rosalie at work before an easel in a column of bright light provided by a large skylight. The best light in the house was probably in this room, Carol supposed, so she had to do her painting in this unconventional location. But the children were quite young and she doubted that the Rookes, given their reserve, had ever entertained much. And anyway, why was she wearing her judgmental police hat? Who even cared where Rosalie painted?

Carol moved quietly onto the porch and stopped to observe her. Seated on a stool, bent forward in rapt concentration, she appeared smaller and thinner than Carol's memory of her, the sandy blond hair pulled back into a ponytail. A paint-smeared pinafore tied loosely at the waist over her clothes, she was intently brushing tiny delicate strokes onto a corner of her canvas. Beside her a rickety table was laden with trays of paint tubes and jars bristling with brushes, the wall behind her hung with canvases presumably drying. On the floor more canvases, undoubtedly dry and finished, leaned two or three deep. Further into the room a round coffee table and two matching end tables were visible, scattered amid pieces of leather furniture—sensible choices, Carol thought, in a home with small children.

Turning to the tray beside her to gather more paint on her brush, Rosalie's glimpse of Carol was simultaneous with the jerking up of her head. She slid from the stool, reaching to untie her pinafore as she came to the door.

"Rosalie," Carol greeted her, "thank you for seeing me on such short notice. I see I've interrupted your work."

Rosalie tossed her smock in a corner on top of an assortment of building blocks, plastic trucks, coloring books, and games. She turned to Carol, her revealed clothes a concession to the heat: thin cotton drawstring pants and a faded pink sleeveless top. She reached to take Carol's hand. "I appreciate you driving all the way out here. Ian always spoke so highly of you."

"And me always of him," Carol said, moved by the warmth of Rosalie's greeting. "I'm so sorry, Rosalie. He's a great loss to all of us."

"Please come in." She led the way to a corner of the living room where two armchairs of soft beige leather faced each other. "How about you get comfortable while I get us some tea."

"If I could use the bathroom…"

"Of course," Rosalie said, gesturing down the hall.

"…and then I'd quite like to look at your work, if I may."

Rosalie looked shyly pleased as she glanced at her canvases. "With the children at their grandparents I've been working all hours. Pat Bourke's being so kind to me—she's arranged for a venue willing to show a few of my pieces and I want to give her plenty of choice."

"She's a good contact," Carol said, nodding.

"I'm lucky to know her. I need to make a living now. And I need to get my mind off…" She turned and headed for the kitchen.

In a bathroom confined to adults—absent of bathtub toys or any other evidence of small children—Carol noticed a half dozen bottles lined up on the counter as she washed her hands. At a glance, various vitamins, but a distinctive prescription container stood out among them. She picked it up. The container seemed full, its label made out to Ian Rooke, prescribed by a doctor here in Galston. *Effexor*, she read. She pulled her phone from her jacket pocket and used its search engine to look up the name, then took a photo of the bottle. Also the name of the prescribing doctor. She pocketed the prescription bottle and returned to the living room.

She took her time looking over Rosalie's work. It was a distance from Bourke's dismissive description of flowing robes and mist-shrouded trees, but there was indeed an ethereal quality common to all of it, a feathering of edges as if the reality portrayed in the work was either part of or dissolving into an indeterminate spiritual realm. She had no way of judging the quality of the art, but she found it interesting. Would she have one of these in her own house? Maybe, but not today. Not with her own life actually imitating this art, the reality she knew and had taken for granted disintegrating into an unknown.

"I find your work quite appealing, absorbing," she told Rosalie who had appeared with a tray of tea and biscuits.

"Thank you. That's lovely of you to say."

They made themselves comfortable with mugs of tea, Carol leaving the biscuits untouched. She felt as if she could never eat again.

Rosalie said, "I know you're here as part of the investigation into Ian's accident. I'll tell you everything I know."

"His mood," Carol said immediately, seizing the opening. "He seemed withdrawn, preoccupied, distracted—"

"Not unusual for Ian," Rosalie said with a faint smile that bordered on a grimace.

"He was on a very big case," Carol pointed out.

"Don't I know it. I was so busy keeping the boys out of his hair—" This time her expression was pure anguish. "Had I known, I'd have let them do whatever they wanted with his hair. Poor little Gordie, he's got asthma you know, and he's needed the inhaler three times. He's about to turn six and you'd think he'd be too young to understand what's happened but he *knows*."

Carol met Rosalie's pale blue eyes and shook her head in wordless sympathy.

"Carol—sorry, I mean no disrespect," she said hastily, "Carol is how Ian always referred to you. So proud he was to see you get your promotion."

"Of course you can call me Carol."

"I know you're investigating whether Ian drove off that road deliberately. I can tell you all the ways I know he didn't. I know it was an accident."

Carol nodded and said encouragingly, "Tell me."

"He was in a good place. Cheerful. Busy as he was, he put it all aside to be with the boys and with me." She dabbed at her eyes while at the same time managing a ghost of a chuckle. "He

told me a long time ago there were times in his life when he felt
so bad he'd thought about ending it and once, when he was a lot
younger, he'd actually tried it and found out the hard way there
was no way he could ever find the courage to off himself."

Carol reached into her pocket. "Did he take these because
he was still feeling bad?"

Rosalie's eyes widened at the sight of the prescription
container and then they began to darken with ire.

"It was sitting right there on the counter in the bathroom,
Rosalie," Carol told her. "There is no way I'd ever search your
bathroom. It was there in plain sight."

Rosalie closed her eyes for a moment, whispering, "Jesus."
Then she said, "So stupid...I never thought...but then we've
never had police visitors. Only friends..." She looked at Carol
with a touch of defiance. "There's no reason you shouldn't
know. Now that he's gone. He had to keep it a secret. He knew
he'd not have a police career if anyone knew he suffered from
depression."

With this blundering answer Carol saw what Bourke meant
about Rosalie Rooke not being good at subterfuge. She defined
what a superior officer had described to her years ago as "dumb
honest." She said gently, "That must have been very hard on
you both."

"We always got through it. It was worst when he felt it
coming on. The medication always helped him. He hadn't had
one of those...slides is what he called them, for a long time."

Again Carol held up the prescription container. "But this is
new. Newly prescribed."

"He felt one of his slides coming on again just as he got
this huge case. He thought maybe he wasn't up to doing his
job anymore, this was it—he just couldn't do it anymore. But
then it went away." She gazed at Carol with wide, ingenuous,
trusting blue eyes. "He told me he felt so much better, he didn't
even have to take any of the pills. It had to be the truth because
believe me, his depression wasn't ever something he could just
will away. If you look in there—" she pointed at the container,
"—you'll see it's a full container."

Carol nodded and handed it over to Rosalie.

Rosalie put it on the tea tray and continued, "Answer me this: why would he go to his dentist if he intended to kill himself? He came back from there in such a good mood I asked if the dentist had given him laughing gas." She smiled sadly. "He joked that Dr. Bower had extended the cleaning to a fluffing of his spirits."

"Dr. Bower's here in Galston too?"

"Yes, just up the road."

"I appreciate all this, Rosalie. For giving us a more rounded picture of Ian."

"I need to see about getting his superannuation released. Right from the day Gordie was born Ian was a saver, and we bought this little place so we could put money aside for their education. But with Gordie and Allan my responsibility now, the life insurance will be a godsend."

Glancing at the artwork around her, Carol could only agree. Survival in any part of the art world was chancy at best. "I'll do what I can to move that along."

She rose. "Rosalie, I'll let you get back to work, I'm sorry for the interruption. Thank you for seeing me, for sharing with me some of your life with Ian."

Rosalie walked with her to the door, took Carol's arm and turned her. Her eyes brimming with tears, she said, "Ian thought the absolute world of you."

Carol felt moisture gathering in her own eyes. And said with certainty, even though she had no way of knowing it, "You gave him the happiest years of his life, Rosalie."

She gripped and released Rosalie's hands, and took her leave.

She sat in her car for some moments, feeling a wry, perverse pride that with her world disintegrating around her she had given no sign of it to Rosalie Rooke; she had managed to conduct a meaningful, perfectly professional interview.

She drove on into the Galston shopping village, wishing again she could spend the day here, especially in Swane's Nursery amid its ornamental gardens. She loved the atmosphere of this close-knit semi-rural community on the outer fringe of the Sydney metropolis.

She took out her phone, called the office of Dr. Michael Bower. A recorded message gave a contact number to ring for dental emergencies. Carol did so and spoke with the answering service, explaining who she was and asking if he had five minutes he could spare to see or speak with her. Bower returned her call immediately.

"Chief Inspector, I assume this would be about Ian Rooke?"

"It would. We're putting together a picture of the last few days before his death, and I understand he came in to see you. I've just spoken with his wife and she mentioned he came home from his appointment in an unusually cheerful frame of mind."

"He did? Glad to hear it. He was a fine chap, he—"

"Can you tell me anything about your conversation with him?"

"Same as always. We talked about our kids. Both of us have a son with asthma, you see."

"So, nothing comes to mind, nothing different from any other conversation?"

"Well, he'd just got an EpiPen for Gordie and was a bit puzzled as to how it was effective against a severe asthma attack…"

"And what did you tell him?"

"Adrenaline. It's mainly just plain old adrenaline."

"And that was it?"

"That was it."

"What was his mood? Up? Down?"

"Same as always, as I said. Chief Inspector, I was not his friend, I only cleaned the man's teeth."

"Thank you for your time, Dr. Bower, and if anything else comes to mind will you call me?" She gave him her details.

Then it occurred to her that there was someone else she should try to see if at all possible, as soon as possible. Again she picked up her phone.

EIGHTEEN

Surveying her surroundings, Carol took in the credentials on the walls in Jayleen Smith's office with interest. The minimal yet tasteful furnishings, the crystal box and the orchid emerging from river stones on the glass table drew her approval.

The small, slender woman seated opposite her had been quietly watching with calm blue-gray eyes until Carol finished her assessment. Then she said, "Please call me Jayleen, Chief Inspector. I'm afraid you'll have to put up with me having lunch while we talk." A sandwich with an unidentifiable filling between slices of brown bread sat on a paper plate on the end table beside her, a small bottle of water near the plate. "I have somewhere to be afterward, and this the only time I could give you."

"Of course," Carol said, settling herself more comfortably in the upholstered chair across from Jayleen Smith. "I'm very grateful you could find a few minutes for me and appreciate how very unusual it is that you would be willing to see me on a Sunday."

"It is. But as I told you, next week is impossible—I'm fully booked. I happened to be here in my office doing some catch-up when you called. And besides, anything for the Sydney police." When Carol did not respond to this wry, half-smiling allusion to Jayleen's environmental run-ins with law enforcement, she said, "That you would call my answering service on a Sunday is quite unusual. I could only infer that this is of special urgency. I can offer you water—"

"I'm fine."

"You said it was police business. Which begs the question why you're not consulting your own police psychologists. Let me guess," she added before Carol could speak. "It's a matter with enough confidential and consequential aspects that you deem it necessary to consult an outsider."

Carol looked at her in appreciation for her grasp of the situation and that she did not have to search for careful words to compose an answer. "That's correct."

"I remind you that all of us in my profession are bound by stringent rules of confidentiality."

"I've been a police officer a long time," Carol said evenly. "Long enough to not put blind trust in anything. Plus, there are circumstances that do allow you to break that confidentiality."

"The breaking of confidentiality rules apply to me as well, Chief Inspector," Jayleen said with just a touch of sharpness. "I follow our rules around mandatory reporting to the letter."

"Understood. This comes nowhere near that. I need to ask, have you had much experience with clients consulting you about depression?"

"Years of it. I have a practice full of such clients."

Carol nodded. "So that's what I need to ask some very specific advice on—depression. And suicide."

Jayleen sat back and crossed her legs, the movement intersecting with a slant of sunlight from the plantation shutters that illuminated her deep green pants. They blended nicely with a pale green shirt, and Jayleen's gray-streaked hair added to an appearance and demeanor that invited Carol's trust. And confidence. She could see why Sybil was seeing this therapist.

"Tell me more," Jayleen said, and picked up her sandwich.

"We're trying to assess whether a death was an accident or suicide." Carol continued slowly, "The individual ran off the road in what could well be an accident. But it could have just as easily been suicide." She began embroidering as she went along, to disguise identifiable facts of the case. "She was a high-functioning professional who suffered intermittent but deep bouts of depression all her life. She appeared to be in good spirits in the days leading up to her death and everyone around her confirms she showed no signs of depression, made no allusions to suicide. Early in her life she did have thoughts of suicide and made one attempt, nothing since."

"How long since that attempt? At a guess," Jayleen added, seeing Carol's hesitation.

Piecing together her conversation with Rosalie Rooke, she said, "Probably three decades."

"So what makes you suspicious of suicide now?"

"Grossly unprofessional behavior that was highly uncharacteristic, in fact inexplicable, during the week or so before her death. Behavior that would normally have been distressing and unacceptable to...this individual. It was as if she'd lost it," she concluded.

Jayleen inspected her as she finished a bite of her sandwich. "I'm suspecting this was a colleague of yours but I don't expect or want you to answer that. Was she on medication?"

Carol kept her face judiciously blank. "According to her... husband, she was. But intermittently. She'd felt herself on the brink of depression again and got a prescription filled a week before her death."

"Do you know the medication?"

"Effexor. None of the pills were taken. The husband claims she didn't need them, she'd pulled out of it. He contends that after all their years of marriage she couldn't fake normalcy if she tried."

"He's not wrong. But he's not right, either. Here's what I can tell you. Quite a surprising number of suicides occur when people suffering depression are not actually depressed."

At Carol's quizzical expression, she asked, "Have you ever suffered a depression you thought you'd never come out of?"

Other than right now? "No," Carol said.

"Most of us haven't. We've been depressed, but not like that. It's a very dark, very painful world most of us can't really fathom. Fortunately, medications like Effexor can lift and pull many sufferers out of there. But the descent into it becomes increasingly hard, increasingly dreaded. The thought of depression recurring can be as bad as the depression itself. Suicides often occur not because the person is depressed but because they know all too well they're about to be. About to suffer one of those slides and they can't bear another journey into that darkness. Your woman who drove off the road, if she'd made that decision to not go there again…during the last day or two of her life, it would not be strange if she'd appeared happy, at peace with herself."

"Thank you," Carol said, "that's very good information. Another topic, if you have just a few more minutes?"

Jayleen had finished her sandwich. She glanced at the clock behind Carol and then nodded.

"You must know I'm partnered with a client of yours, Sybil Quade."

"I never reveal the names of my clients."

"Understood. But I do know she's seeing you. I'm wondering if you could see me as well. Or perhaps the two of us. I think I'm going to be needing some professional help of my own."

Jayleen Smith contemplated her, drumming her fingers on the arm of her chair. Finally she said, "Like you, Chief Inspector, I'm in a profession where I have to follow the rules. Please forgive me if my answer sounds like an evasion or a redirection. I encourage you to pose the questions you just asked me to your partner. I believe you'll find that's the very best place to start."

Carol nodded. "I believe you're right. Thank you. I'll think about all this." She rose. "I appreciate this favor of your time. It's been invaluable."

"That's all that matters to me." Jayleen smiled. "You could repay me by taking it easy with the cuffs the next time you people arrest me for protecting the environment."

Carol smiled back at her. "That's asking a lot."

Before she opened the door of Jayleen's office, Carol said, "I want to tell you something I would like you to consider privileged information, even though you might well wonder why or how it would be privileged."

Jayleen raised her eyebrows. "Right. Consider it privileged. And that would be...?"

"Watch tonight's *Shipley Report*."

* * *

Carol got into her car and switched her phone back on. There was another message from her aunt. It had come in ten minutes ago. The first one had been left as she made her way up to Galston and had simply said, *"Dear, call me as soon as you can."*

The latest one reminded Carol of this morning's phone call with Madeline Shipley, the tones in her voice she had never heard before. She had never heard this tone of voice from her aunt.

"Carol. Come home. Now. It's important. Urgent. Don't call me back, just come home."

She called her back. "Aunt Sarah, what's going on?"

"Carol, come home. This instant." Her aunt hung up.

Now what? What else could possibly be happening on this most hideous of all hideous days? Carol pulled her car into the heavy weekend Darlinghurst traffic.

Half an hour later, letting herself into her house, Carol could hear her aunt moving around in the kitchen, could smell something tomato-based—pasta sauce, probably. She stopped to gather herself into at least a semblance of normalcy, suddenly and sharply glad that her aunt would soon be leaving the country and that her son was in Europe. He, at least, would not be witness to the coming disgrace.

"Is that you, dear?" called Aunt Sarah from the kitchen. "I'll be right out. I'm just fixing a bit of lunch."

The idea of food was repellant. And her aunt's voice sounded much too unperturbed, much too normal to warrant her anxiety-ridden trek through Sydney traffic. Carol flung herself onto the couch, waiting for her aunt in rising irritation.

Aunt Sarah emerged, wearing her customary overalls, and seated herself comfortably in an armchair, raising her slippered feet up to the ottoman. Her face and her voice solemn, she declaimed. "Your career is not over."

"Sybil called you," Carol said, instantly, acutely, and, she realized, irrationally resentful.

Just get over yourself. They're the two women you love most. Who love you.

"Of course she did, Carol," her aunt confirmed. "Of course she would. And," she said in a tone of rebuke, "you should have included me in the goings-on when you were here this morning."

She swung her feet down from the ottoman, rose to her full height and reached into a commodious front pocket of her overalls. She withdrew an envelope, placed it on the coffee table in front of Carol, returned to her chair.

Carol stared at the envelope, a stark white oblong on the teak coffee table.

"It's my handwritten account of what happened," said Aunt Sarah. "I know it has to be written out and signed to be legal."

Carol could not bring herself to ask: *What do you mean?*

"About the death of your mother. My sister."

Carol continued to stare at the envelope.

"I overheard you with her that night," her aunt continued in easy, quiet calm. "What Vi asked you to do. It was her right to go, it was her right not to suffer. But she was wrong to ask you. She should have known you couldn't do it. I made her understand that, I made Vi understand that you couldn't do it, given your oath as a police officer."

"Aunt Sarah—"

Her aunt threw up a silencing hand. "Then Doctor Yates came in, and your mother made the same request to him in my presence. He told her he believed it was her right, and like you, quite rightly said he couldn't do it. He looked straight at her and told her he was sorry but all he could do in good conscience was sign a death certificate. That told me all I needed to know. After he left I told Vi I was in the same boat as you and Doctor Yates—" Her eyes widened as she looked at Carol. "There was no way I could kill my own sister!"

Roiling with memory of her own last moments with her mother, Carol managed to say, "No. Of course not."

Aunt Sarah heaved a heavy sigh. "But there was something I *could* do, Carol. I rolled her tray of drugs over to her. Asked if she knew which pills to take and the dose. Vi told me she did. I told her it was all up to her. I would leave the room for an hour. She asked me to count the Demerol in the bottle so I would know if she'd done it or was just asleep. I kissed her, held her. We didn't say anything more. Then I went away."

Aunt Sarah's eyes sparkled with tears and her shoulders heaved in another sigh. "I came back and Vi was asleep. Pills were missing. Ten or so, I think, probably all she could manage to take. I held her again until she died in my arms a few hours later, peacefully and painlessly. I rolled the tray of pills back where they belonged. And I left her like that."

Carol's eyes stung with moisture as her aunt continued softly, "In all these years since, not one day has gone by that I haven't missed my sister. At the same time I have not had not a single minute of regret. It was what she wanted and it was her right to do it." Her aunt looked at her from out of her own tear-streaked face. "I hope you can understand, I hope you can forgive my part in…"

"I'd forgive you anything. But there's nothing to forgive. Thank you, Aunt Sarah."

Her aunt nodded and swallowed audibly, and after a moment continued in a low, shaky voice, "Leanne came in and found her. Screamed out your name, and I came running. You didn't answer, you were passed out on your bed. I called Doctor Yates and then saw to you, but you were in the shower by then and I told you to get dressed."

"I remember that, I remember you…" She shrank inside as she relived her mind screaming, *I didn't do this! Please God I didn't do this! I didn't kill my own mother!*

"Doctor Yates came over. Examined Vi. Didn't even look at me except in the general way he told all of us how sorry he was. Said we should call a funeral home, he'd be signing the death certificate for natural causes."

Her aunt pointed at the envelope. "Every detail of what happened that night and my role in it is in that envelope. So, you'll call Madeline? Tell her you have this?"

"That's what you want?"

"That's what I want."

Her aunt put her feet back up on the ottoman. The smile of peace and acceptance that spread across her face transformed it into an expanse of benevolence. "Your wonderful mother made her own choice and is resting in peace with it. Now, how about I get on with lunch."

"Not for me. I have to get back."

"First call Madeline."

Carol got up, picked up the envelope. "I have to get back to the office, Aunt Sarah."

"Tell me this is not an evasion, Carol. Promise me you'll call Madeline. Or," her aunt said staunchly, "I will."

Carol met her aunt's determined, unblinking stare for a long moment. "Aunt Sarah, I promise."

* * *

Hours later, when Carol finally let herself into Sybil's house, Sybil was already at the door.

"I haven't been able to reach you all day! What's happening? Did you call Madeline again?"

"No."

"*What?* You promised! You *promised* Aunt Sarah!"

"I had to. Or she'd have called Madeline herself." Carol managed a faint smile. "I didn't say *when* I'd call."

She went directly into the kitchen. Pulled out of her shoulder bag the white envelope containing her aunt's confession, ignited a burner on the stove.

"What are you doing?" Sybil demanded, coming into the kitchen behind her.

"What it looks like I'm doing," Carol said, and held a corner of the envelope over the flame until it ignited. She carried the burning paper over to the sink while it fully engulfed, then dropped it into the sink. She completed the operation by washing the charred remains down the drain.

She turned to Sybil. "I won't risk it being found."

Watching an array of expressions flood Sybil's face—astonishment, confusion, and finally, alarm—Carol calmly said, "Do you really think so little of me? Did you imagine for even one moment that I would actually let my aunt do this? Let her destroy herself and end all the good work she's doing that means so much to her?"

"Carol, she didn't kill your mother, all she did was make it—"

"In the eyes of the law, anyone enabling someone to kill herself is the same as killing her."

"You can't take the blame for what you didn't do!"

Carol turned on her savagely. "So I should throw over a cliff the one woman who's loved me unconditionally all my life? I don't even believe she did what she says she did! I don't think she could. She loves me. I have every reason to believe she made it all up and she's doing it for *me*. So I should go ahead and have my wonderful aunt expose herself and my mother and the humane doctor who helped us—I should betray them all to save my bloody *career*? Bad enough the death of my own mother will be open slather on a scandal show for the entire country to see—I won't do this, it's not *worth* it to me! I'd rather have everybody in the country blame just *me*! Can't you understand I'd never be able to live with myself?"

"Madeline—" Sybil's fists were clenched white. "*I'll* call her—"

"It will do you no good to ask her not to do her job. Any more than if someone asked me not to do mine."

Sybil took this in, swallowed and said in a more reasonable tone, "It's Aunt Sarah's choice, not yours." She pointed at the sink. "When she finds out, there'll be other confessions where that one came from."

"Once the story breaks, it's over."

"I just can't let you—"

"You have to," Carol said raggedly. "You just have to. I know what you're trying to do, you and Aunt Sarah. There's no saving me from this, Sybil. You can see that, can't you? I need to preserve what's important to me. Aunt Sarah. You. What little I can salvage of my mother's privacy. My son's."

She reached blindly for Sybil, grasped her hands. "I just need you to help me through what happens after Madeline breaks this story. Once I hear what's broadcast, I'll have to call David and deal with this with him. Will you help me, just be here for me? I need to be with you to hear this broadcast." Carol said desperately, "I need you. Like I've never needed anyone before in my life."

Tears glittering, Sybil pulled Carol into her arms.

NINETEEN

Aunt Sarah arrived at Sybil's house by taxi five minutes before *The Shipley Report*'s seven o'clock starting time. She bustled in silently, brushing past Sybil, casting a glance at Carol that combined disapproval, anxiety, and anguish. Sybil poured her a glass of sherry, and without a word they arranged themselves around Sybil's television—Aunt Sarah in an armchair, Carol on the sofa beside Sybil, who reached for and grasped her hand, and held it on the narrow strip of sofa fabric between them.

Carol had declined the offer of her usual scotch, a decision she was beginning to reconsider. As the minutes ticked their way toward seven o'clock the heat over the surface of her body was approaching scalding.

The hour-long program opened with its usual prologue, a barrage of split-second flashes, a photographic montage down through the years of Madeline Shipley featured against the Sydney Opera House, Uluru, and other iconic Australian backgrounds, in the company of Nicole Kidman, Hugh Jackman, Cate Blanchett; past and present prime ministers; assorted other actors, sports stars, musicians. Then a three-dimensional block of gold and green stripes appeared and broke open, its segments darting together to construct *The Shipley Report*, the three words angled on an upward trajectory as if they would rocket off the side of the screen.

There was not the usual voice-over excitedly delivering teaser headlines of what would be featured on the show, Carol noted. Madeline intended to have this go off like a time bomb in prime time on this Sunday evening to a national audience. Rising nausea added to Carol's miseries.

Madeline appeared on screen, seated alone in a forest-green armchair, an empty matching armchair across from her, her head down as she sorted through papers. The papers were as unusual as the absence of voice-over. Madeline, like most, worked from a teleprompter if needed and prided herself on thorough preparation that allowed her free-form interviews, and on her facility for pursuing her guests into any rabbit hole they fled to. The image of Madeline dissolved into product logos as an announcer listed in stentorian tones all the sponsors who proudly presented Australia's premier, trailblazing commentary and news program.

The screen blanked momentarily, then a camera moved slowly in on the striking star of the show. Tonight her copper hair was set off by a coffee-colored dress, form-fitting but long-sleeved, the famous cleavage concealed in favor of a round neckline decorated with a thin row of bronze beads.

"She's pretty conservatively dressed tonight, for her," Aunt Sarah quietly observed.

As the camera closed in for a headshot, a copper chain came into view, suspending a beaten copper disk nestled just above her breasts.

Carol's breath caught: she had given it to Madeline years ago. For the first time this day she felt a glimmer of something that was far less than hope, but yet a lessening of her apprehension.

Madeline's gaze rose from her papers and with a perfunctory smile she looked directly into the camera. "Good evening. I'm Madeline Shipley. Our program begins with a story exclusive to *The Shipley Report*. And, as it happens, especially relevant to a topic we've been covering in our series on *Motives for Murder*: mercy killing. Tonight you will hear from a woman who has brought to us a truly shocking accusation against a well-known member of the New South Wales Police Force. I now present to you the guest who will tell you the story she's given exclusively to us. Leanne Gordon, welcome to *The Shipley Report*."

A panoramic shot revealed a figure moving out from the shadows into the bright light of the set. Carol heard a low growl, then a hiss from her aunt.

Carol's first impression was of white. A plain white scoop neck dress, white low-heeled pumps, hair streaked with whitish gray.

"How virginal," Sybil muttered. "How first-confessional."

Leanne Gordon made her way to the armchair opposite Madeline, who rose to greet her. The woman's birdlike, wary body language was eerily familiar, awakening in Carol images of her around her mother's bed; and as she came fully into view, fresh memory of those last days of her mother's life.

Leanne appeared surprised by the hand Madeline thrust toward her in greeting but she took it gingerly and shook it. She sat down, perched on the edge of the armchair as if prepared for flight. Blue eyes behind rimless glasses looked earnest, ingenuous, almost unfocused. But lines were forming on both sides of her lips as they thinned into a line of determination.

"Thank you for bringing your story exclusively to us, Leanne. And of course you'll call me Madeline." She loosed a smile that all but melted Leanne back into her chair under the beaming warmth of it. The trademark Shipley charm, Carol thought. Designed to disarm all possible resistance. But you would have to be very naïve to appear on this show and not know that between the snake charmer and the cobra, Shipley was both snake charmer and cobra.

"Before we begin with your story, I'd like to ask you just a few questions about yourself."

As Leanne's eyes began to widen in uncertainty, Madeline's face softened into an expression of beguiling kindness. She leaned toward her reassuringly. "Nothing too personal, I assure you, Leanne. Our audience would like to learn a little about the woman who's brought us this important story—I'm sure you understand it will help them with the context of your story. Now, you are a registered nurse?"

"Yes. For twenty-six years." The voice was girlish, quivery.

She looked and sounded, Carol thought dismally, utterly credible.

"And when was it that you came to the household of Violet Ashton in your professional capacity?"

Carol cringed at this naming of her mother; Sybil's fingers tightened around hers.

"That would be 1996."

"Tell us what brought you to the Ashton household."

"I was hired to look after Mrs. Ashton—they chose me from a staff of twelve at my agency," she added with a touch of pride.

"How many people were in the Ashton house at that time?"

"Her daughter, Carol, Mrs. Ashton's sister, Sarah. Including Mrs. Ashton and me, four of us."

"A doctor was in attendance as well, yes?"

"Doctor Yates."

"You told me he was very attentive, yes?"

"Yes." Leanne Gordon was relaxing under these innocuous questions. "He came to the house just about every day."

"How remarkably kind of him." Madeline smiled into the camera and shook her head. "Highly unusual back then and unheard of today unless you're wealthy. I take it they were they friends?"

"I have no idea. I just know that like me, he was doing everything he could for her."

"For how long did you provide care to Mrs. Ashton?"

"A month."

"A month. So, not very long at all."

"No, she was quite ill."

"Quite ill," Madeline echoed. "She was suffering?"

Leanne nodded, her blue eyes widening, a sorrowful look coming over her face.

"Suffering, I take it, that couldn't be fully controlled by medication?"

"Well, it was end-stage cancer, of course. She was dying."

"In agony with her dying."

Wherever Madeline thought she was going with this, Carol thought, it was a dead end.

Leanne's sorrowful demeanor began to alter. "Whatever pain she was in, no one had the right to kill her!"

"I would *never* suggest that *anyone* has the right to murder *anyone*," Madeline declared, raising both hands in wounded protest. "Leanne, I'm just trying to make the circumstances clear for the audience waiting to hear your story."

But Carol had seen a micro-expression flash across Madeline's face: keen anticipation. The cobra was coiling.

Leanne nodded, mollified; but she was sitting forward again, tension in her body.

"Murder is one thing. Suicide another. So tell me, Leanne," Madeline said in an easy, casual tone, as if they were sharing a confidence, "do you think Violet Ashton had the right to take her own life?"

"Look," Leanne said, her face and voice gathering suspicion, "I don't know what's going on here, I don't know about all this politics stuff, and that's not what I'm here for and that's not what happened. I came here to tell my story—"

"And we want to hear it. But it's an easy question anyone can answer. Did she have a right to take her own life?"

"Suicide is a sin," Leanne answered forcefully.

Madeline nodded. "No matter how much pain we're in, how much we're suffering?"

"It's God's will. God's plan. God's will for us must be done."

Carol had no memory of Leanne being so inordinately religious. Which didn't mean she hadn't been.

"If anyone can answer the question," Leanne suddenly flung at her, "then it's only fair that you do too."

"Good one," Carol muttered.

But Madeline appeared unruffled, nodding acceptance of the challenge. "Do we have the right to take our own life? My personal belief is that we all should have agency over our own bodies and that includes the time and manner of our death."

"I thought so," Leanne said sternly. "Now I'd like to get on with—"

"But I always listen respectfully to opposing views. Anyone who's watched this program over all our years on the air knows that *The Shipley Report* has welcomed points of view from everywhere on the political spectrum, no matter how extreme. On this issue I respectfully disagree with you."

"Well, I don't respectfully agree with you," Leanne returned vehemently. "If it's a sin in God's eyes, then it's wrong, it's a sin."

Madeline answered with an agreeable nod. "Just one more question before we get into your story, Leanne. Mrs. Ashton died twenty-one years ago. Why are you just now coming forward to tell us what you believe happened?"

Leanne sat perfectly still and took a breath.

It'll be a lie, Carol thought. She'd seen this body language in any number of interrogations down through the years.

"I was always suspicious about how she died."

That I can believe, Carol thought.

"It's bothered me ever since. I just couldn't live with it any longer."

"I see. Leanne, just one more thing…" Madeline sat back and contemplated her. The silence stretched and stretched, became electric. Then she picked up her notes, pulled out a document and appeared to be studying it.

It was a tactic Carol well understood. She'd used it herself, sometimes truthfully, sometimes as a bluff, to convince an interview subject that she was holding incontrovertible confirmation of a fact. And it was working on Leanne, whose apprehensive, unblinking stare was frozen on Madeline.

Madeline said, "We've learned that you're a member of the Cherished Life Church. Would you confirm that?"

"Oh my God," Sybil uttered from beside Carol, clutching and squeezing her hand.

Leanne's body remained frozen, and Carol's rapt attention was drawn to Madeline: she cast a single burning glance directly into the camera and touched the copper disk above her breasts.

Leanne finally spoke, saying coldly, "Why would that matter?"

"Do you deny it, Leanne?" Madeline asked courteously.

"Of course not. I'm proud of it."

"Why would it matter, you ask. I posed this question to you because this would be the Church led by Canon Armitage."

"Crikey!" Aunt Sarah crowed, pounding the arm of her chair.

"Yes," Leanne said, gripping the arms of her chair and lifting her head in defiance. "The finest man I've ever known in all my life."

"Tell me the truth as the God-fearing Christian woman you say you are: did Canon Armitage ask you to come to us with your story?"

Leanne hesitated. "I wanted to do this."

That the hesitation was fatal could be seen in the victorious expression that galvanized Madeline's face. The cobra was about to strike.

Madeline raised her voice in the unmistakable tone of confrontation that had made her famous: "This would be the same fine man making headlines all over the state for staging a failed attempt on his own life."

"That story is simply not true," Leanne flung back, matching Madeline's voice in volume. "He never staged *anything*," she proclaimed, looking away from Madeline and wide-eyed into the camera. "The media's made all that up. It's a crazy person who did that."

Madeline lowered her voice enough to say reasonably, "Perhaps a crazy person did do it. Let's assume that's true. That crazy person happened to be caught and arrested on the scene by two police officers, one of whom is named Carol Ashton. And you do know that, don't you Leanne. You do know that Carol Ashton is the daughter of Violet Ashton."

"I don't see why that—"

"Is it possible," Madeline continued relentlessly, "is it possible that this very same fine man, Canon Armitage, decided to use you to get himself off the front page and off the Internet where he's being endlessly ridiculed? Get the subject changed at any cost? Decided he would go to any length to salvage a reputation that's being reduced to tatters? Including using yet another member of his own congregation to plant a false story about a well-known and highly respected Chief Inspector in our police force?"

"*It's not false! She did this!*"

"Indeed? Then lay out the proof you brought us."

"You have it!" She jabbed an accusing finger at Madeline. "I *gave* you my list of discrepancies between Mrs. Ashton's medications and the written instructions from Dr. Yates—"

"Ah yes. Dr. Yates. Who happens to be conveniently dead. But not conveniently enough." She plucked a paper from amid her sheaf of notes and waved it at the camera. "We've examined these so-called handwritten instructions—and also examined archived medical records from his practice. This handwriting bears no resemblance whatever to any handwriting of his. A bit sloppy on your part, Leanne—but then you and your canon had very little time to throw this tale of yours together, didn't you. Only a few hours to fabricate these so-called notes from Dr. Yates."

Leanne's rapid headshakes were like a dog shaking off rain. "It doesn't matter! I saw her do it with my very own eyes!"

"Your very own eyes," Madeline repeated, her face, her voice brimming with contempt. "I assume your very own eyes would refuse to believe a sworn statement by a key witness present at the scene, the highly reputable Simon Sykes, that Canon Armitage did indeed stage his farce of an assassination attempt. You actually expect us to believe that your unsupported contention is good enough to warrant destroying the reputation of a woman who has served this city with distinction for many, many years—"

"But I *saw* her! I saw her do it! You tricked me into this, this—"

"You're the one who came to us, Leanne. And we're very glad you did so we—"

"You're just another enemy of our church that's only trying to save lives," Leanne spat. "Another of the devil's minions attacking God's will and the sanctity of life. You're just another unbeliever—"

"What I believe in above all else, Leanne, is finding the truth wherever I can as best I can. You know what's worst about your story? That the media I'm a part of has become so debased, so without principles, that you and your canon felt confident any of us would willingly allow you a platform to destroy the reputation of a police official who's spent her life protecting us. You and your canon actually believed we'd run with a story that can't be proved, has no eyewitnesses, no official documentation of any kind, no merit whatsoever. My profession has a lot to answer for, but not all the media is as pliable and irresponsible as you and your canon Armitage believe us to be."

She was shaking a finger at Leanne Gordon, who had been all the time attempting to talk over Madeline's rising voice. "My investigative team has spent an entire day looking into every aspect of the death of Violet Ashton. Let me be the first of many in the city of Sydney to call you out as a dupe, if not a liar. And most of all to call out Canon Armitage for putting you up to this travesty."

She glanced offstage for an instant and nodded. "I see we're about to have a commercial break." She turned back to her guest. "Time now for you, Leanne Gordon, to get the hell off my set."

Leanne Gordon leaped to her feet as if to lunge at Madeline who half rose to readily meet her. But two security men instantly appeared and Leanne only waved in disgust as she turned and stalked off.

A close-up of Madeline Shipley, fingering her copper disk as she glared after her guest's departure in clear contempt, dissolved into an aquamarine vista of the Great Barrier Reef and an advertisement for Queensland tourism.

Carol, Sybil, and Aunt Sarah sat in stunned silence.

Carol's mobile shrilled. Carol could not move, could not summon the effort of silencing it. Sybil finally seized it, looked at the caller ID.

"You'll want to take this." She handed the phone to Carol, picked up the remote control and muted the television.

Carol read the caller ID: *M. Shipley.*

Carol answered the call, demanding without preamble, "Madeline, why didn't you tell me? This has been the most unspeakably hellish day of my entire life."

"Carol, I knew what I'd be putting you through. But I also knew if I told you what we'd learned about her, you'd arrest her. For perverting the course of justice or some slap on the wrist charge that wouldn't do a thing to discredit her story—and would probably enhance it."

"I—" Carol searched but could find nothing to offer in rebuttal.

"I have thirty seconds before we're back from commercial." Her voice picked up a teasing note as she added, "Here I was actually thinking you might thank me."

"Thank you," Carol managed, her voice breaking. Then she began to laugh. "You're right," she gasped, barely managing the words, "thank you, Madeline." Her peals rose toward such hysteria that Sybil grabbed the phone from her.

"Madeline, it's Sybil. As you can hear, it's either laugh or cry here. Aunt Sarah and I are the ones crying. Thank you from the bottom of our hearts for this. She owes you. We all do."

"She deserves the best taking care of, Sybil. I'll be expecting you to do the rest from here on."

Madeline clicked off just as the commercials faded into a close-up of the smiling star of *The Shipley Report.* Who was again fingering her copper disk.

TWENTY

One day ago at this hour, Carol had thought the walk to her office the morning after *The Shipley Report* aired would be through a gauntlet of silent stares ranging from pitying to censorious. Instead she was greeted by showers of applause, congratulatory calls of "Great outcome, Chief Inspector!" from office doorways and handshakes from colleagues and staff. She deflected the curious and those with specific questions with shakes of her head and murmurs of, "I'm still absorbing it all myself."

She had left instructions that she would not take calls from the press, from anyone other than police personnel. David, with whom she had yet to speak beyond a cryptic email from him— *What was this crazy woman ON about?*— but would call when the time difference allowed.

She proceeded to her office where she was greeted with an exuberant, crushing hug from Mark Bourke, and, taking his example, a less physical but wholly affectionate embrace by Anne Newsome.

"The low profile yesterday," Bourke said, peering keenly into her face, "you knew this was coming down."

Carol delivered her prepared answer in as casual a manner as she could muster to her acutely observant colleague of many years. "In some dimension, yes, Mark. But you never know how anything might play out on live TV—especially on *The Shipley Report*."

"Must have been sky-high anxiety," he said in a neutral tone that told her he was bothered that she had not shared any of it with him.

"There was no help for it. Nothing anybody could do. I drew on all my years of practicing a stiff upper lip," she quipped, hoping this would mollify him.

"Nice to have friends in high places," Anne lightly observed. "I wonder if La Shipley would have been as kind—" She broke off awkwardly.

"To someone else in the same situation?" Carol finished for her. "Hard to imagine. But it's safe to say you're right, Anne, I'm very lucky."

"It's luck you've earned and deserve," Bourke told her with renewed warmth in his face.

But he knew as well as she did that worthiness had nothing to do with it. Any number of worthy people had been obliterated by the rabid judges and juries of the media. It had been pure luck that she knew the right woman in the right place at the right time. But she replied to this gallantry with her own warm smile.

"How about that headline in the papers this morning?" Bourke gloated. At Carol's puzzled look, he marveled, "You didn't look at any of the papers? You amaze me. Pretty much everybody's got the same one: *Get the hell off my set.* You've become bloody famous, Carol."

For a day, she thought.

"And Shipley even more so," Anne added. "As if she needed to be. As for Armitage, the phony hypocritical bastard—"

"This should put him and his collection of acolytes in the same bin with that American crazy Fred Phelps and his Westboro so-called church," Bourke finished.

Carol nodded but felt no desire to bask in a triumph that felt hollow in its every dimension. The only piece of yesterday's turmoil that felt real was the night with Sybil, their fierce and inexhaustible passion born of explosive relief and reprieve, as if the two of them had survived a bloody battlefield. It had left her physically and emotionally replete, echoes of it still in her body. "Let's get up to date, shall we?"

"Les Upton first," Bourke said. "He's champing at the bit to meet with us."

Thinking it odd that she had yet to hear from the commissioner, Carol picked up her phone and punched in Upton's number. "Les, we're ready for you."

Moments later, iPad in hand, two neat folders under an arm, one red, one blue, Les Upton entered with an exuberance unusual for him. It wasn't just gladness for her—clearly he'd found something significant in his scrutiny of the Denby family holdings and finances.

After he'd clumsily expressed his own variation of "Glad they nailed that woman," and she'd given her obligatory response, he told her, "I know you're flat out. I'll get right to the good stuff."

He carefully placed the blue folder on her desk, and handed Carol the red one. "Reports on the Denby companies," he said, gesturing at the folder on her desk. "Lots of paper here I've yet to go through, but I can tell you Harland Denby built himself a first-class enterprise. Professional management and oversight, impeccable business practices apparently, including large charitable grants. Seems like he was an upstanding fellow."

His wife was just as upstanding, Carol thought dolefully. She doubted their good works would survive them, most regrettably Greta Denby's sponsorship of services vital to women. With the Denby offspring in charge...

"Even though I'm still working on everything, I found a piece that's really interesting." Upton flipped open the plastic cover on his iPad, shifting from one foot to the other as it powered up and he located his file.

"Sit," Carol told him, pointing to a chair between Bourke and Anne Newsome.

Upton obeyed and directed a few finger jabs at the screen, propped the tablet on the desk, then addressed the three of them. "I've been looking at the trust fund allowances set up for Thalia and Kenneth Denby. Thalia's managed to live quite nicely on her hundred and twenty-five thou a month. Doesn't even draw down all of it."

"That would be what, a million and a half a year?" Anne said.

Carol silently thanked her for her math skills.

"Kenneth not so much," Upton said. "He's spent it right down to the penny and is in debt besides."

"That's what we understand," Bourke said, his crossed arms indicating his dismissal of what he'd heard so far.

"Interesting thing is, the only actual *things* he buys of any consequence are pricey cars. Even though he's wrecked two of his autos, he'd be hard-pressed to spend more than two months' allowance replacing them, and that leaves ten more months in the calendar year."

"No guessing where the money's gone…we understand he's an *entrepreneur*." Bourke's voice dripped with sarcasm. "Are you telling us that doesn't cover the rest of his allowance?"

"No, in fact it does. And he's actually got a few ventures paying back a bit in royalties, four games with enough followers to have forward potential. Then we have *Krazy Koalas*, *Wacky Wombats*, and *Killer Kangaroos*."

"Where?" Bourke joked, raising his arms above his head in mock terror.

"Where happens to be exactly the question," Upton said, his features sharpening with anticipation as he continued. "They were initially capitalized for a quarter million each, with another fifty thousand every three months—"

"Given that Harland Denby's been dead, what, going on two years, that means about a million and a quarter to these three entities?" Anne queried.

"Give or take," said Upton.

"Will somebody please clue me in," complained Bourke. "What are *Krazy Kangaroos* and the rest of them?"

"*Krazy Koalas*," corrected Upton. "Computer games. Big dollars these days if you happen to strike the public fancy." He pointed to his tablet. "Here's one example of these three games in particular."

Carol saw a row of acrobatic cartoon koalas forming the letters *KRAZY KOALAS*. Beneath the flashy heading was the message: *Website Under Construction. Check Back Soon.*

"All three creations have similar websites."

"They're inaccessible? After all this time?" Anne shook her head. "With so much money invested? Kenny isn't checking on his own creations? Even he can't be that dumb."

"He isn't," Carol said, having put Upton's facts together. "He doesn't even know about them."

"Exactly," said Upton, looking at her in appreciation. "Everything's been done to make them legal but they begin with the paperwork that set them up and end in three dead websites. It's all in that red folder."

"You're telling us the money's gone elsewhere? Been embezzled?" Bourke said, staring at the website.

"Which would point right at Frederick Lowell," Carol said, thinking the man had the nerve of a daylight burglar. He'd sat right in this office and told her that Greta Denby's greatest fear was that Kenneth Denby would quite easily be swindled in one of his many business ventures. It had been happening right under her very nose, the perpetrator her most trusted advisor.

"Exactly," Upton said again. "He's directly, entirely responsible for the direction of Kenny's funds. And we've just nailed him."

"So Kenny's not the sucker we all thought he was," Bourke offered.

"I wouldn't go quite that far," Anne said.

Carol smiled at her protégé. "Nor would I. Lowell recognized a dupe when he saw one."

"That's all I have," Upton said, picking up his iPad. "I'll leave it with you."

"Thank you, Les," Carol said. "This is great work."

Smiling at her and at the echoed compliments of Bourke and Ann, Upton ducked his head and left the office.

Anne jumped to her feet. "Shall I proceed with Frederick Lowell?"

"In a minute," Carol said, gesturing her back to her chair.

"Right," Bourke said, nodding at Carol. "We may have a lot more here than embezzlement. That document Lowell gave you when he was here, Carol. Do you have it handy?"

Carol opened the file drawer next to her and plucked a labeled folder out of its neatly arranged contents. A system, she remembered, that she had learned from Ian Rooke. She pulled out the sheet of paper Lowell had left with her with its handwritten notations.

"No numbers, just statements as to what Greta intended. According to Lowell. An enhancement of Thalia's allowance—a tripling of it with the expectation that she would continue her mother's charitable good works. A lowering of Kenny's by one hundred thousand a month—"

"Lowering?" Anne exclaimed. "A million and a half a year to three hundred thousand is an ax chop." She added, "That would impact the two hundred thousand a year that Lowell's been siphoning off Kenny's allowance. Make it far more noticeable."

Carol looked from Bourke to Anne. She said wryly, "In between the discredited assassination attempts on the canon and on my character, I've been asking myself why Lowell was so willing to turn over basically useless information since any changes would be null and void with Greta Denby's death. Why he was so anxious to confront me with an unprovable claim of bias against Ian Rooke about Kenny Denby."

"I reckon he was trying to nudge us toward his sitting duck," Anne suggested. "Clever bastard was actually giving Kenny a motive by defending him."

"If Kenny did get stitched up for this," Bourke contributed, "Lowell could maybe cover his own tracks about both Kenny and Greta Denby's death. Bottom line, this gives Lowell a motive for her murder."

Carol looked at her trusted team of two with pride and satisfaction over how well they meshed and collaborated. She addressed Anne. "Get started on a task force. Search warrants for Lowell's home, office, bank records, confiscation of any and all electronic records. We have no evidence connecting him to Greta's death yet, but we do have probable cause for embezzlement. So arrest him while you're at it."

"Done," said Anne, and left the office.

Carol directed her attention to a broadly grinning Bourke. "What?"

"Just imagining Anne cuffing that pompous ass and marching him through his law office."

Carol's phone rang. Smiling at Bourke's imagery, she answered, listened to the announcement of the caller, said, "Yes, of course."

"Chief Inspector, are you alone?" the commissioner said. "I need to speak with you privately."

Covering the receiver she looked at Mark, mouthed "Hindley," indicated he should remain seated and silent, and put the phone on speaker.

"I am, sir."

Hindley rumbled, "What did you know about this business on TV last night and why didn't I know about it?"

Carol smothered a smile. He was not about to utter the name of the show or the woman who had derided his appointment to Commissioner as pure political payola and continued her sniper attacks at every opportunity. "I was given word that someone had come forward regarding the death of my mother. That's it. I was as surprised as everyone else at what played out during the program last night."

His voice rose. "You had no idea that the Shipley woman would name Simon Sykes as a witness against Canon Armitage?"

Bourke raised both hands and she raised both eyebrows. Then chided herself for her surprise that concern for himself would trump any jeopardy to one of his officers or his department. She understood why she had not heard from him earlier. He'd been busy with damage control.

She replied definitively: "I had no idea she'd name Simon Sykes. Absolutely none."

His voice rose further. "How did the Shipley woman get this information from his police interview?"

Carol rolled her eyes at Mark Bourke. "Sir, how does she get *any* of her information?"

"You need to find whoever it was that leaked this," he barked.

A fool's errand, she thought, but offered mildly, "It could well be someone in the Crown Prosecutor's office. Madeline Shipley has sources everywhere. It could have been Sykes himself."

"Goddammit," Hindley hissed with exasperation. "It goes without saying that I've had to cut Sykes loose."

Bourke silently clapped.

"Why on earth," Hindley complained, "didn't he just let this stupid publicity stunt of Armitage's go and not involve himself and this office? Why provide bloody *evidence?*"

"According to his statement he was roped in at the very last minute," Carol said, and continued evenly, "he wanted no part of it and he felt telling the truth was his duty."

She watched in amusement as Bourke delivered his own eye roll. Simon Sykes's stock-in-trade was opportunism and with the capture of Douglas James Fulton at the Kirribilli house he'd known a dead loser when he saw one. Sykes's willingness to cooperate in his police interview and statement was pure self-preservation, devil take the consequences.

"It's a bloody disaster, Chief Inspector. Just between us, that damn Shipley woman is about to reveal Canon Armitage as a major contributor to the Premier. The money involved is already being donated to appropriate charities, of course, but who knows how much blowback there'll be. I know you know the woman. Given the stakes, can you do *anything* to stop her?" His voice took on an unctuous tone she'd never heard from him before. "The Premier, I assure you, would be very grateful."

Desperation, she thought. The Premier's people would have already tried. "If I could, Commissioner, don't you think I'd have stopped the story involving me? With my career on the chopping block? I had absolutely no idea where she was going with whatever it was she'd learned."

Bourke was up on his feet, dancing silently around the office. Simon Sykes would not be the only casualty. Hindley, with his very public association with Sykes and cooperation with

Armitage, would have lost the trust and support of the Premier, whose ruthless discarding of anyone or anything damaging or no longer useful to him was as legendary as Hindley's.

"Well, I'm glad *you* came out of it so well, Chief Inspector," he grunted. "We hardly need another black mark against the department. Any news to put us in a more positive light?"

Meaning yourself. "We should have a disposition of the Ian Rooke matter within a day or so. We're making progress on Greta Denby."

"Hmmph," Hindley uttered. He disconnected.

Bourke strode to Carol's desk to lean down and exult, "He's a puff of smoke. With the enemies he's made, we should start an office pool for how many days—maybe hours—before we see the last of him."

* * *

Carol was not as annoyed as she might have been at Kenneth Denby's tardiness. Had he been on time she'd have left him cooling his heels until she received the report from Les Upton and taken the call from the commissioner. But his scruffy faux-poor appearance in faded shorts and a dingy T-shirt, along with his patently insincere "Sorry I'm late" as he sauntered into her office in the wake of the officer escorting him, ignited her anger.

Contemplating his insolent manner after the stresses of the previous day, she gave in to a reckless impulse to put into words exactly what she was thinking. "You're not in the least sorry," she said flatly.

"You're right, I'm not." Hands in his pockets, he strolled over to a chair across from her and slumped into it. "You ordered me here. I had better things to do."

"Better things than cooperate in the investigation into the death of your own mother?"

He blinked at Carol's scathing tone. "It doesn't matter whether I'm here or not. Mum won't be any less…dead." His voice cracked on the last word.

Carol looked over to Bourke, who was frowning at her. She didn't blame him for wondering why she was ignoring the nonconfrontational strategies they'd agreed upon. She wasn't quite sure herself—but after her first exchange with Kenny, a gut feeling had persuaded her that there was something desperate behind the obnoxious front.

Bourke was about to join in when she silenced him with a single warning glance, then fixed her eyes on Kenny. He returned her stare. She let the silence build, then leaned across her desk and said, "See yourself as a bad, bad bloke, do you? You're just a pathetic yobbo swanning around in your fancy sports cars. People put up with your infantile antics only because you have family and money."

"I know," he tossed back. "So what."

"So, since you've clearly decided to be no help to us, I won't waste any more of your valuable time."

"I could report you for speaking to me like this," Kenny said, but without conviction. He was sitting very still and regarding her with a level gaze.

"I'm sure you'll receive tons of sympathy," Bourke said sarcastically.

Kenny jerked his head in Bourke's direction. "Why does he have to be here?"

"Inspector Bourke is a member of the team on this case."

"Otherwise I'd be doing something more constructive," Bourke said. "Like sharpening pencils."

Carol smothered a grin. "Let me offer you a deal," she said more amiably. "If you step away from your shock-jock act for a few minutes and answer my questions with something other than trash talk, I'll trust you with information we've uncovered that may have a considerable impact on your life."

"Impact on my life?" He sat up. "What the—"

"Your mother did not die a natural death. Murder is a distinct possibility. The inquest opened and then almost immediately adjourned. The coroner is collecting more evidence. You and everyone in your household are suspects."

"What the hell's going on here?" he demanded.

"Why don't we begin with you telling me if there's any reason why your mother's death wouldn't be murder. Did she ever mention suicide? Was there any time when she told you or if you ever believed she might want to kill herself?"

He did not answer. She did not speak or move as he sat blinking rapidly and rhythmically, as if absorbing a new set of data clicking into place. Into the silence of her office he finally stated, "No. My mother never wanted to kill herself." Then he bit his lip. Then tried but failed to prevent his face from falling into an expression of utter misery as he added tonelessly, "And to answer your follow-on question of whether she'd have told me if she did, she would not have. But I would have known."

She said quietly, "You loved her."

Somehow, the question ambushed him. His body collapsed into the chair. Defenseless against his overwhelming emotions, his face crumpled, and he ineffectually scrubbed at tears with his knuckles. He blubbered, "I can't believe what you're telling me. It's for sure somebody actually *killed* her?"

Carol realized: He's been in shock, he's barely been holding himself together. He's only just realizing what's happened.

"Mum's *gone* and I don't know what to do. Why would anybody kill my *mother*?"

A child, Carol thought. A child refusing to leave childhood, to be anything other than his mother's baby. She decided with certainty that he'd had nothing whatever to do with the death of Greta Denby.

She met Bourke's astonished eyes and said, "How about you get Mr. Denby some tea?"

Bourke nodded his understanding that from here on the interview would be more productive without his male presence. Carol knew he would take his time making the tea, if he did so at all.

As Bourke unobtrusively took his leave, she asked gently, "Are you okay to talk to me, Mr. Denby? Will you help with some information about that night when you lost your mother?"

He sat clutching the arms of his chair; she sat in a stillness of waiting.

At his gulp and shrug which she took as a yes, she plucked a question from her list of facts unsatisfactorily explained by either Rooke's investigation or her own. "Would you explain to me why the alarm system was off at the house?"

"My fault—and Thalia's too, because she came up with the idea," he snuffled.

"Sergeant Newsome noted that when you came home late you tripped the alarm and then couldn't remember the code to silence it."

"An act," he blurted, then again gripped the arms of the chair as if to steady himself. "Just an act. For Thalia and me. A game to get the bloody thing shut off. But if somebody got into the place and did this to Mum because of me—"

"That's very unlikely," Carol assured him. "Camera surveillance appears to be overlapping and thorough."

He shook his head. "Not like you think. There are ways through it." He stopped to swipe his tear-streaked face. Carol handed him a box of tissues from her desk drawer.

He blew loudly then went on, "Thalia and I, we've always covered for each other. The place is wired and monitored like a prison. Dad put all that in to protect everybody from all the crazies out there. But all those cameras, alarms, spotlights, electronic tracing of when we came and went—we just wanted to be like regular people."

As if there's anything regular about you or your sister... "Why would it be necessary to disarm your alarm system?"

"Mum. She never looked at surveillance tape—the alarm monitor in her room flashes when somebody comes in. We couldn't have her upset, not when she needed everything in her to get well." He swiped at his eyes and dabbed at his nose. "Mum didn't know about Thalia and she was always at me about how I spent my money and—" He broke off.

"What about Thalia?" Carol inquired offhandedly.

He shrugged. "She likes to party. Me, I just had to get out of the house, it was too much sometimes to see Mum so sick. It helped to take a car and just go driving off anywhere."

Not much wonder, she thought, that he wrecked two cars.

"Sometimes I went gaming with my mates. Thalia..." His voice firming, he continued, "Weekends, my wild Teflon sister's out most of the night. Parks down there by Iris's place so nobody can see her come in at five in the morning or whenever."

"And your mother would have been upset by this behavior? Both of you are adults."

"Upset? Blown a gasket." He was recovering more of his composure. "Mum was on my case anyway. I could never make her understand how you have to product-test new games while they're in beta, how it takes money to develop them. But if you get a hit, get that big one like *Grand Theft Auto* or *Minecraft*..."

"And Thalia?"

He looked away and cast pained glances around her office while she waited. His eyes softening as they settled on the photo of Carol's son, he said slowly, "Thalia was always the star. First for Dad, then Mum. Mum thought she was spending all her time looking out for the organizations Mum cared about. Thalia told her she was—I told her to. I mean, that's what Mum needed to hear."

"But she wasn't?"

"No. Well, look...mostly no. She did some stuff, did what she had to. To make it look like she was."

Carol remembered Thalia's reluctance to fulfill the commitment to Dr. Valdez's event. "How did you feel about that, Mr. Denby?"

"Kenny, call me Kenny, okay? I would have done better than her, I could see the good in it. But she's the one who needed to, it's women's stuff, shelters and all, why wouldn't she care? I thought it was okay though, about Thalia, I mean I don't blame her, everything changed for her when she wasn't working with Dad in the business anymore. Look, Mum came to all this charity stuff late, just a few years back and full bore after Dad died. I suppose you know Mum herself was pretty wild when she was young, till she met my dad." Carol nodded sagely as if she did know. "How fair was it to expect us to..."

"Right," said Carol. "That night, Kenny, what time did you get in?" she asked as she picked up her pen and made a quick note on her desk pad.

"I was there for dinner, Bea fixed spaghetti, one of my favorites. Mum was feeling pretty good and I didn't go out at all that night."

Carol noted this new information about Greta Denby's state of mind and body. "And Thalia?"

"She was there too. We both stayed in."

"Who else was there?"

"Everybody. I mean, the usual people who come and go most days. Dr. Valdez, Mr. Lowell, they had dinner with Mum in her suite. Bea, Iris, Thalia, and me, we were out on the terrace."

"Why was Mr. Lowell there?"

He shrugged. "He pretty much comes in and out all the time. We're his primary client, you know. It helped Mum, keeping busy with reports on the business, her foundations—"

"I can well understand it gave her a lot to think about beyond her illness. Did she have any reason to look at anything to do with the allowances for you and Thalia?"

"No," Kenny said, looking puzzled by the question. "She fussed over what we did with our money, especially me, but Mr. Lowell told Mum right in front of us that we had a right to our independence, we needed to be responsible for our own money. I didn't think he had it in him."

"How did your mother react to that?"

He was recovering his composure, engaged by her questions, and managed a brief grin. "Furious. Like I told you, she had her own ideas about what we should be doing with our lives."

Carol was piecing together a portrait of an autocratic woman of wealth and power juggling control of the disparate areas of family businesses, societal beliefs, and commitments, her offspring orbiting out of her domination, her health sliding ever faster downhill. But she held a powerful weapon, the purse strings reaching to every corner of her empire. The motive for her murder seemed the classic one: money.

"Was that the reason you asked Bea Parker to intercede for you with your mother?"

His face twisted in pain, apparently at the last memory he held of his mother, one of confrontation. Then it darkened into a scowling pout. "Bea told you that?"

"Kenny, information comes from various sources during an investigation. She seems very securely in your corner."

"Bea's the only one who gives me any credit. The only one who sees how many hours I spend developing each game, all the graphics, conduits, pathways..."

"Like *Krazy Koalas, Wacky Wombats,* and *Killer Kangaroos?*"

He smiled at her uncertainly, disbelievingly. "You're a gamer?"

"You know these games?"

"No. I can't believe I've never heard of them—such great names. Whose are they?"

"Yours, apparently."

He gaped at her.

She picked up her phone and hit two digits. "Mark," she said crisply, "would you come back in? We need to explain the existence of Mr. Denby's games to him."

TWENTY-ONE

The conference room door opened quietly and Anne Newsome entered, her face somber, eyes clouded.

Carol's eyes lingered on her as Mark Bourke, focused on the computer screen in front of him, inquired perfunctorily, "How did the Lowell arrest go down?"

"He was thunderstruck. Stunned when we cuffed him. You'd think we'd just laid our dirty peasant hands on royalty. Kept insisting it was some kind of mistake."

Carol looked down at the table to conceal a sympathy Anne Newsome neither wanted nor needed. Someone like Lowell, with his protestations and incredulity, his assumption that his status and privilege would protect his victimization of a hapless target like Kenneth Denby, made visible that crucial difference between police officers and predators: empathy. An arrest like Lowell's was not part of the usual criminal activity that made up the bulk of police activity. No surprise that Lowell's utter cluelessness that his freedom was gone, his life as he knew it was over, would rouse discomfort in so honorable a person as Anne Newsome.

Anne was saying, "You've never heard such declarations of innocence. He's still maintaining he only borrowed the money."

Bourke chortled, then looked up when no one joined him. "He'll find lots of other people claiming innocence where he's going."

Anne smiled thinly. "I did ask him if he'd borrowed the money then why hadn't he paid any of it back yet. I've never seen such *arrogance*—"

Carol nodded her agreement and encouragement, understanding that Anne's withering contempt, aside from its focus on a deserving transgressor, was a necessary restoration of self-protection.

"—like anything he did was automatically okay if he did it. He told us Kenny Denby would say it was all okay."

"Who knows, maybe he will," Carol mused, remembering Kenny's anguished disbelief at this fresh new loss, a gross betrayal by someone he held close, took for granted, unconditionally trusted. She told Anne, "He was shattered about Lowell. I'm not sure he believes it or wants to. Even when we showed him Les Upton's evidence."

"No one can be that much of a dunce."

"More bereft child than dunce," Carol said mildly. "Take a seat, Anne, we need your brain. Mark and I are assessing evidence." She waved a hand over folders, reports, and photos covering much of the table and parts of the whiteboard attached to the wall. "I reviewed all the documents yesterday afternoon while I was waiting to see whether Madeline Shipley was going to put my head in a guillotine."

She had commandeered this room to organize and lay out everything connected with a case relatively self-contained compared to most homicides. Bourke had already written on the whiteboard the six names of everyone at the Denby estate in the hours before and after Greta Denby's death, adding a photo of the dead woman.

Carol had pieced together her own theory about this crime. But first she had to confront the reality that before any arrest, the gravity of a murder charge meant it had to be considered from every possible angle. The Crown Prosecutor would accept no less than that high bar of proof beyond a reasonable doubt, every element of evidence cross-checked and airtight. *Who* murdered Greta Denby was only the first question to be answered. The far stickier matter was proving it beyond that reasonable doubt.

Mark Bourke closed his computer screen, rose and strode to the whiteboard. "What about tradespeople?" he said. "They're all over the estate every day of the week."

"Yes," Anne said. "Here's your mail, Mrs. Denby, now how about you be a good girl and take this Nembutal."

Carol and Bourke exchanged grins. Clearly Anne's promotion had given her a lively boost in both confidence and cheek.

"Right," Bourke said amiably. "Not much motive there. So let's take everybody one by one as to who does have motive, least likely first. According to most mystery novels," he joked, "that'll be our killer."

"Eduardo Valdez," Anne said promptly. "He could have just signed off on a natural death. He'd have to be crazy to kill Greta and then demand an autopsy."

"Then call him crazy," Carol said crisply. "Because he had everything to lose by signing that death certificate. Look at it from his perspective, Anne. He's just got a toehold in Australia, he's got himself a darling of the media in Greta as his patient, tons of publicity. Her dying from the cancer he's treating would torpedo it all. Having her death a murder takes his treatment right off the table."

Bourke whistled, circling Valdez's name with a red marker pen. "Truly devious. See that the treatment was failing. Kill the patient and then have the brass balls to demand an autopsy to prove it's murder. Now *that* would make for a good mystery novel."

"He'd have to be brass-balls-confident he'd get away with it too," Anne said, staring at the name on the whiteboard. "I'll stick with my instinct that he is what he is, a true believer, absolutely certain his treatment would help Greta. He's a bit of a jackass but there's something about his belief in his treatment that feels genuine."

Carol's impression of him did not match Anne's, but Anne had seen more of him when Ian Rooke had the case. She conceded the point and added, "He's been treating her for some time. Maybe he knew her death was early for the progress of the cancer and her overall condition. She obviously felt well enough to dine with Lowell and him that night. And then she ordered a snack later." She selected the autopsy report from among the documents on the table, held it up to point to a paragraph. "The pathologist confirms the diagnosis of ovarian cancer, but without a prognosis, and I see from your notes that you checked with her, Anne."

"I did. According to her, how long Greta might live was inconclusive due to individual factors. Although she would have been experiencing considerable discomfort, pain even, her body condition and the spread of the cancer, although very extensive, didn't necessarily mean that death was imminent. And from what we've learned, I'd say Greta demonstrated considerable will to live." Her voice became wistful. "I'd like to think Eduardo Valdez actually has a treatment that might help. Maybe someday he'll contribute to beating this bastard of a disease."

"I'd like to think that too," Bourke said with an apologetic glance at Carol that she did not miss. She knew he was regretting his withering condemnation of the methods of compassionate suicide on that flash drive in view of what he'd learned about the nature of her own mother's death on *The Shipley Report*.

"But I also still like him for this," he argued, inscribing another circle around his name. "Carol's made a great point that he's got more to lose than any other name on this board. If he assessed that Greta had passed the point of no return with her cancer, he definitely had motive. Certainly he had opportunity. More than anyone else in the house he had the means with his access to medication."

"Well, that last one's debatable, Mark," said Carol. "You can get anything today. Right over the Internet."

"True. But she had to swallow the stuff and he had her trust. The big question about anyone else is how they could get Greta to take anything that wasn't ordered for her by Valdez. All the medication is accounted for, the totals in the pillbox all match up, so does what's left in the prescription bottles, plus the chart Bea Parker kept. It had to come in from an outside source."

"I have my own theory about that," Carol said, "but let's look at the circumstances. We know Greta was given a toasted cheese sandwich—"

"Which she had two or three bites of," said Anne. "Confirmed by the pathology report."

"And coffee with lots of cream, brought to her by Thalia," Carol continued. "Both of which we can discount as sources because she had those around nine. Time of death occurred sometime after midnight and before four. So Bea Parker couldn't have awakened her for her midnight meds if Greta had taken the Nembutal at ten—it's too fast-acting."

"If we're to believe Bea Parker that she actually did give her the midnight meds," Bourke said.

"Right," Carol said. "And Iris Kemp didn't confirm that she either saw or heard Bea at that hour."

"Bea Parker," said Anne, jabbing a finger at her name on the whiteboard. "She of the mysterious behavior the morning she found Greta dead. Very mysterious behavior, for a nurse."

"Didn't touch her, check her pulse," Carol reiterated. "According to Iris, she ran around like a hen with her head cut off, hysterical over the meds she'd given Greta."

"More than strange, all that, despite any adjustments Valdez might have made in the medications," Anne said, and began looking through the crime scene photo file. "Because the meds were all presorted into clearly marked compartments in a big plastic pillbox." She found the tab and opened the file to a photo of the large pillbox sitting on a shelf in Greta Denby's dressing room. "She had nothing to do with counting out the pills that night, supposedly just gave Greta what was already there. Very odd behavior for a nurse."

"But a registered nurse—we checked," Bourke said. "Solid record except for the inconvenient fact of two women recently dying in unnatural circumstances under her watch."

"Playing devil's advocate with you two," Carol said, "a close friendship with a patient can poke a hole through that detachment medical professionals try to pull over themselves."

Bourke said, "My guess is she behaved that way because she saw the same big elephant in the room we did—she was the last one to see Greta alive, she had another woman die on her, and she gave her those last meds. The midnight dose was always a heavy one compared to those during the day—to help her sleep through the night without pain."

"But what motive would she have?" mused Anne.

"That very friendship," Carol replied, thinking of her mother's last hours. "Bea Parker appears to be a sort of control freak—her behavior about what Iris could and could not do for Greta for instance—so maybe she needs to feel some control over her environment—"

"—or has an exaggerated sense of self-importance," Anne said acidly.

"And maybe she'd seen enough of Greta's suffering," Carol continued. "It's also possible Greta confided in someone that she'd lost faith in her survival, and that person might have been Bea."

"Plausible," Bourke conceded, tracing a slow, seemingly reluctant circle around Bea Parker's name.

"Iris Kemp," Anne said. "What motive would she have?"

"The same as Bea Parker times five," Carol said, tapping her gold pen on the table for emphasis. "For her politics. That report Sykes sent us about her run-in with Canon Armitage. We have only her word it was just over abortion. We haven't looked all that hard into her background—she may hold a fervent belief in mercy killing. Iris was a longstanding friend, so close that Greta provided her with a rent-free flat. Iris might well be the one Greta confided in. Her death might even be collusion between the two the night Greta died. Surely she had opportunity—she could have given her the Nembutal after Bea came in to administer the midnight meds."

Shaking his head, Bourke circled Iris Kemp's name, muttering, "It's a mystery novel all right. Agatha bloody Christie."

"Kenny," Anne said. "Easy motive there if Lowell was right about Greta losing patience and disemboweling him financially."

"Equally easy to discredit that motive, given the source is Lowell," Bourke said.

Carol remained silent; she had already disqualified Kenny Denby as a suspect, but was not about to encourage her team to do the same.

"If he's the child Carol says he is, he's capable of the same irrational behavior as a child," Anne argued. "We know his mother had issues with him. We know he has no censor around how he behaves—he says and does whatever he feels like at the moment. Maybe this was death by tantrum."

Bourke grinned. "You make as good a case as there is for him, Anne. But I can't see Kenny feeding his mother pills or his mother doing anything but laughing at him if he tried to."

"Okay, least likely," Anne conceded. She grinned back at Bourke. "Until we arrest him."

"Powder puff that he is," Bourke grunted, "he'd last twelve minutes in jail."

"We could put him in with Lowell," Anne said dourly.

"Thalia," said Carol. "What have we got there?"

"A double life hidden from her mother," Bourke said. "She got tired of waiting for her inheritance."

An eye roll from Anne conveyed her opinion of this theory. "She wasn't even spending the allowance she got."

"There's a monumental difference," Carol pointed out, "between the million and a half Thalia was drawing down and the multimillions making up the Denby fortune and all that goes with it. What else have we got?"

Bourke tapped on Thalia's name with his marker pen. "Her mother found out she didn't give a damn about the organizations Greta was funding and supporting."

"Entirely possible," Carol said thoughtfully. "Someone in the household might have put the wind up to Greta as to what she was actually doing with her life." But she could not imagine who would want to further distress a sick woman with cruel and disillusioning news about her daughter. Or why they would do such a thing.

"Even if that happened, what would Greta do about it, really?" Bourke argued. "I can't imagine she'd disinherit her daughter, do anything more than find somebody else to look after her interests."

"Thalia seems to have had more access to her mother than Kenny," Carol observed. "Much as Greta might have loved her son, it seems to me she'd be far more likely to trust something Thalia gave her."

"Or maybe Thalia overpowered her, forced Nembutal in some form down her throat. Any of them could." Anne shook her head over her own point and indicated the autopsy report. "But there was no sign of struggle."

"Which doesn't mean there wasn't," said Bourke, pointing at the photo of Greta mounted on the whiteboard. "Tiny and frail as she was, any of the men could have held her down without leaving a trace of a struggle."

The women too, Carol thought, but let her team continue with their theorizing.

"Well, Valdez wouldn't have to, as she'd happily take whatever he gave her," Anne said, "and I can hardly see either Kenny or Frederick Lowell physically forcing anything on anyone."

"Ah yes, we finally get to Lowell," Bourke said, circling his name with a flourish. "Our number one suspect."

"Okay, so how would he even get to Greta at that hour? Do we know that he actually left after dinner?" Anne said.

"The cameras picked up both him and Valdez leaving. But according to Kenny," Carol added, "there's a way through the surveillance. Lowell would know that as well as anyone in the family. And he'd know how to navigate the other alarm systems."

Bourke gave an impatient shrug. "Right. We agree he has motive—covering his tracks about embezzling Kenny's funds, maybe circumventing whatever Greta had in mind for changing her will the morning of her death. If she in fact had anything in mind—we have only his unreliable word for that."

Carol started to disagree, changed her mind in favor of listening.

"I'm not sure I'm with this idea of him covering his tracks," Anne said, looking at a note on her pad. "The man's an experienced lawyer. He'd know the Denby finances would be looked at in a murder investigation."

"He couldn't know there'd be an autopsy calling the death a murder," Bourke countered. "He couldn't know we'd have a Les Upton looking beyond the obvious wills and financial statements into the fine print."

Carol finally spoke up. "I do believe Lowell about the meeting Greta had set up with him the morning of her death."

She flipped her notebook back several pages, then told her team, "I did some research yesterday into ovarian cancer. Greta had a classic recurrence—it almost always recurs after remission," she said in answer to the question on Anne's face. "Whatever her hopes from Valdez, this cancer made it odds on that she was dying—it was inevitable. But someone couldn't wait for that to happen and that *has* to be the reason for this murder. The only conclusion that makes any sense—to me at least—is she was changing something crucial in her will."

"Then that makes it Kenny," Anne said. "If we're to believe what Lowell gave us in his notes of what he claimed Greta wanted."

"We'll question him on that, but we all know he had his motives for giving us that so-called list. Lowell may or may not know anything about what Greta wanted to change. But I do think she told someone, and that someone killed her to prevent the changes."

"What you say makes sense, Carol. But we're still at square one. We don't know who and we have the same problem we've had all along—the delivery of the Nembutal."

"I have a theory about that," Carol said, "but first, what about that flash drive in the aspirin bottle? Any ideas?"

"Some clumsy insurance," Anne offered. "Really clumsy."

"A just-in-case," Bourke agreed. "A stupid attempt to plant an idea that Greta had looked into suicide and was trying to cover it up. Why would she put it on a flash drive instead of just keeping it in a file on her computer?"

Carol nodded. "I suspect this murder was impulsive. But I don't think it was clumsy or stupid. I think it was cunning."

She reached for the crime scene photos and took some time searching for the group she wanted. Bourke came over from the whiteboard to sit beside Carol as Anne collected and stacked folders to make a sufficient space on the table for Carol to spread out the extensive sequence of photos she'd selected.

"In this first group are the medications taken from Greta's suite for analysis." Carol indicated fourteen photos forming a circle. "To be administered in varying doses at different times, some of them as rarely as every second day, which is why Bea Parker kept her chart of what was to be given to Greta and exactly when. All the pills tested out in our lab. They are exactly what they're supposed to be."

She picked up four photos of a large plastic pillbox, one of them the overview Anne had selected earlier, the other three close-ups of its segments.

"The pillbox has three days of medication in twenty-one compartments—Greta took medication seven times a day. At eight in the morning, at ten, at one, four, seven, ten o'clock, and midnight. The largest amount was at midnight, designed to get her through the night asleep and pain-free. It contained all Dr. Valdez's stuff, as well as oxycodone and Stilnox, which I'm sure helped to interact fatally with the Nembutal."

She pointed to the three other photos. "As Anne said, each compartment is labeled with the time the meds are to be given."

Bourke and Anne inspected the photos while Carol searched for another. "Here's what's interesting…"

She pushed everything away in favor of a close-up photo of a scattering of pills and capsules, placing it equidistant between herself, Bourke and Anne.

"These represent the final medications Bea Parker would have given Greta." She pointed with her pen. "Nine all told, and notice the number of large capsules. Five. A herbal mixture to build up the immune system that Valdez orders directly from New Zealand—it's not available here." She placed the pen precisely on the photo showing the entire array of medications.

"It's this bottle. The others are time-release meds that match up to these other two bottles." She pointed those out.

"Okay," Bourke said. "Whatever I'm supposed to be seeing here, I'm not seeing."

Staring at the photo, Anne said slowly, "The capsules pull apart."

"Exactly," Carol said.

"Got it!" Bourke jerked up in his chair and bounced a fist off the table. "Whoever killed Greta used her own medications. Took the stuff out and put in powdered Nembutal. Five capsules I assume would be enough for a fatal dose."

Anne picked up the photo, held it by its edges between both hands. "So anybody could come in at any time during the day or evening and substitute capsules filled with Nembutal for the midnight meds, and neither Greta nor Bea would know the difference."

"Unless it was Bea herself," Bourke said.

"Brilliant, Carol," Anne told her with a wide grin, "just brilliant."

Plain common sense and logic, Carol thought, but remained prudently silent.

"But still, who?" muttered Anne.

"Now that we have Lowell in our cozy confines, we'll talk to him about what he actually knows," Carol said. "But I believe we have better priorities. Greta's will—I want to get back to that. We found nothing in the house relating to anything she had in mind—"

"Which a killer probably would take, if that was the motive and if there was anything lying around," Bourke said.

"Tell me what you think, brain trust," Carol said to her team. "Would she have given Lowell instructions about her will just off the top of her head?"

"No way," said Anne. "Not if she was making significant changes, given the dimensions of the Denby empire. For sure she didn't come up with them the day before she died."

"Her computer," said Bourke. "She might have notes. Even messages."

They had arrived at exactly the place where Carol wanted them.

"This is what I want done today," she informed them. "We have an existing search warrant for the Denby home as a crime scene, so I want the whole place selectively searched again. Any pill bottle anywhere that we didn't collect is to be taken and fingerprinted. I want the clothes everyone wore the three days before Greta died. I want every existing computer or tablet collected and our tech is to get right on this and restore every deleted file she can find. If it hasn't been done already, I want Greta's pillbox fingerprinted. I want phone records for everybody on that whiteboard, including Greta, dating back at least a month."

As Bourke and Anne gathered up the notes they'd made of Carol's instructions, she told them, "We'll meet here again first thing in the morning. I fully expect we'll make an arrest sometime tomorrow."

Bourke frowned. "Carol, this all won't be done by tomorrow."

"The computers better be."

"Yes ma'am," Anne said with a mock salute.

"Well, an arrest tomorrow sure sounds good," Bourke said.

"You doubt me," Carol said with a grin.

"Never." Standing, he grinned back at her. "We've still got Ian Rooke too. Our final report is due in to Hindley. I gather the interview with Rosalie yesterday brought nothing new."

Carol said firmly, "We'll have a disposition on Ian tomorrow as well."

TWENTY-TWO

Sybil and Carol sat on the deck of Sybil's house watching a cloudless evening sky mutate into ever deeper blues over an equally darkening ocean. A breeze transporting an almost tropical warmth lifted fine blond strands of Carol's hair as she raised her face to inhale the smell of the sea. Her eyes were closed and she lay back with an easiness in her body, ankles crossed, tranquility replacing the usual tension in her face.

It had been an extraordinary evening. A truly extraordinary two days, Sybil reflected, ever since that warning call from Madeline Shipley. She gazed intently at the face of the woman relaxing beside her, drinking in the classic contours, sculpted by shadows, of the face she had held in her hands and savored with her lips the previous night, remembering intimacies she had performed on the body of this woman she loved.

I so love you and always have. I loved you even when I wanted to believe I didn't.

They had had an almost silent dinner on the deck, Sybil sensing the need to let Carol emerge from the still-echoing shocks of *The Shipley Report*, and her day at headquarters, letting her lead the conversation when and where she wished. Carol had refused her usual scotch, needing, she said, to keep her head and thoughts clear for a significant day tomorrow. Sybil had not inquired into the nature or definition of "significant."

Carol opened her eyes, caught Sybil gazing at her, and her face softened with the slow smile that never failed to spread warmth throughout Sybil's body.

Carol gestured to the darkening sea and its line of white surf. "I don't know how you could ever have thought about selling this house, much less agree to do it," she told her.

Sybil stared at her in astonishment. "But it's no less hard for you. Tit for tat for your place and how much you love it."

"Not anymore." Carol's tone, and face, had instantly hardened. "There's something wrong with me that I ever did. My mother suffered and died there. My mind won't let me go anywhere near what happened to you there. It's become a house of horror."

Amazed, Sybil spoke carefully into this raw confession. "What's brought out all this feeling, Carol?"

"The avalanche that's just all but buried me." Carol's voice was sharp with self-reproach. "What you've been going through all this time. The waking, walking ghost of my mother. Aunt Sarah leaving tomorrow. All of what I went through yesterday, second only to when you were attacked as the worst day of my life." She shook her head. "It turns out Madeline was quite the catalyst."

"I'll always be grateful," Sybil offered, trying to digest all this.

"Sybil, quite honestly I don't want to even walk through the door of my house ever again."

Sybil reached to her, took both her hands. "Maybe you should give it some time." But she knew Carol, knew she would have already made up her mind.

As Carol vehemently shook her head, Sybil squeezed her hands, and said, "Then don't do it. Be here with me. Sinker and Jeffrey will sort out their respective territories. Have someone pack you up and move everything to storage for now. How does that sound?"

"Good. Actually, really good. I mean it," Carol said, her face clearing. "I truly love it here." She smiled at Sybil, joked, "It could be good to exchange cockatoos for seagulls."

She took her hands from Sybil's. "I want to talk about something else. I'd like your thoughts about one of my cases."

Then she laughed. "To answer the question on your face, no, hell has not frozen over."

"You've never…"

"I know. I'm beginning to reconsider some of those 'nevers.' Something else happened yesterday that helped, which I'll tell you about. But right now I'd really like to have your perspective on a report I need to give to the commissioner tomorrow. Regarding my colleague, Ian Rooke."

"Ah yes." Sybil sat back, pushing aside her roiling reactions to all that Carol had told her, ordering herself to listen, to focus. "His car went into Galston Gorge. Leaving a wife and two little boys." She was very glad she'd not had any wine; she was acutely aware this was a key moment between them.

Carol nodded. "The surface facts are pretty simple. He was driving home to Galston about nine o'clock on a weeknight, in light traffic. His car went off the road on one of those curves that—"

"I know the road. Had he lived in Galston long?"

"Years. So he knew the road well. Of course you're aware he'd been working on the case I've taken over. The theory is, he fell asleep at the wheel…"

Sybil watched Carol turn away and drum slender fingers on the table next to her, discomfort in her face. She waited.

"The car was every bit the smashup you'd imagine. But it didn't burn, so we were able to check it out mechanically as best we could—no problems that we could find. Ian wasn't wearing a seat belt. His window was down." She looked over at Sybil.

Sybil suggested quietly, "The window being down would help him stay alert, I would think. But the seat belt doesn't make sense. Not on that road and not for a cop. Unless he was too tired and distracted to be bothered?"

Carol nodded. "Exactly what I told myself. A couple of other things bothered me, though. His mobile phone was in the glove compartment."

"But wouldn't he have Bluetooth?"

"Yes. But he hadn't used the phone in days and putting it in that glove compartment was as if it didn't matter to him anymore. Which was odd, to say the least, considering the high profile case he was working on. Also very unlike him, he hadn't done some pretty basic investigation on the Denby case. And there were no case files in the car."

"I can attest to how odd *that* is," Sybil mused with a faint smile. "The file room at police headquarters couldn't be more cluttered than your study when you're on a big case."

"Yes, you should see it now." Carol immediately looked as if she regretted the reference.

Sybil did not change expression to convey she was intent on the matter at hand, and Carol continued, "There was a needle puncture in his thigh. Which no one can account for, including the pathologist, including his wife."

"So, what are you thinking, Carol?"

"Before yesterday I wasn't actually thinking anything beyond none of it added up. There was no rationale to any of this behavior, none of it matched up with the man I thought I knew. Until I talked to Rosalie, his wife, and went into the bathroom in his house. Until I found out from Rosalie about a visit Ian made to his dentist."

Carol sat forward, elbows on the knees of her track pants, hands clasped as she stared out to sea. "This is what I know now. Ian had a lifelong illness he kept a close secret from everyone. Recurring acute depression. I found that out from a prescription bottle sitting in plain sight in his bathroom. I learned from his wife that he'd felt himself descending into another of those black holes. I found out from a psychotherapist I respect that suicide often happens not when someone is depressed, but when they know they're about to be sucked back into that particular inner circle of hell. I found out from his wife that Ian had made one attempt at suicide years ago but couldn't go through with it. I found out that just a few days earlier Ian talked to his dentist and came home from the visit as if the world had been lifted. I found out from the dentist that his son and Ian's had asthma in common, and they'd talked about an EpiPen being the emergency treatment for severe asthma attacks. Ian learned from him that the main ingredient is adrenaline. Which can't be picked up in an autopsy, as Ian well knew from all his years in homicide. I also figured out why Ian might have taken off his tie that we found in his car, what he did with it."

She turned to face Sybil. "Here's what I believe happened. Ian decided he couldn't withstand another bout of depression, couldn't inflict himself on his wife and family again, couldn't compromise the big case he'd been assigned. His life was insured for seven hundred thousand dollars. He and Rosalie had savings. She would get his police pension. But he couldn't risk another failure of courage, or worse than that, badly injure himself instead of dying. That visit to the dentist was key because he knew the adrenaline would take care of the courage. So before Ian started up Galston Road, he tied his tie around his thigh to restrict his circulation. No seat belt—to give himself two chances, either be crushed in the car or thrown to his death. Just before he got to that curve, he rolled down his window, jabbed himself with the EpiPen, threw it out the window, ripped off the tie, and in the surge of adrenaline that zapped his system he took himself over the side."

Sybil winced, closed her eyes briefly against the images. "It all makes sense. It accounts for everything."

Carol sighed, looked away. "Not everything. If only it did. He's left a widow and two fatherless children. A wife who loves him with all her heart and stood by him through all his bouts of depression and doesn't believe for an instant that he killed himself. A wife who has absolutely no idea that her carelessness about his medication, her unwitting honesty over what she told me yesterday, has stabbed a knife into the heart of what Ian so carefully planned. There's also the fact that he was a deeply respected police officer with a sterling reputation. The fact that his life insurance will be invalidated by suicide and I'm not sure how his police pension might be impacted."

Sybil put a hand to her chest as she absorbed the impact of these facts and the anguish on Carol's face. "Does anyone but you know what you learned yesterday, Carol?

She shook her head. "Not yet. Just me and his dumb-honest, totally admirable wife."

Again she looked into Sybil's eyes. "So tell me, my darling. If you were the one to make the determination on an official report about what happened to Ian Rooke, what would you do?"

Speaking as a human being... But she managed to choke off those first words to utter instead, "I'd declare it an accident."

Carol nodded. "I thought that's what you'd say. But I needed to talk it out. What I told you is a virtual certainty, but conclusive proof would be to send a search team up there to look for an EpiPen in the bush. Specifically, a child's EpiPen."

"Is that you're going to do?"

"Right now I'm somewhere between what you say and the oath I took as a police officer—"

She broke off, and stared at Sybil, stricken. Sybil knew they both realized she had applied to Ian Rooke the very words she'd spoken to Sybil about why she couldn't help her mother die.

Carol cleared her throat. "Tomorrow morning," she said emphatically, decisively, "I'll write an official report of accidental death and submit it over my signature. Not involve anyone else in the doing of it." She grimaced. "Not that anyone will question it, Sybil. Whatever the truth is, none of the higher-ups really want a Detective Inspector of the New South Wales Police written up as a suicide."

"I believe it's the right thing to do," Sybil said firmly. "God knows his wife's entitled to his pension. She deserves every penny. No one knows better than you and me the toll police work takes on everyone around you. As for his insurance, it would be payable sometime, anyway."

"That's not justification. But it is a comfort," Carol said with a wry smile.

"I'd always hoped you'd one day trust me," Sybil said. "I expected nothing like this."

"You mean that I'd put my career in your hands with what I've just told you? It's yours. All of me is yours."

They sat in silence, Sybil, close to tears, staring into the blue-black ocean, the lights beginning to sparkle around the shore.

"The psychotherapist I mentioned seeing," Carol said quietly. "The one who gave me the information about Ian's depression…"

"Yes," Sybil responded, expecting to be told who it was among the police psychologists Carol had been mandated to see over the years.

"It wasn't one of ours," she said. "I needed to explore the ramifications of what Rosalie Rooke told me. Confidentially. I didn't want to risk notes being put in any file that didn't deserve to be there."

"I understand," Sybil said.

"Jayleen Smith was good enough to give me an appointment."

Sybil sat perfectly still, so nonplused she wasn't sure how to react.

"While I was there I asked about seeing her on my own behalf. You're right, Sybil, she is very impressive and I finally understand I need to work some things out about myself. I need to figure out what it is that's been driving me all these years."

Sybil gaped at her. "Hell *has* frozen over. Who *is* this person sitting next to me? What's come over you?"

"You," Carol said. "You've come over me. Realizing how close I've come to losing you, that I'm lucky beyond lucky to even have a chance to have you back in my life. I need you to know that Jayleen refused to answer me. She said I'd have to speak to you, it was all up to you."

"Well of course you can—"

"I was thinking…we could go as a couple?"

"Whichever way it works," Sybil managed to say. She threw her hands up. "I'm not sure I'll know what to do with this new Carol."

"I'd like to think I can be a better old Carol." She reached for Sybil's hands and took them in hers. "As for what to do with me…my darling woman, it's been a long hard day and I'm about to say my four favorite words."

"Let me guess," Sybil said impishly. "You are under arrest?"

Carol laughed uproariously, the sound bringing an explosion of joy to Sybil.

"Let's go to bed," Carol said softly, her hands releasing Sybil's to gently, warmly cup her face.

"Yes," Sybil whispered, her hands covering Carol's.

TWENTY-THREE

Mark Bourke and Anne Newsome joined Carol where she stood with arms folded, staring fixedly through the one-way window of the interview room. She had been observing the room for the past fifteen minutes.

Carol asked, "All told, how long have we had her in there?"

"Maureen and I picked her up about three. So, just over an hour," Anne answered. "I brought her tea when you said, at the half hour mark. She thanked me. She didn't seem the slightest bit ruffled or annoyed." She cast a glance through the window. "Still doesn't."

"A very cool customer," Carol agreed, watching the motionless figure sitting at the metal table, a meditative gaze fixed on the plain gray wall across from her. "This may take a while."

"Carol, are you sure—"

"We've discussed it, Mark," she cut him off. "Thoroughly. A solo act has the best chance. With you and Anne observing and coming in only strategically. Nothing I've seen in the past fifteen minutes surprises me—how she's behaving pretty much confirms my own assessment of what we'll be dealing with."

"All set then, Carol?" Anne inquired.

"I'd like to observe her a few more minutes. Would one of you fetch me two more cups of tea? But not in paper cups, this time I'll need them to be a bit more special than that. Along with everything else about this interview."

* * *

Bourke held open the door of the interview room as Carol entered, a ceramic mug in each hand. Then he closed it behind her.

"Ah, how very welcome a sight," Thalia Denby said, accepting one of the mugs, her fingers lightly touching Carol's in the exchange. "You as well as your tea."

"My apologies for the wait," Carol said with an easy smile. "It's been that kind of day."

Thalia set down her mug and held out both hands, palms up. "At least I'm not in handcuffs."

"Should you be?" Carol took a seat opposite her in the gray, stark room.

"I've had them on a few times. And not just for fun and games in the bedroom. As you undoubtedly know." With a slow smile, Thalia fingered a thin gold bracelet set with diamonds. "I prefer to make a better fashion statement."

Carol reminded herself that Thalia Denby's high degree of poise and aplomb was rooted in an abundance of wealth and privilege. But as an alluring waft of perfume reached her she felt the woman's physical magnetism like a force field.

"Handcuffs or not," Carol said, "I need to advise you that our conversation is being videoed. And that you are not obliged to say or do anything unless you wish to do so, but whatever you say or do could be used in evidence."

"My, my. Against whom?" Thalia said, picking up her tea.

"Do you understand these rights?" Carol asked courteously.

"It would take a dimwit not to. Of course I understand these rights. I know you talked to Kenny yesterday. He didn't say anything about you putting him through this rigmarole."

Carol raised her own hands palms up. "It's up to Kenny to tell you what he wants you to know."

"Well, he most certainly told me about Frederick Lowell. I don't know who's more distraught, Kenny or Bea. Bea came to us on Lowell's recommendation, you know, so she's hysterical about him being a personal reflection on her. Kenny's acting like he's been kicked in the balls."

"What do you think about it?"

"Honestly..." Thalia shook her head and contemplated her over the rim of her mug of tea. "I'm dumbfounded. Truly. You've arrested him, I hear."

"We have."

"I didn't think the smarmy little bastard had it in him. I feel really bad for Kenny. My little brother's never been the fuckup other people think he is, but Lowell's made him look the part, made him look like the world's biggest fool. Unbelievable that it's the faithful family retainer who did this to him. On top of everything going on around my mother—police all over our house yet again yesterday, taking God knows what—Kenny's just beside himself. Is Lowell why I'm here?"

"We'd be happy to hear anything you know about that," Carol said, sitting back in her chair, picking up her own tea as if this were a normal conversation.

"Nothing. Is this why you've had me waiting more than an hour? To ask this question about Lowell so I can say, 'nothing'?"

Carol smiled. "I didn't imagine you'd have much to offer about him. He covered his tracks very well."

"I guess it took your investigation into Mother's death to expose him."

"That's quite possibly true."

Thalia Denby set down her mug and inspected her with cool, dark, appraising eyes. Carol set her own tea aside and sat still and silent under the scrutiny. She had dressed with care this morning, in a round-necked gray silk top under a summer-weight navy jacket with matching pants, one of the outfits she preferred for court, simple, stylish apparel that she would not have to adjust or think about. Thalia Denby's crisp cotton shirt, cream-colored with white lace edging its collar and cuffs and forming a seam across her shoulders, draped elegantly over beige pants. The shirt undoubtedly cost more than much of Carol's wardrobe. The bracelet and ear studs alone were probably worth more than the contents of her jewelry case.

"When this is over, much is possible," Thalia murmured, her insinuation unmistakable.

Carol did not respond. *We must look like a pair of well-feathered birds in this grim room,* she thought. *Instead of what we are: two sword fighters sizing each other up with everything at stake and equally confident we'll come out ahead.*

She broke the silence. "I'd like you to take me through that last day with your mother. I know it's difficult to take yourself back there. Just anything you can remember, can share with me."

"Share with you and the camera, wherever it is," Thalia said with a sweep of a hand, "and whoever's looking in through that one-way window."

"The world is full of nosy eavesdroppers," Carol countered with a brief smile. "Let me ask another question. From the members of your household I've spoken with, I have a sense of what your mother was like. Would you tell me a little about your father?"

"Ah." Thalia's face instantly lightened. "No difficulty there. My father was, above all, smart. Smart as hell. Sharp smart, whip smart, wise smart. Principled, too. A great businessman."

"I see he was a great loss to you."

"You have no idea."

"Tell me more."

"Why?" Thalia was not hostile; she looked genuinely curious. "He's been gone for well over two years—he's not any part of this."

But he is. "He was a loss to this country as well as to you and your family. For all that he built, he was an exceptional man."

Thalia nodded. "My father was decisive, bold. Everything he did—it happened because he was *bold*."

A trait you inherited in spades, Carol thought.

"Not enough people appreciate how well-earned our family's wealth is, thanks to him..." Thalia's eyes were distant and softened by admiration as if she were gazing at Harland Denby somewhere over Carol's shoulder. "It's come from good jobs for Australians, all those jobs he created in our economy."

"Did you work with your father?"

Her face closed. "Not in any official capacity."

"But in an important way. From your observations of him and how he conducted himself in business, you had to."

She conceded this with the briefest of nods. "As a trusted sounding board."

"As his presumptive heir?"

"Mother was always his presumptive heir."

The suddenly clipped, terse tone interested Carol. "Iris told us you and your father were very close."

"Is that so. Maybe you should be asking Iris all these questions."

Carol held up both hands. "I'm sorry to upset you."

Thalia grimaced. "It's just that I miss him. Every day. The whole world changed when he died."

With Thalia Denby braced and fully expecting her to ask in what manner the world had changed, Carol deliberately abandoned the follow on for a tangential question. "Your mother and father seem to have had a very strong marriage."

"Yes. But tempestuous." For the first time Carol saw Thalia Denby smile. "You undoubtedly know this was the second marriage for them both. They were chalk and cheese— incompatible but for some reason they clicked. Dad truly loved her."

No mention of love the other way around, Carol noted. And it's Dad for the father but not Mum for the mother.

Thalia shook her head. "Politically, he was ultra right wing Liberal, she was ultra left wing Labor. Dinner conversation at our house was like the Israelis and the Palestinians."

Carol was smiling. "And whose side were you on?"

"Dad's, of course. It was always Dad and me versus Mother and Kenny. I think Kenny sided with Mother so it wouldn't be three against one."

Carol veered tactically away from the topic. "I do need you to tell me what you remember that last day. How did your mother seem to you overall?"

"The same as most days." Thalia drummed her fingertips briefly on the metal tabletop and Carol noticed nail polish in variegated shades of glossy coral. From her earlier observations of Thalia, she had noted that she was not a fidgeter, revealing little through body language. "She was in pain. Putting a brave face on it as usual."

"Was her pain medication insufficient, in your opinion?"

"How would I know? The only opinion I have any right to is of Valdez's so-called treatment."

"Why? What exactly did you know about his 'so-called treatment'?"

"A concoction," she said contemptuously. "Nothing but a bunch of vitamins and herbal extracts. All you have to do is take a look at the bottles."

"Did you ever sit down with him for an explanation of the theory around his treatment, its research basis?"

"*Of course* I did. Do you take me for a simple judgmental fool? I did ask, and I could have been listening to some New Age zealot or spirit guide. His research consists of all the ways we fell off the trail to good health ten thousand years ago."

"If your father had been alive, do you think he would have made a difference in her cancer treatment?"

"Yes I do. Well…" Thalia's dark eyes narrowed. "Then again…maybe no. What an interesting question." She reflected for some moments, again drumming her fingers. "I don't think so, actually. They both had wills of iron, but I think his belief would have given in to hers if he thought her belief would help her more."

"But your belief didn't give in." When Thalia shrugged and remained silent, Carol said, "Were you aware she was taking an opioid for the pain, aside from whatever else he'd prescribed?"

"Certainly, or I'd have screamed the place down. It would take a monster to refuse medication for cancer pain." Thalia leaned forward, clasped her hands together on the tabletop, gazing at Carol. "I'm no judge of how effective the painkillers were or weren't. All I knew was the face of my mother. It was gray and pinched, I knew she was in no way pain-free, but she didn't want to be drug-addled, either. She'd been like that for weeks."

"Did anyone else in the house share your view of her pain?"

"To be honest, we didn't talk about it all that much, anything to do with her condition. Too hard. Mother's suffering created a constant level of anxiety, it was a difficult subject for us all."

"I can well understand that," Carol offered. The same had been true in her household about her own mother. "In view of everything you say about where your mother was in her illness, was the request for an autopsy a surprise?"

"A shock."

"Dr. Valdez was very shocked that she had died."

"That *dickhead*," she spat. "Whatever Pollyanna pap he was selling, he was blind if he didn't see she was going to die, she was *dying*. Of the cancer that recurred despite his whiz-bang treatment."

"You would rather no one found out about the fatal overdose?"

"I'm not saying that at all. But I would rather not have had the Four Horsemen of the Apocalypse descending on our lives and swarming our home and making Mother's death hideously worse for all of us."

Carol nodded, and lifted the last three fingers of her left hand; then heard what she expected, a knock on the door of the interview room. Followed by Bourke's entrance. He bestowed a perfunctory, expressionless nod on Thalia as he placed a folder at Carol's elbow. "Information you requested, Chief Inspector."

"Thank you," she said in dismissal.

Thalia Denby had not seen Bourke before, and she surveyed him with a raking glance as he turned and left the room. Carol placed the folder beside her.

"We found something in your mother's room that we're trying to understand," she said. "In an aspirin bottle in her bathroom cabinet."

Thalia looked at Carol quizzically.

"A flash drive."

"How very odd," Thalia said. "Was there anything on it?"

"A presentation on methods of painless suicide apparently copied from a website." Carol waited; Thalia didn't respond. "Would you have any idea who might have put such a thing there?"

"The only answer that makes any sense would be my mother."

"A treatise on methods of suicide? With her belief in the treatment she was receiving?"

"My mother was a realist." She gave a brief, wry smile. "About most things."

"Did she share any of these doubts about her prognosis with you?"

Thalia hesitated. "To my knowledge, she believed in Valdez's course of treatment."

"Why hide the flash drive in an aspirin bottle? Or anywhere?"

"To hide any doubt she may have had from the rest of us. That seems obvious."

"Not to us. Why put something on a flash drive that she would have on her computer?"

Thalia blinked rapidly, then said in a calm, flat voice, "Perhaps she was planning to send it to someone else—how would I know? My mother only rarely used her computer. Mostly to look at the gallery of family photos on it. Which is why I want it back."

"Yes. So you said. But your mother knew the basics of using a computer?"

"Of course."

Carol did not miss the swift glance Thalia had taken at the closed folder. "Searching the web, composing documents?"

"Of course."

"It appears to us more likely that someone put that drive in the bottle to suggest the possibility of suicide in case something about her death invited police inquiry."

"I think that's absurd."

"I agree with you, actually. I think it's also quite stupid," Carol said. "Clumsy and stupid."

Thalia picked up her tea, inspected its contents, took a few sips. And glanced again at the folder.

"It strikes me as an impulsive act," Carol bored in. "For that very reason, stupid. What do you think?"

"I think you're the police and your job is exploring various possibilities."

"Yes," Carol said, thinking it was a good answer. "I understand your mother had an appointment with Frederick Lowell about changes to her will the morning of the day she died. What can you tell me about that?"

"Nothing. I'm not surprised he had an appointment to see her—he saw her all the time, at least several times a week, and he was there for dinner the night she died. But changes to her will? Did you hear about these so-called changes from the oh so reliable Fred Lowell himself?"

Carol ignored the question. "Would your mother have told you if she'd been making any changes?"

"Certainly."

"Would that be because you're next in line to control the entities your father built?"

"That would be because I'm her daughter."

Another good answer. "So you would know."

"As I said."

Carol opened the folder. She removed the first two items, photographs of Greta Denby's pillbox and of the individual pills in one of its containers, closed the folder, and placed the photos on the table.

"I expect you recognize these—"

"Indeed."

She took her gold pen from her jacket pocket and tapped on the photo of the individual pills. "This is a reproduction of the last dose your mother was scheduled to take at midnight. Can you identify these pills individually?"

"Not hardly. Not outside their pill bottles."

"They're actually quite distinguishable." Carol pinpointed them with her pen as she spoke. "These are solid pills, these are capsules."

"So what?" Thalia's elegant shoulders lifted in a slight shrug. "Why would I know what was what?"

"Because otherwise, why would a fingerprint of yours be on the pillbox?"

Thalia looked astonished. "That's impossible."

"Nevertheless...the lab made a positive match." It was a bluff to gauge her reaction.

She shook her head as if cudgeling memory from it. "I guess I must have given her some pills at some point. Maybe I just moved the pillbox—there was often a lot of clutter around."

"Isn't that Bea Parker's responsibility?"

"Of course." Thalia added with irritation, "If I was in Mother's room and it was time for her pills I probably gave them to her. I just don't remember that I ever did. Any fingerprint of mine could have been on that pillbox for who knows how long."

"That's true."

"I would imagine there are other prints on there besides my own."

Carol did not respond to this. She pointed out the five capsules in the photo of the individual pills. "Do you recognize any of these?"

Thalia reached for and pulled the photo closer to her without asking permission, and scrutinized it for some time.

"Maybe," she said.

"What are they?"

"Valdez's junk." She pointed. "These are from New Zealand, I think."

"Do you know the name of them?"

"Why would I?"

"Perhaps because you ordered the same thing?" Not taking her eyes off Thalia's face, she slid the folder over in front of herself but did not open it. "You can erase your search history of websites you visit, but not email and not files, even when you delete them. Not unless you actually know how to clean a hard drive. And with our technicians, sometimes not even then."

"I see," Thalia said in a casual tone that belied the tension that froze her face.

Carol opened the folder and withdrew a sheet of paper. "We found in your deleted email this record of a shipping notice from the lab in New Zealand for capsules your mother was taking. They were shipped directly to you four days before she died."

"I remember now," Thalia said evenly. "It's an immune system booster. I ordered it for myself. Because of all the stress."

"We found no such bottle beyond the one in your mother's suite prescribed by Dr. Valdez."

"You must have. Your people would have collected it along with everything else you swept up yesterday."

Carol said, tapping the closed folder, "It's not on the inventory list."

"Then you must have collected it the first time your people came to the house." Thalia eased back into her metal chair and looked at her, her face slowly softening into an incandescent smile of disarming blamelessness.

Thalia's weapon of physical magnetism had dissolved. Intent on her quarry, Carol felt no effect. They had stopped circling each other, had entered the heart of the battle between them. Gazing intently into Carol's face, Thalia again drummed her fingers. "I'm beginning to think you're trying to actually pin this on me."

"We're not trying to pin anything on anyone. We're gathering and assessing facts as we do with every investigation."

"What other facts can I help you assess, Chief Inspector?" Thalia asked.

"Do you have any suspicions around who did this to your mother, or why?"

The answer was prompt. "I think Mother did this to herself."

"How would she have gained access to a drug like Nembutal?"

"She had to have help. Of course."

"If it was what your mother intended, why wouldn't she have taken an overdose of the oxycodone and Stilnox she was already being prescribed?"

Thalia's well-shaped brows pinched slightly together. "Maybe somebody knew something else would be more effective…easier for her."

"Any suspicions as to who that would be?"

"I think it was Valdez."

"Valdez." Carol did her best to convey the incredulity expected from her. "He helped her die and then called for an autopsy?"

"Yes. Because Mother had given in but retained her faith that his treatment would help others. He called for the autopsy so he wouldn't be exposed for the fraud he is."

"That's a bit convoluted," Carol observed.

"Isn't that the beauty of it?"

"She did very much want his cancer treatment and research to continue after her," Carol said, and added quietly, "but then you knew that, didn't you."

Thalia's fingertips, about to begin another drumroll, froze. "On what basis do you conclude such a thing?"

"From several documents we found in the deleted files of your mother's computer."

Carol again opened the folder and extracted six pages fastened together and held them up.

"This is what we found on your mother's hard drive. The changes she was planning to make in her will. Changes of considerable dimension affecting the entire Denby holdings, changes she'd been thinking about and working on over a period of weeks. The changes you claim she would have discussed with you, her daughter. Did she discuss these changes with you?"

Thalia Denby did not look at the documents. She fixed Carol with a cold, steady stare. "Since this conversation or interview or exchange of views or whatever you call it has taken on what appears to be accusation, I exercise my right to say nothing further until I've spoken with a lawyer."

Carol nodded. "As is your right."

"I assume I'm free to go."

"No."

Thalia rose to her feet. "I insist on leaving and I demand a lawyer."

"And you shall have a lawyer. You are in police custody and I remind you that this interview is being video-recorded. I state for that record that I will ask you no more questions, nor will I expect you to say another word in response to anything I say as I lay out for you what we now believe happened to your mother, and our evidence. Please sit down."

Thalia sank back into her chair.

Holding her dark, flat stare, Carol steadily recounted the facts. "According to the documents we recovered, your mother began discussions with you eighteen days prior to her death. There are notations about your objections to her plans and a few revisions she made accordingly. But she made no substantive changes to her intentions toward the estate she would leave after her death. The companies were to be liquidated in orderly fashion, the proceeds to go to designated charitable organizations throughout Australia for services to women, and in support of Dr. Eduardo Valdez's cancer research."

Thalia Denby exhaled an audible breath.

"We believe that five days before your mother's death, because your mother remained intractable, you placed your order for the herbal extract from New Zealand. We believe you obtained from a local source Nembutal in powder form. When you learned that your mother's meeting with Frederick Lowell was imminent, you acted. You removed the herbal extract from the New Zealand capsules you ordered so there would be no inconsistency with the quantities in your mother's supply. You then filled them with Nembutal, replaced the pills already in your mother's pillbox with the ones containing Nembutal. Probably wearing gloves, judging by your surprise that we would find a fingerprint. Sometime after midnight, you entered your mother's room and deleted every file you could find about the proposed changes to her will."

"This is utter fantasy," Thalia stated, her face an icy mask.

"As for motive...you couldn't live with your mother's plans for your father's achievement."

There was an involuntary, almost inaudible utterance through tightened lips. Carol thought she heard "Destruction…"

"Up until then you were obeying your mother about involvement in her interests, you were keeping your actual behavior and intentions a secret only because you knew her death would return control of the Denby holdings to you and you could take over what your father built. There was only one reason your mother had to die before her appointed time: because she intended to change her will and destroy your plans."

"You'll never prove any of this theory," Thalia stated.

"It's the facts that will prove it. We found the file copied to the flash drive with the methods of suicide in a deleted file on your computer. Placing it in that aspirin bottle was your attempt at insurance, but then you had no reason to expect an autopsy— this would simply be the death of a dying woman, like so many other cancer deaths. On your mother's computer, her changes to her will are annotated with numerous references to you and quotes of your comments and objections."

Carol removed two reports from the folder. "Forensics will also prove our case. The only key on your mother's computer that holds anything other than her own fingerprints is the delete key. With each file you deleted you gave us a stronger imprint on that key, a clear, eight-point image of your index finger. We've just completed testing on clothing you wore during the three days prior to your mother's death, clothing identified by dated security camera footage on the estate. The pocket of a pair of red shorts has tested positive for Nembutal, residue from the capsules you concealed to carry them into your mother's room."

Thalia Denby said nothing. Nor did Carol, as she watched the color in her face recede into pallor.

Carol raised a hand in signal, and stated, as Bourke and Anne Newsome entered the room, "Thalia Denby, I am placing you under arrest for the murder of Greta Denby. You have requested a lawyer and I repeat to you your rights: You are not obliged to say or do anything unless you wish to do so but whatever you say or do may be used in evidence. Do you understand?"

She stared at Carol. "It was a bloody sorry day when Inspector Rooke died. This travesty would never have happened."

He did what he did exactly so this would happen.

She held Thalia's stare with a hot satisfaction that she had won their sword fight and Thalia knew it.

Thalia asked carelessly, "Will you be putting me in the cell with Fred Lowell?"

"He bailed out this morning," Anne Newsome informed her coldly as she seized one of Thalia's wrists and snapped on a handcuff.

"This will never happen," Thalia said to Carol. "You do know that, don't you?"

Perhaps not, Carol thought. With enough money to buy the best legal talent in Australia, and a defendant with the advantage of charismatic allure, even film of Thalia stuffing pills down her mother's throat might not be enough. But she would be ruined by the accusation—if nothing else. Madeline Shipley and all her equivalents in social media would put the evidence against her though endless speculation and all but chemical analysis.

"If it does happen," Carol said quietly, "you do understand what you've done to your father's legacy? Since your mother never got to change her will, your brother Kenny will be caretaker of what your father built."

But Thalia only smiled as Anne finished cuffing both her hands securely behind her. "Did you know that my brother Kenny has a genius IQ? And an abiding interest in robotics? He'd just have his main chance to blow everything sky high or be the Steve Jobs of Australia."

"Assuming," Carol said acidly, "that he ever recovers from the premeditated murder of his mother by his monstrosity of a sister and the betrayal of everyone he's ever trusted."

In a contemptuous tone she told Anne, "Take her."

"With pleasure," Anne said. As Bourke held open the door of the interview room, she jeered, "Please excuse my peasant hands," and propelled Thalia Denby through it with a forceful shove.

TWENTY-FOUR

Madeline Shipley answered Carol's call with a cheerful, "What can I do for you, Carol? Have I not done enough?"

Carol laughed. "More than enough, Madeline. Which is the purpose of this call. I owe you—"

"Carol, listen," Madeline interrupted eagerly, apparently with an agenda of her own. "There's been so much feedback and commentary—to the benefit of us both. I've learned how to do this job over the years and I'm good at it. But sometimes it actually becomes apparent what we go through to put a story on air and get it right. Not to mention last-minute complications like your aunt lobbing in. Did you know she called me an hour before we went to air?"

"No I didn't," Carol uttered, closing her eyes and shaking her head.

"I guessed not. She tried out a confession on me."

"That woman," Carol sighed. "Clearly you didn't believe her."

"Aunt Sarah? Everyone knows she'd walk through fire for you. Clearly not. Would you?"

"Of course not," Carol obediently replied.

"I told her she had zero credibility. But Carol…" Her voice dropped into a more serious, more intimate tone. "I must say, even with knowing Leanne Gordon was lying through her teeth, I felt something a bit off about all this, about that night with your mother…"

"This is what I know—and all I know," Carol said immediately into the questioning pause. Madeline had earned a right to the facts. "That night my mother begged me to end her suffering, help her die—"

Madeline gasped. "How *awful* to ask you to do something you couldn't possibly do."

"That's what I told her—I couldn't. But I grabbed a bottle of bourbon and got so drunk that I have no idea what actually did or might have happened."

"Well, if anybody did something, it couldn't have been you. Even drowned in alcohol that conscience of yours would have been operational."

The certainty in this dismissal by someone who'd known her for many years was so comforting, so relieving that for several moments she did not trust her voice to reply.

"Carol, has it ever occurred to you that maybe it was Leanne Gordon herself?"

"Leanne Gordon?"

"The research for our series on mercy killing—we saw how people tend to discount the impact of someone suffering on the person taking daily care of them, even if that person is a so-called stranger. Maybe she acted as an angel of mercy before she got religion and decided to make you a sacrificial lamb to save her canon."

"Well, it's possible," Carol conceded, remembering her team's similar speculations about Bea Parker. "But it seems a real stretch."

"Stretchier things have happened. About your aunt, I wouldn't put it past that clever old soul to know more than she's letting on."

"Yes," Carol said thoughtfully, "maybe I shouldn't either." Then, "Madeline, I have a newsworthy purpose in calling you.

It's about an arrest we've just now made in the Greta Denby case."

Carol tore her phone away from her ear as Madeline let out a shrieking whoop. "You're giving me a *scoop*? *You*? How is this *possible*?"

"I owe you," Carol said simply. "But I need you to understand it's to be a one-time thing."

"Agreed, agreed. Between arrest and trial, this figures to be one of the major ongoing stories of the decade. I'll mark you paid in full."

"The Crown Prosecutor was here to witness the interview and arrest and she's signed off, so it's a go. But we both know I've had more than one slam-dunk arrest go up in smoke, there's always unpredictability."

Madeline sighed. "That's a freight train we both have to avoid every day of our working lives. Okay, Carol. I agree to your terms. Now...I'm all ears."

"That consensus choice of your psychics—they were right."

"Thalia Denby?"

Again Carol had to tear the phone away from her ear.

* * *

Getting up from her desk, Carol tucked her mobile into her jacket pocket. She had gone into her office immediately following the Thalia Denby arrest and closed her door for privacy to call Madeline. She now opened it and Bourke immediately marched in past her.

"The way you put all those pieces together...the way you built that interview, it was masterful," he crowed. "A real cat and mouse act."

There was no mouse anywhere in that room, Carol thought, only cats. But she smiled her appreciation at Bourke.

He slung himself into a chair and crossed an ankle over a knee, hands behind his head, exulting in this aftermath of the Denby case and the final disposition she had filed on Ian Rooke. "At one point I thought we might even get a confession out of her."

"I never did," Carol said, perching on the side of her desk, arms folded. "She's much too smart."

"If she was all that smart she'd have known better than to answer even one question of yours."

"She did know better, Mark. But she thought she could handle me easily enough. The biggest advantage we had was the Jupiter size of her ego. We got the lies and inconsistencies we were looking for. The Crown thinks she can work with them along with our evidence."

Bourke said wryly, "Anne's convinced she'll get clean away with it."

As am I. Cynically familiar with the influence of money and fame over the justice system, she suspected that by the time Thalia Denby's phalanx of lawyers and expert witnesses were through with all the evidence, it would lay all but pulverized on the courtroom floor. But like America's O.J. Simpson case, regardless of outcome the court of public opinion would rule. And would leave the stain of matricide on Thalia Denby's privileged hide, a stain she could never expunge. Not to mention contempt from women all over the country when Greta Denby's thwarted changes to her will were introduced into evidence.

Bourke said, "Yesterday when we were putting the evidence together I got the feeling something had already put you onto her."

"You're not wrong, Mark. I saw no grief in her. She was the only one Anne and I talked to who showed no sense of loss, not a trace. Couldn't even manage the pretense. We knew there had to be a reason to murder a dying woman and it had to be connected to changes she planned for her will. Those deleted files—motive and proof. Everything Thalia Denby learned from her father, all that grooming and training to one day take over from him—he suddenly dies and she gets slammed into the brick wall of her mother. Greta's changes would demolish the Denby empire, end all her own aspirations. This wasn't a murder for gain, it was rage and frustration."

"Well, it sure ranks up there with the strangest if not most selfish motives I've ever run across. What a bloody tragedy Greta never got to change her will. You don't have to be a feminist to see how blind Thalia Denby is. Her father's companies would still remain intact, just not controlled by Thalia. All those jobs she bragged her father created. And aiding the women of our country could have been a great next stage for the Denby fortune."

Carol sighed in gloomy agreement. "The whole thing's a calamity, Mark. Thalia Denby detonated a bomb, and the damage..."

"What do you reckon our odds are for conviction?"

"Carol! Mark!" Anne Newsome rushed through the doorway without her usual warning knock. "Can you bloody well believe it? Madeline Shipley's just now come on the air with breaking news about the arrest!"

"There's your answer, Mark," Carol said with a laugh. "She's just gone on trial in the media. I for one don't like those odds."

"In this case the media may be a good thing," he said, and grinned back at her.

But Anne, oblivious to their exchange, was stalking around Carol's office, hands on her hips, consumed by vexation. "How in hell does she *do* it?" she fumed. "How does the bloody woman *get* her information?"

"One can only wonder," Carol said as the desk phone rang and the phone in her pocket buzzed with the first of many calls she would be fielding that day.

FINIS

Her arm in Sybil's, Carol leaned into her for comfort as she watched Aunt Sarah at the Qantas counter completing her check-in for her flight to Rio de Janeiro. They stood aside from the rapid current of travelers in the buzzing, teeming International Terminal in Sydney Airport, not far from the coterie of companions who had also checked in. All of them, including Aunt Sarah, wore vibrantly colored overalls.

Sybil pointed at the group and chuckled. "Just look at that feisty little band. People in the Amazon will think they've been invaded by a flock of rainbow lorikeets."

"I just hope she can stay out of trouble," Carol said soberly.

"She won't. But she'll be all right. And you know that."

"I'll miss her, Sybil," Carol lamented.

"We both will. But you'll be very busy working with a new commissioner on all those plans of yours around diversity, busy with the renovations making my house our house." She smiled. "Busy with our therapy appointments." Her smile grew. "And really busy making sense of all this to David when he gets home from Europe."

"True, all true," Carol said, and kissed her on the cheek. "It was mass confusion when I spoke to him on the phone. All he could say was 'What? What?'"

"You two," said Aunt Sarah as she came bounding up to them, tucking her boarding pass and passport into a capacious carry-on constructed of quilted patches emblazoned with CRONES OF THE WORLD—UNITE. "You're such a nice sight, all arm-in-arm. I'm leaving you in good hands, Carol dear."

"Yes you are," Sybil said.

"Aunt Sarah," Carol said sternly, "I spoke with Madeline. I know all about your last-minute phone call, what you tried to pull off."

"That woman was so *rude*. She all but laughed at me." But her aunt looked more amused than annoyed. "It all worked out anyway, didn't it."

"Not exactly," Carol said. "Aunt Sarah, now that you're off to who knows where for who knows how long, and we have only these last few minutes together...I want the truth. Whatever it might be. I respect that my mother had a right to end her life and I'm at peace with however it happened. So how about you finally tell me what you actually know."

Her aunt looked at her earnestly. "Yes, I can finally do that now. It was Dr. Yates. He gave her a handful of pills. Your mother told me after she'd taken them."

Carol gaped at her. "Why on earth didn't you say so straightaway? Instead of rigging up all the drama around that confession of yours?"

"Because he's been dead for years, dear," her aunt said. "What good would it do to put it on him if he wasn't here to confirm what he did? Leanne Gordon would still have crucified you. If Madeline had let her do it."

"Why did you never tell me?"

Her aunt looked uncomfortable. "Well, it was such a hard time for us both and you never asked, we just never spoke of it. Carol dear, I didn't know what you did or didn't know about that night, and I figured, just leave well enough alone."

"Secrets." Sybil's voice was just audible over the relentless cacophony in the airport. "Is there anything more destructive than the secrets we keep?"

"I'm glad to finally know," Carol said simply. "Thank you, Aunt Sarah."

Aunt Sarah's traveling companions were approaching. She kissed Sybil on both cheeks and gathered Carol into the pillowy warmth of a full-bodied hug. Then held her at arm's length and addressed both of them: "You take best care of each other."

"We will," Sybil said.

"We will," echoed Carol.

Her throat closing, Carol watched her aunt stride off, her companions surrounding her in an eddy of bright color, toward her departure gate and her continuing quest to help save the world.

When she could finally speak, Carol said, "I feel sad and glad."

"Me too," Sybil said thickly, gazing after the group.

"There's so much good in our future, Sybil. It's been so long since I've felt anything but cynical about my career—and now that Hindley's on his way out I have so many ideas about what I might actually be able to accomplish in this new role of mine."

As Aunt Sarah, with a final wave, was swallowed up in a sea of travelers, Carol took Sybil's hand and waited until she turned to look at her. "Above all else, I'm excited about us."

"I am too, my darling. Anything and everything that happens from here on—we'll do it all together."

Carol squeezed Sybil's hand. "Let's go find ourselves a sunset to walk into."

AFTERWORD

Katherine V. Forrest explained how she became my *Lethal Care* co-writer. She didn't mention how gracefully she met the challenges of that role.

It was my good fortune that Katherine had edited many of the Carol Ashton novels, and so was very familiar with the personalities and motivations of the main characters and the web of relationships that had developed over the sixteen-book series.

Knowing the main characters—Carol, Sybil, Aunt Sarah, Mark, Anne—was an advantage, but as the novel already existed in partial form, she had to tackle an entirely new cast whose lives were weaving the intricate plot. And on top of this, Katherine had to shape her writing to blend with my spare style.

Working with Katherine, the dearest of friends as well as my co-writer, has been one of the great joys of my writing career. Thank you, Katherine, for all you have done for me—and for Carol. You are truly the Goddess of Co-Writing!

Claire McNab
Los Angeles, CA
2017

Bella Books, Inc.

Women. Books. Even Better Together.

P.O. Box 10543
Tallahassee, FL 32302

Phone: 800-729-4992
www.bellabooks.com

Printed in the USA
CPSIA information can be obtained
at www.ICGtesting.com
JSHW022126111023
49953JS00001B/3